OXFORD WORLD'S CLASSICS

THE SHADOW-LINE

JOSEPH CONRAD was born Józef Teodor Konrad Korzeniowski in the Russian part of Poland in 1857. His parents were punished by the Russians for their Polish nationalist activities and both died while Conrad was still a child. In 1874 he left Poland for France and in 1878 began a career with the British merchant navy. He spent nearly twenty years as a sailor before becoming a full-time novelist. He became a British citizen in 1886 and settled permanently in England after his marriage to Jessie George in 1896.

Conrad is a writer of extreme subtlety and sophistication; works such as 'Heart of Darkness', *Lord Jim*, and *Nostromo* display technical complexities which have established him as one of the first English 'Modernists'. He is also noted for the unprecedented vividness with which he communicates a pessimist's view of man's personal and social destiny in such works as *The Secret Agent*, *Under Western Eyes*, and *Victory*. Despite the immediate critical recognition that they received in his lifetime, Conrad's major novels did not sell well, and he lived in relative poverty until the commercial success of *Chance* (1914) secured for him a wider public and an assured income. In 1923 he visited the United States, to great acclaim, and he was offered a knighthood (which he declined) shortly before his death in 1924. Since then his reputation has steadily grown, and he is now seen as a writer who revolutionized the English novel and was arguably the most important literary innovator of the twentieth century.

JEREMY HAWTHORN was born in 1942 and is Professor of Modern British Literature at the Norwegian University of Science and Technology, Trondheim. He has published two books and a number of articles on the work of Joseph Conrad, and among his other published works are *A Glossary of Contemporary Literary Theory* (4th edition, London: Arnold, 2000) and *Studying the Novel* (4th edition, London: Arnold, 2001). He has edited Conrad's *Under Western Eyes* for Oxford World's Classics.

MARA KALNINS is the General Editor of the Works of Joseph Conrad in the Oxford World's Classics series. She is a Fellow of Corpus Christi College, Cambridge, and Staff Tutor in Literature, Board of Continuing Education.

OXFORD WORLD'S CLASSICS

For over 100 years Oxford World's Classics have brought readers closer to the world's great literature. Now with over 700 titles—from the 4,000-year-old myths of Mesopotamia to the twentieth century's greatest novels—the series makes available lesser-known as well as celebrated writing.

The pocket-sized hardbacks of the early years contained introductions by Virginia Woolf, T. S. Eliot, Graham Greene, and other literary figures which enriched the experience of reading. Today the series is recognized for its fine scholarship and reliability in texts that span world literature, drama and poetry, religion, philosophy and politics. Each edition includes perceptive commentary and essential background information to meet the changing needs of readers.

OXFORD WORLD'S CLASSICS

JOSEPH CONRAD

The Shadow-Line

A Confession

Edited with an Introduction and Notes by
JEREMY HAWTHORN

OXFORD
UNIVERSITY PRESS

Great Clarendon Street, Oxford OX2 6DP
Oxford University Press is a department of the University of Oxford.
It furthers the University's objective of excellence in research, scholarship,
and education by publishing worldwide in

Oxford New York

Auckland Bangkok Buenos Aires Cape Town Chennai
Dar es Salaam Delhi Hong Kong Istanbul Karachi Kolkata
Kuala Lumpur Madrid Melbourne Mexico City Mumbai Nairobi
São Paulo Shanghai Taipei Tokyo Toronto

Published in the United States
by Oxford University Press Inc., New York

First published as a World's Classics paperback 1985
Revised edition 2003

British Library Cataloguing in Publication Data
Data available

Library of Congress Cataloging in Publication Data
Data available

ISBN 0-19-280170-8

1

Typeset in Ehrhardt
by RefineCatch Limited, Bungay, Suffolk
Printed in Great Britain by
Clays Ltd., St Ives plc

CONTENTS

GENERAL EDITOR'S PREFACE

Conrad is acknowledged as one of the great writers of the twentieth century, but neither in his lifetime nor after have his works been available in authoritative texts. This was partly because Conrad himself revised his writings at several stages (in manuscript, typescript, and proofs), partly because many of his works appeared in different versions (slightly so in the English and American editions, significantly so in serial and book form), and partly because he himself continued to revise them for subsequent publication. Moreover he was involved in still further revision of the texts when his works were issued in the collected editions of Doubleday and Heinemann in 1921, though the extent of his involvement varied considerably from work to work. Like many authors, he also suffered from the well-meant, but often misguided, editorial efforts of his publishers who not only imposed their own house styling but sometimes changed his grammar, spelling, and punctuation, and even altered whole phrases. The textual history of Conrad's works—the revisions they underwent and their transmission and publication—is therefore an intricate and complicated one. A scholarly edition of the *Letters and Works* is currently being prepared by Cambridge University Press and six volumes of the *Letters* as well as two novels have been published to date.

In the absence of authoritative texts which accurately incorporate Conrad's corrections and revisions and which remove the editorial interference, house styling, and printing errors of his publishers, the base-texts for this new Oxford World's Classics edition must be the British first editions. These editions are important because they are what Conrad originally expected to be published, because they were the texts which first shaped his reputation as a writer, and because they are free of later layers of editorial interference. As late as 1919, when Conrad was correcting copy for a limited Collected Edition, he still affirmed their importance: 'I devote particular care to the text of the English Edition always and it is to be considered the standard one' (letter to Fisher Unwin, 27 May 1919). At the same time, however, they are themselves flawed by numerous misprints and some idiosyncratic house styling. The present edition therefore aims to correct such errors in order to restore Conrad's idiom and distinctive prose style.

In this edition the following emendations have been made silently throughout: (*a*) obvious spelling errors and typesetter's mistakes have been corrected; (*b*) inadvertent omissions have been supplied in the case of incomplete quotation marks, final stops, apostrophes in colloquial contractions (e.g. 'o'clock') and the stop following a title (e.g. 'Mr.'); (*c*) the convention of hyphenating words such as 'to-day', 'to-night', 'good-bye' has been dropped in accordance with modern usage; (*d*) inconsistencies in punctuation inside or outside quotation marks have been standardized and other inconsistencies—such as hyphenated words—have been regularized in accordance with Conrad's most frequent practice in each work; (*e*) paragraphs have been indented throughout in accordance with modern conventions and a few typographical details—such as display capitals, chapter numbers and headings, and running titles—have been regularized. However, where the sense of a phrase has been occluded or where there is a controversial reading or some specific textual difficulty, the editor of each volume will record the editorial emendation and explain the adopted reading briefly in the Note on the Text or in an explanatory note where the reader may also be directed to further reading on the issue.

Each volume has an Introduction which seeks to relate the work to Conrad's life and other writings, to place it in its literary and cultural context, and to offer a cogent argument for its relevance both to his time and ours. Although Conrad is a modern writer, his specialized terminology is not always familiar to contemporary readers nor are the literary, historical, and political allusions always clear. Explanatory notes are therefore supplied but it is assumed that words or expressions found in a good dictionary will not need to be glossed. Appendixes in most volumes will also provide material useful to the reader, such as a glossary of nautical or foreign terms, maps, or important additional texts. Conrad's own series of prefaces and Author's Notes (the latter written between 1917 and 1920) are reprinted as an appendix to each volume.

Finally, any work on so major a figure as Conrad must be deeply indebted to the research of many scholars and critics, but I would like to express my gratitude especially to Jacques Berthoud, Jim Boulton, Andrew Brown, Laurence Davies, George Donaldson,

Donald Rude, J. H. Stape, and Cedric Watts for sharing their expertise, and to Judith Luna of Oxford University Press for her unfailing encouragement and advice.

Mara Kalnins

Corpus Christi, Cambridge

ACKNOWLEDGEMENTS

Many friends and colleagues have helped me in the production of this edition. Domhnall Mitchell, Terence Cave, Stephen Donovan, Paul Goring, and John Stape have scoured libraries in search of material or information for me. Gordon Williams helped me with some specific queries. Jakob Lothe and Ruth Sherry have been always ready to talk about problems, while my wife Bjørg has been, as ever, consistently supportive. Mara Kalnins has been a meticulous and helpful General Editor, and Judith Luna of OUP has answered many queries expeditiously and helpfully. A number of individuals answered my queries about the meanings of technical terms while I was compiling the Glossary. After the first World's Classics edition of the novella was published in 1985, Mr Seiji Minamida, Captain D. E. Mitchell, and Captain D. C. Thomas wrote to me with comments on my notes. My former colleague Professor John Corner, now at the University of Liverpool, was able to answer some of my questions on the basis of his years in the Royal Navy. My thanks to all of these—none of whom is responsible for any errors in what follows.

I am indebted to Yale University Library for having granted me permission to quote from Conrad's manuscript of *The Shadow-Line*, the property of the Beinecke Rare Book and Manuscript Library.

INTRODUCTION

The ship, this ship, our ship, the ship we serve,
is the moral symbol of our life.[1]

Autobiography and Fiction

Joseph Conrad wrote the above words in 1918, two years after the publication of *The Shadow-Line*, but they express a belief that is exemplified in everything he wrote concerning ships and the sea. *The Shadow-Line* is one of a group of Conrad's works, written at different times in his life, which draw on his experiences during his third trip to the East in 1887 8.[2] Conrad had sailed from Amsterdam to Java, but was injured by a falling spar during the trip and ended up spending six weeks in hospital in Singapore. Afterwards, he signed on as mate of the *Vidar*, which traded among the islands of the Malayan archipelago, signing off four and a half months later, just as the narrator of *The Shadow-Line* signs off his ship at the start of the story. He was offered his one and only command on a seagoing vessel shortly after this, and travelled from Singapore to Bangkok on the *Melita* to take over as captain of the *Otago*, an iron barque. After a short stay in Bangkok he sailed to Sydney, calling in at Singapore to replenish his supply of medicine.

This relatively brief period provided Conrad with experiences which appear, in different forms and with different emphases, in *Lord Jim* (1900), 'The End of the Tether' (1902), 'Falk' (1903), 'The Secret Sharer' (1910), 'A Smile of Fortune' (1911), and *The Shadow-Line* (1916). They are also referred to in the non-fictional *The Mirror of the Sea* (1906).

On a number of occasions Conrad used the word 'autobiography' in connection with *The Shadow-Line*, and clearly its

[1] Joseph Conrad, 'Well Done' (1918), in *Notes on Life and Letters* (Dent Collected Edition, repr. London, 1970), 188.

[2] For the information that follows I am indebted to Norman Sherry, *Conrad's Eastern World* (London: Cambridge University Press, 1966).

basic plot corresponds quite closely to Conrad's own experiences. Moreover the names of many of the characters in the tale resemble, or are identical to, many real people with whom Conrad came into contact during 1887–8.[3] Captain Ellis *was* Master Attendant at Singapore (Conrad had used the name Eliott in *Lord Jim* and 'The End of the Tether', and in his manuscript of *The Shadow-Line* he uses both names, opting finally for Ellis—perhaps because the real Ellis was now dead). There *was* a John Niven who was engineer on the *Vidar*, and moreover Conrad's first mate on the *Otago* was a Mr Born, who appears as Mr Burns in a number of Conrad's works in addition to *The Shadow-Line*. In *The Mirror of the Sea* he is known as Mr B——, and of him Conrad reports that he was: 'of all my chief officers, the one I trusted most . . . He was worth all his salt'.

In 'The End of the Tether' Captain Eliott refers to a certain Hamilton as 'the worst loafer of them all', and forces him to accept a command he does not want. The difference between this last detail and the account of the way in which Conrad's narrator in *The Shadow-Line* obtains his command despite the Steward's attempt to give it to Hamilton should alert us to the fact that in none of these stories can the reader assume that the text is 'exact autobiography', as Conrad inadvisedly described *The Shadow-Line*.[4] Although a considerable body of personal experience lies behind this work, Conrad transformed not only certain external facts of the first voyage of the *Otago* under his command, but also

[3] I have again relied on Sherry below.

[4] In a letter to John Quinn of 24 December 1915 (written very shortly after he completed the first draft of the work), Conrad explained: 'The next production is a sort of autobiography—a personal experience—dramatised in the telling' (Frederick R. Karl and Laurence Daries (eds.), *The Collected Letters of Joseph Conrad* (Cambridge: Cambridge University Press, 1983–), v. 543). Norman Sherry refers to two letters written by Conrad in 1917 to his agent J. B. Pinker and to his friend Sidney Colvin. Both letters refer to *The Shadow-Line* as autobiographical, and the identical term 'exact autobiography' appears in each letter (see Sherry, *Conrad's Eastern World*, 211; the letters are also reproduced in G. Jean-Aubry, *Joseph Conrad: Life and Letters*, ii (London: Heinemann, 1927), 181, 182). In a letter to Helen Sanderson Conrad commented: 'it is a piece of as strict autobiography as the form allowed,—I mean, the need of slight dramatization to make the thing actual. Very slight. For the rest, not a fact or sensation is "invented." ' See Jean-Aubry, *Joseph Conrad: Life and Letters*, ii. 195. Jean-Aubry dates this letter to '1917'.

some of his personal experiences during that trip.[5] In particular it is striking how different the tone of *The Shadow-Line* is from that of many of the previous stories which used the same set of experiences. There is little doubt that a major factor here is the date of *The Shadow-Line*'s composition. Although the story was written in 1915, and first published in 1916–17, Conrad's earliest recorded reference to it (as *First Command*) comes in a letter written on 14 February 1899 to his publisher William Blackwood, concerning the stories he has planned, which include 'A Seaman' (perhaps 'Typhoon') and *First Command*: 'These are not written. They creep about in my head but [have] got to be caught and tortured into some kind of shape. I think—I think they would turn out good as good as (they say) *Youth* is.'[6] The 'torturing' took him almost sixteen years, and it is tempting to speculate whether this was because of the pressure of other work or a result of some less material problem—some psychological block. Such conjecture is necessarily inconclusive, but had *The Shadow-Line* been written in 1900, it is certain that it would have been a very different work. In September 1915 Conrad's older son Borys had enlisted and had become a second lieutenant, and although Conrad had been writing *The Shadow-Line* since the beginning of the year, he had certainly been very conscious of the war even if its threat to his own immediate family only became unavoidably clear a few months before he completed the manuscript. Frederick Karl quotes the comment Conrad himself wrote in Richard Curle's copy of the novel:

> This story had been in my mind for some years. Originally I used to think of it under the name of *First Command*. When I managed in the second year of war to concentrate my mind sufficiently to begin working I turned to this subject as the easiest. But in consequence of my changed mental attitude to it, it became *The Shadow-Line*.[7]

[5] For example, according to Sherry, by no means all the crew of the *Otago* went down with malaria; John Snadden, the previous captain of the *Otago*, was apparently on good terms with Mr Born (Burns), was neither mad nor a bad captain, and did not even throw his violin (which he did possess) overboard! See the comments on Snadden and Born in the explanatory notes for pp. 46 and 44.

[6] William Blackburn (ed.), *Joseph Conrad: Letters to William Blackwood and David S. Meldrum* (Durham, NC: Duke University Press, 1958), 54. See also *Letters*, ii. 167.

[7] See Frederick R. Karl, *Joseph Conrad: The Three Lives* (London: Faber, 1979), 770.

Thus, although Conrad's use of the ship as 'the moral symbol of our life' is constant, his 'changed mental attitude' ensures that *The Shadow-Line* is rather different from those other works that are built on the same set of experiences from 1887 to 1888. In particular, the consciousness of evil and of death that permeates *The Shadow-Line* is not to be found in the much earlier 'Youth' (1898). Although the latter is based on a different set of experiences in Conrad's life, like *The Shadow-Line* it too is concerned with the passage from youth to maturity. This concern with evil and death, together with the far more crucial role allotted to older men such as Captain Giles and Captain Ellis, makes *The Shadow-Line* a far more profound work than stories such as 'Falk' and 'A Smile of Fortune', more comprehensive in its view of the human condition, more reflective in tone and outlook.

Isolation, Collectivity, and Tradition

As with other stories in which Conrad writes about a young and inexperienced sea-captain, he fully exploits the productive tension between isolation and collectivity that the narrator's situation affords him. The ship as a symbol of 'our life' functions collectively; as such it can be used to demonstrate that interconnectedness of social life that is—in the everyday world—concealed and unapparent. But Conrad is clear that collectivity is not democracy:

> My sensations could not be like those of any other man on board. In that community I stood, like a king in his country, in a class all by myself. I mean an hereditary king, not a mere elected head of a state. (p. 51)

Like the young captains of 'Falk' and 'The Secret Sharer', the captain in *The Shadow-Line* feels his isolation very sharply, and in all three works this paradoxical blending of community and isolation offers Conrad the perfect opportunity to explore what are essentially philosophical questions concerning the existence of evil and the basis and function of morality. The novella is also a study of the dawning of self-consciousness, a self-consciousness that is associated with the 'shadow-line' dividing youth and maturity but one that is also brought about by isolation and responsibility:

In the face of that man [Mr Burns], several years, I judged, older than myself, I became aware of what I had left already behind me—my youth. And that was indeed poor comfort. Youth is a fine thing, a mighty power—as long as one does not think of it. I felt I was becoming self-conscious. (p. 45)

This view of the difference between youth and self-conscious maturity has subtly altered from the one offered in 'Youth', in which the perspective of age is given but the emphasis is on the experience of youth. In *The Shadow-Line*, however, it is human maturity, the self-consciousness of the individual occupied with his life and place in the scheme of things, that is the point of focus. As in 'The Secret Sharer', the young captain suddenly becomes conscious of his identity as something not given, but (at least in part) still under construction. It is not accidental that there are many echoes of *Hamlet*—especially from the great soliloquies—in *The Shadow-Line*. Hamlet's sense of conflicting isolation and responsibility, his shocking perception of the depth of evil in the world, and his subsequent musing upon the place of humanity in a seemingly immoral (or amoral) universe: all of these offer direct analogies to the situation of the young captain in *The Shadow-Line*. The corrupting desperation induced by inaction, along with the constant awareness of the presence of disease, are further factors which bind *The Shadow-Line* to *Hamlet*. In 'The Secret Sharer' the young, isolated captain's insecure sense of identity is objectified through the appearance of a 'secret sharer' or double, who represents what are potential alternative courses of development open to him. Talking to him on one occasion, the captain feels 'as though I had been faced with my own reflection in the depths of a sombre and immense mirror'. In *The Shadow-Line* the captain actually does see himself in a mirror, and he recognizes that this 'other' is 'not exactly a lonely figure', for 'He had his place in a line of men whom he did not know, of whom he had never heard; but who were fashioned by the same influences, whose souls in relation to their humble life's work had no secrets for him' (p. 44). Against his isolation, in other words, he is able to set the community provided by a specific tradition: his captaincy will (like that of the narrator of 'The Secret Sharer') involve a search for identity, but one that is not entirely lonely. He imagines a 'sort of composite soul, the soul of command', whispering to him: ' "You, too!" it seemed to say, "you, too, shall taste of that peace and that unrest in a searching intimacy with your own self . . ." ' (p. 43). Here the isolation and the sense of belonging to a supportive tradition are finely balanced. That 'searching intimacy with your own self' leads the captain to keep a diary in order to be able to commune with himself, much as Conrad had done in the Congo and as his character Razumov, in *Under Western Eyes*, also does when faced with social and moral isolation. For R. L. Mégroz: 'There is no earthly reason for those "notes". They are simply a continuation of the skipper's narrative.'[8] But this is to overlook the thematic importance of the narrator's self-communion: the 'earthly reason' for the notes is, among other things, that they inject a note of psychological realism into the narrative, reminding us that a combination of extreme stress and isolation typically produces forms of talking to oneself.

Like many of Conrad's sea stories, *The Shadow-Line* is the story of a test, a test which enables the protagonist to find the self which, at the start of the tale, he has so conspicuously lost. Like the captain in 'The Secret Sharer' he experiences a sense of horrific inadequacy: 'Now I understand that strange sense of insecurity in my past. I always suspected that I might be no good. And here is proof positive. I am shirking it. I am no good' (p. 88). He is able to pass this test, however, thanks both to his own moral strength and inculcated modes of behaviour and response, and—crucially important—the help of others. The self-sufficiency of 'Youth'—and of youth—has passed. After days drifting in a ship with a diseased crew the captain is ready to accept defeat and

[8] R. L. Mégroz, *Joseph Conrad's Mind and Method* (London: Faber & Faber, 1931), 230.

death, but the cook Ransome confirms, when asked, that he thinks the captain ought to be on deck. The captain responds, and the reader is told that 'The seaman's instinct alone survived whole in my moral dissolution' (p. 89). It is Ransome's catalytic initiative here, along with the accumulated instinct of years as a seaman, that save the captain, just as earlier it was Captain Giles's benevolent prompting that secured his captaincy. The episode clearly demonstrates Conrad's belief in collaborative work as a moral force, a force that builds up habits of application that survive moments of personal despair. Such habits of application enable the individual to transcend egoism and to collaborate creatively with other human beings. It is a familiar Conradian theme, explored in both 'Heart of Darkness' and *Nostromo*.

Christianity and the Supernatural

Ransome is the 'housekeeper of the ship' (p. 85); his name suggests Christ's redemptive role in Christian theology[9] and at several points he is described in Christlike terms:

It was a pleasure to look at him. The man positively had grace. (p. 60)

That man noticed everything, attended to everything, shed comfort around him as he moved. (p. 99)

The association is not forced, and is arguably not even dominant so long as the reader remains concerned only with Ransome as a single character. But the symbolism becomes more apparent when it is noted that Captain Giles is described rather like a benevolent God, who admits that few things are done in town that he cannot see the inside of (p. 32), and who with his 'big, paternal fist' (p. 22), and in his general role as protector, functions as a somewhat more sympathetic divinity than the

[9] Stephen Land's discussion of *The Shadow-Line* cites Matt. 20: 28: 'Even as the Son of man came not to be ministered unto, but to minister, and to give his life a ransom for many.' The verse sums up Ransome's willingness to sacrifice himself for the ship's crew. Jakob Lothe cites both this verse, and also the very similar Mark 10: 45. See Stephen Land, *Conrad and the Paradox of Plot* (London: Macmillan Press, 1984), 216; Jakob Lothe, *Conrad's Narrative Method* (Oxford: Oxford University Press, 1989), 131.

'Deputy-Neptune' Captain Ellis. Along with the young captain the reader must 'wonder what this part of the world would do if you were to leave off looking after it, Captain Giles' (p. 32). Moreover the work contains a good steward and a bad steward, and two straightforwardly evil characters: the dead captain and Hamilton. In a deleted passage from that part of Conrad's first draft of the work that was dictated to a typist (see the Note on the Text, p. xxxv), the antithesis of good and evil represented by these characters is made explicit: 'I could no more forget Captain Giles than Mr. Burns to [*sic*] forget the late Master of the ship and my extraordinary predecessor.'[10] The work is riddled with biblical and Christian allusions: words such as 'sin', 'devil', 'evil spell', 'spiritual strength', 'advent', and 'miracle', recur time and time again, and at one point the captain even feels that he has grown a pair of wings on his shoulders. This has led many critics to doubt Conrad's disavowal in his 'Author's Note' of any supernatural meaning. A very early reviewer noted a central ambiguity: 'The first thing that strikes you is Mr. Conrad's elfin power of mingling the natural with the supernatural . . . all these suggestions, experiences, and episodes might be ascribed equally to natural or supernatural causes. The artist reserves his judgment and we reserve ours.'[11] But in a letter to his agent J. B. Pinker Conrad wrote: 'By the way the title will be: *The Shadow-line* it having a sort of spiritual meaning' (letter dated ?18 March 1915, *Letters*, v. 458). Of course, 'spiritual' is not the same as 'supernatural'. Even so, the repeated allusions to and echoes of both *Hamlet* and Coleridge's 'The Rime of the Ancient Mariner'—both works containing explicitly supernatural elements—suggest that Conrad's disavowal should be treated with a certain caution. Moreover writing to Helen Sanderson Conrad noted: 'Strangely enough, you know, I never either meant or "felt" the supernatural aspect of the story while writing it. It came out somehow and my readers pointed it out to me.'[12]

[10] MS, *The Shadow-Line*, typed section p. 17.

[11] Unsigned review of *The Shadow-Line, Nation*, 24 Mar. 1917. Repr. in Norman Sherry (ed.), *Conrad: The Critical Heritage* (London: Routledge & Kegan Paul, 1973), 307.

[12] Jean-Aubry, *Joseph Conrad: Life and Letters*, ii. 195.

There are, nonetheless, sequences in the novella in which Conrad's claim that he was more concerned with 'the world of the living' than with the supernatural seems fully justified. The following passage counsels a concern with this world rather than the next and even throws doubt on the existence of any supernatural agency that keeps a 'reckoning' of human lives:

'You, too!' it [a 'composite soul of command'] seemed to say, 'you, too, shall taste of that peace and that unrest in a searching intimacy with your own self—obscure as we were and as supreme in the face of all the winds and all the seas, in an immensity that receives no impress, preserves no memories, and keeps no reckoning of lives.' (pp. 43–4)

Conrad certainly contradicted himself when referring to his own religious belief or rather the lack of it. Zdzisław Najder suggests that Conrad adapted his position according to whom he was talking or writing, and that he moved closer to an acceptance of (Catholic) Christian belief around 1921—several years after the writing of *The Shadow-Line*.[13]

The Shadow-Line certainly warns against placing one's confidence in divine or supernatural help at the expense of personal responsibility and hard work, as the captain's mildly ironic description of the medicine chest and its contents suggests.

I went into the spare cabin where the medicine chest was kept to prepare two doses. I opened it full of faith as a man opens a miraculous shrine. (p. 65)

I believed in it [quinine]. I pinned my faith to it. It would save the men, the ship, break the spell by its medicinal virtue, make time of no account, the weather but a passing worry, and, like a magic powder working against mysterious malefices, secure the first passage of my first command against the evil powers of calms and pestilence. (pp. 72–3)

Indeed, Norman Sherry has suggested that Conrad makes explicit use of a genre that has traditional associations with the supernatural.

Conrad transforms the story of his first command . . . to the dimensions of the traditional folk-tale, with the narrator as the traditional

[13] Zdzisław Najder, *Joseph Conrad: A Chronicle* (Cambridge: Cambridge University Press, 1983). See especially pp. 459–60.

folk-hero who is given certain responsibilities, well defined and in a definite tradition, and a task to carry out within the area of these responsibilities. Before him was the state of evil and enchantment which he, by his example, his wisdom, his determination, has to break through. In *The Shadow-Line* all these elements are present—the comparison with the Ancient Mariner, during the calm, is apparent. Even the captain who takes the narrator to Bangkok, in his surliness, is a folk-tale figure, and Captain Ellis is seen specifically as the good fairy.[14]

In the light of Sherry's remark it is ironic that Conrad, commenting on the difficulty he had writing while he was at work on *The Shadow-Line*, noted: 'To sit down and invent fairy tales was impossible then'.[15]

Guilt and Expiation

Like many Conradian heroes, the young captain of *The Shadow-Line* is tormented by guilt, particularly about his failure to check the contents of the medicine chest at the start of the voyage. Critics have argued over the justice of the captain's self-accusations: Stephen Land asserts that the captain is apathetic and 'shows a tendency to sit idle in his cabin when he should be on deck', concluding that he, 'is therefore right in taking upon himself the responsibility for the problems of the ship'.[16] Most critics, however, deem the guilt unwarranted or disproportionate. Daphna Erdinast-Vulcan relates the captain's guilt to his 'need for a coherent frame of reference, for a "truth" to be got out of life', and she argues that '*The Shadow-Line*, no less than 'Heart of Darkness' and *Under Western Eyes*, traces the quest of the protagonist for that "sovereign power" which would author and authorize him'.[17]

[14] *Conrad's Eastern World*, 289.

[15] From letter to Sir Sidney Colvin, 27 Feb. 1917. Jean-Aubry, *Joseph Conrad: Life and Letters*, ii. 182.

[16] Land, *Conrad and the Paradox of Plot*, 214.

[17] Daphna Erdinast-Vulcan, *Joseph Conrad and the Modern Temper* (Oxford: Oxford University Press, 1991), 136, 128.

Some of the captain's guilt is indisputably excessive.

And I felt ashamed of having been passed over by the fever which had been preying on every man's strength but mine, in order that my remorse might be the more bitter, the feeling of unworthiness more poignant, and the sense of responsibility heavier to bear. (pp. 96–7)

If, as T. S. Eliot has suggested, Hamlet's equivocation lacks a convincing 'objective correlative',[18] then so too does the captain's sense of guilt. He received a letter from the doctor letting him know that the medicine chest had been checked, and the concealed theft of the quinine by the previous captain could hardly have been predicted. Besides, the captain appears not to feel any guilt for a potentially graver dereliction of duty: his decision to take a sick man with him as mate when specifically warned against doing so by the doctor, thus putting the ship and the whole crew at risk.

The echoes of Coleridge's 'The Rime of the Ancient Mariner' were picked up by the novella's earliest reviewers[19] (not surprisingly, given that publicity material released by the publisher of the English first edition drew attention to the parallel: see the explanatory note for p. 38). A concern with disproportionate punishment and guilt, along with the presence of Christian motifs, clearly links the two works. This may suggest that Conrad is presenting the reader with symbolic portrayals of original sin, a concept that, by relating the condemnation of all mankind to the transgression of Adam and Eve, necessarily brings to mind the issue of disproportionate effects arising from causes unthinkingly initiated. Perhaps the 'enchanted garden' that one enters once the 'little gate of mere boyishness' is closed behind one (p. 3) can be related to the Garden of Eden, a place of tests and temptations—and disproportionate punishments—as well as of potentialities and pleasures. Moreover the Christian doctrine may itself be interpreted as a religious projection of human horror at the devastating results of apparently minor transgressions or omissions.

[18] T. S. Eliot, 'Hamlet' (1919). Repr. in T. S. Eliot, *Selected Essays* (3rd enlarged edn., repr. London: Faber, 1969), 145.

[19] Gerald Gould, review of *The Shadow-Line, New Statesman*, 31 Mar. 1917. Repr. in Sherry, *Critical Heritage*, 310.

Jakob Lothe has drawn attention to the shift from the narrative 'I' in the novella's first paragraph to 'one' in the second, and the generalizing force of 'one' certainly encourages the reader to read *The Shadow-Line* (a 'confession', as its subtitle has it) as both personal account and general commentary on the human condition.[20]

But the captain's excessive self-blame and guilt may also be read as the result of his recognition of his limitations, the inescapable limitations of any human attempt to control human destiny, rather than as a perception of personal culpability. There is a subtly ironic touch in the narrative when the captain is waiting for the ship's first movement:

> 'Won't she answer the helm at all?' I said irritably to the man whose strong brown hands grasping the spokes of the wheel stood out lighted on the darkness; like a symbol of mankind's claim to the direction of its own fate. (p. 63)

Does mankind have a claim to direct its own fate, or is this the sin of pride, the curse of an Adam who believes God to be irrelevant? *The Shadow-Line* suggests that mankind must not rely on magic or benevolent gods but must attempt to determine its own fate. The captain has good luck in getting his command, bad luck in what he experiences on his first voyage as captain. Human beings cannot avoid the blind operation of fate. But the captain rises above bad luck by dedication and by habits of dogged endurance while characters such as Hamilton, Burns, and the old captain are subdued and overcome by circumstances. An important and characteristically Conradian element here is a suspicion of too much intellectualization, too much thought. At the end of the tale Captain Giles remarks that 'a man should stand up to his bad luck, to his mistakes, to his conscience, and all that sort of thing' (p. 108), and he concludes: 'Precious little rest in life for anybody. Better not think of it.' (Other Conradian heroes whose excessive thinking inhibits right action can be recalled—the Jim of *Lord Jim*, for instance, who imagines things so perfectly that he cannot act at all, until too late when his imaginings are seen in their true

[20] Lothe, *Conrad's Narrative Method*, 120.

and misleading form.) The captain is protected from such Hamlet-like inertia by Ransome—simultaneously a Christ-figure and representative of the demands of tradition and collective labour. But the captain is capable of being protected: he has not caught the disease of idleness to which others such as Hamilton have succumbed. Here the fact of his ship's being a sailing (rather than a steam) ship is crucial. Captain Ellis tells him that others are 'Afraid of the sails. Afraid of a white crew. Too much trouble. Too much work. Too long out here. Easy life and deck-chairs more their mark' (p. 26). A suggestive comparison can be drawn with Jim's experience in an Eastern port where he meets white men in hospital living unreal dream-lives, men who had remained to serve as officers of native-owned ships, and who

> had now a horror of the home service, with its harder conditions, severer view of duty, and the hazard of stormy oceans. They were attuned to the eternal peace of Eastern sky and sea. They loved short passages, good deck-chairs, large native crews, and the distinction of being white. They shuddered at the thought of hard work, and led precariously easy lives, always on the verge of dismissal, always on the verge of engagement, serving Chinamen, Arabs, half-castes—would have served the devil himself had he made it easy enough. They talked everlastingly of turns of luck . . . and in all they said—in their actions, in their looks, in their persons—could be detected the soft spot, the place of decay, the determination to lounge safely through existence.[21]

The passage reveals Conrad's shrewd understanding of how colonial ease could corrupt. By contrast the captain of *The Shadow-Line* has qualities that distinguish him from the men who lead unreal dream-lives: he is not blindly loyal to his previous ship because it is a steamship, and in a deleted passage in the manuscript he admits to 'the nostalgia of a deep-water man for the great open spaces between the continents, for the unbroken horizons of my young days'.[22] For Conrad the sailing ship was the moral educator of her crew; the hard work and direct contact with

[21] Joseph Conrad, *Lord Jim* (Oxford World's Classics, ed. Jacques Berthoud (Oxford: Oxford University Press, 2002), 10). Captain Eliott delivers some similar comments in the fifth section of 'The End of the Tether'.

[22] MS, p. 103.

the elements that had not been rendered unnecessary by labour-saving devices both tested and affirmed a crew's strength and solidarity.[23]

Masculinity and Manhood

There is of course one crucial way in which the 'world' of the nineteenth-century merchant ship is quite unlike the world at large. There are generally no women on board (and where there are, as in 'Youth' and *Chance*, their presence is presented as problematic). If the ship is a moral symbol of our life then it would, at first sight, appear to be a masculine and sexless life. *The Shadow-Line* might seem vulnerable to the feminist criticism that this is a vision of a life rendered ideal because it excludes women. While there is no reason to question Conrad's claim that 'Primarily the aim of this piece of writing was the presentation of certain facts which certainly were associated with the change from youth, care-free and fervent, to the more self-conscious and more poignant period of maturer life', or that the 'facts' to which Conrad alludes involve the attainment of 'manhood' through the acceptance of personal and shared responsibilities and the rejection of the corrupting temptations of 'drifting', 'loafing', and rest, nonetheless a number of other issues are raised in less clearly defined forms by the novella. Among these is one that has a clear association with the passage from boyhood to youth: sexuality. In describing his state of unfocused dissatisfaction at the start of the work, the narrator reports that 'The green sickness of late youth descended on me and carried me off' (p. 5). The application of the term 'green sickness' to a man is unusual; indeed the 1914 edition of the *Everyman Encyclopædia* describes it as a sickness 'peculiar to the female sex, and particularly associated with the period of the attainment of puberty'. The events in Conrad's life on which *The Shadow-Line* is loosely based took place when he

[23] A classic source for such opinions is Conrad's *Memorandum* on the scheme for fitting out a sailing ship for the training of Merchant Service officers. This is reprinted in *Last Essays* (1926).

was 30, but Conrad's son Borys, to whom the work is dedicated, was 17 years old when Conrad started the work, and the same *Everyman Encyclopædia* gives the age for the onset of male puberty as between 14 and 16 years old.

Issues relating to sexuality and the female sex permeate *The Shadow-Line* in unclear but vaguely threatening forms. When the narrator leaves his ship the 'mysogynist' John Nieven says weightily, 'Oh! Aye! I've been thinking it was about time for you to run home and get married to some silly girl' (p. 5). The narrator has already told the reader that 'This is not a marriage story. It wasn't so bad as that with me. My action, rash as it was, had more the character of divorce—almost of desertion' (pp. 3–4). If this implicitly defines the abandoned ship as deserted wife, the association becomes explicit when the narrator's new ship, his first command, comes into the picture. Once the reality of his captaincy dawns on him, the narrator's reaction suggests that indirectly this *is* to be a marriage story:

> A ship! My ship! She was mine, more absolutely mine for possession and care than anything in the world; an object of responsibility and devotion. She was there waiting for me, spellbound, unable to move, to live, to get out into the world (till I came), like an enchanted princess. Her call had come to me as if from the clouds. I had never suspected her existence. I didn't know how she looked, I had barely heard her name, and yet we were indissolubly united for a certain portion of our future, to sink or swim together! (pp. 33–4)

In the following paragraph the hints of sexual passion that attach naturally to the description of the ship as 'she' are if anything stronger, with its description of ships as 'the test of manliness, of temperament, of courage and fidelity—and of love'. In Conrad's manuscript the sequence following the paragraph quoted above is even more explicit. (Conrad's deletions are indicated by square brackets.)

> A great revulsion of feeling made me tremble a little. There was some exultation in it and a queer feeling in my breast. It was like having been married by proxy to a woman one had never seen had never heard of before [*sic*].

> A sudden passion of anxious impatience rushed through my veins, gave me such a sense of the intensity of existence as I have never felt before or since. Every fibre of my being vibrated and it seemed to me that life had come to me only then, that I had been dead only a minute before.
>
> It was then that I discovered how much of seaman [*sic*] I was, in heart, in mind and as it were physically—a man exclusively of sea and ships; the sea the only world that counted and the ships like the women in it, the test of [virility] manliness, of temperamen[t] of courage and fidelity—and of love.[24]

Even in the published version, the narrator remarks while travelling towards his ship: 'I was like a lover looking forward to a meeting'. When he first sees her, he knows that 'like some rare women, she was one of those creatures whose mere existence is enough to awaken an unselfish delight' (p. 41).

But if the new experiences of passion, love, and sexuality of early youth are powerfully celebrated in displaced form with reference to the captain's relationship with his 'command', they are suppressed with regard to actual women. There is no 'silly girl', this is not a (literal) marriage story, and the moral and professional collapse of the narrator's predecessor is explicitly associated with, in the words of Mr Burns, his having got ' "mixed up" with some woman' (p. 48). The woman in question, on the evidence of a photograph discovered by the new captain, was 'an awful, mature, white female with rapacious nostrils and a cheaply ill-omened stare in her enormous eyes'. Here is woman as temptress, 'the last reflection of the world of passion for the fierce soul' of the previous captain. If Conrad was thinking as much of his son Borys as of his youthful self as he wrote, then the work's attitude to heterosexual passion—celebrated in displaced form in the captain's relation to his ship, and rejected in literal form with regard to a spouse or the old captain's 'awful' female—may be understandable. The concerned father would perhaps prefer his immature son to divert his sexual energy away from actual women and towards a career.

However heterosexual passion is only one form of sexuality.

[24] MS, pp. 93–4; material within square brackets deleted or missing in the MS.

Captain Giles's startled reaction when the narrator laughs at his exclamation: 'Oh! these nice boys!', seems to convey more than a hint of a possible homoerotic interpretation (see the explanatory note for p. 12), and this takes us back again to Ransome whose significance is more than mundane or literal. His role approaches the Christlike, as noted earlier, but the captain's perception of him also seems to contain erotic hints suggestive of a homosocial attraction:

> Ransome's eyes gazed steadily into mine. We exchanged smiles. Ransome's a little wistful, as usual, mine no doubt grim enough, to correspond with my secret exasperation. (p. 65)
>
> And then I would know nothing till, some time between seven and eight, I would feel a touch on my shoulder and look up at Ransome's face, with its faint, wistful smile and friendly, grey eyes, as though he were tenderly amused at my slumbers. (p. 81)
>
> Ransome gave me one of his attractive, intelligent, quick glances and went away with the tray. (p. 85)
>
> Here a faint smile altered for an instant the clear, firm design of Ransome's lips. With his serious clear, grey eyes, his serene temperament, he was a priceless man altogether. Soul as firm as the muscles of his body. (p. 93)
>
> 'But, Ransome,' I said. 'I hate the idea of parting with you.' (p. 106)

'The Secret Sharer' (1910), a tale based on the same period of Conrad's life as is *The Shadow-Line*, contains comparable hints of an erotic charge between the captain-narrator and his double, the 'secret sharer' Leggatt. But at the end of that tale, when the captain overcomes his doubts concerning his own ability to command the ship, Leggatt slips overboard to strike out on his own. Equally, Ransome's departure from the ship at the end of *The Shadow-Line* may imply that the captain no longer needs a housekeeper, that he can manage on his own.

> 'I must go,' he broke in. 'I have a right!' He gasped and a look of almost savage determination passed over his face. For an instant he was another being. And I saw under the worth and the comeliness of the man the humble reality of things. Life was a boon to him—this precarious hard life—and he was thoroughly alarmed about himself. (p. 106)

The narrator's comments here signal a shift from a symbolic to a realistic portrayal of the frightened Ransome. While 'comeliness' carries a faint but insistent erotic charge, the captain seems to recognize that he may have superimposed a self-interested perception of Ransome on the man's true 'humble reality'. Throughout *The Shadow-Line* the reader's attention is drawn to the intimate nature of the eye-contact between the serene Ransome and the captain, but as the two men part, the narrator reports: 'I approached him with extended hand. His eyes, not looking at me, had a strained expression' (p. 109). Like Leggatt, he is striking out on his own now that the captain has established his authority—and his manhood. For the captain he has indeed become 'another being'.

Structure and Narrative Technique

The structuring device of a ship's passage can be said to form the narrative backbone of many of Conrad's fictional works, but the shape of this backbone in two works of similar length—Conrad's early *The Nigger of the 'Narcissus'* (1897), and *The Shadow-Line*—is strikingly different. The earlier work opens with the crew being mustered and by the second chapter the voyage is under way. Although there are delays and serious difficulties involving both natural and human forces, the novella ends with the ship docked and the first mate preparing to leave it. The plot and the voyage depicted in it share a matching structure: a beginning, a set of complications, and an end.

The Shadow-Line presents us with a much less conventional and predictable structure—both in terms of its collection of broken or incomplete voyages, and also in terms of its more open-ended, modernist plot. The novella opens with the unnamed narrator leaving his ship after a single voyage for no good reason that he is able to formulate. From this point, more than half of the narrative is occupied with the steward's unsuccessful attempt to prevent the narrator from obtaining his first command. R. L. Mégroz notes with some irritation that 'we might well ask why the story has this shape of a cup with an extra large handle'.[25] *The Shadow-Line* ends with the narrator in (the unnamed but implied) Singapore: the very place where the reader first encountered him. If *The Nigger of the 'Narcissus'* involves a journey from A to B, *The Shadow-Line* plots the narrator's progress from A to . . . A. This is of course only part of the story, for if the narrator's geographical movement is circular, his psychological journey to maturity is anything but that. But unlike the voyage in *The Nigger of the 'Narcissus'*, the voyages (literal and psychological) in *The Shadow-Line* remain incomplete: the closing pages of the work anticipate a continuation of the captain's geographical movement and personal maturation. In technical terms *The Shadow-Line* presents the reader with a characteristically modernist deferral of unambiguous closure.

On board his new ship the narrator-captain learns of the meanderings, loafings-about, and pointless attempts to defy natural forces of his predecessor's final voyage, one which for him ended at the bottom of the ocean. The surviving first mate, furthermore, sails the ship not to Singapore—the logical destination—but, for self-interested reasons, to Bangkok. At the close, while many crew members leave ship sick and Ransome signs off (just as the narrator had done on the first page—albeit for different reasons), it is clear that the young captain will set off with a fresh crew at daybreak the following day. The end of the novella signals a fresh beginning for its narrator. Perhaps a further irony is that while the narrator thinks he has finished with the sea, but then discovers that he is actually starting a new phase in his relationship with it, he also finds that his appointment as captain, an event which was a crucial new beginning for him and which he took to be a matter of routine for Captain Ellis the Harbour-Master, was actually 'the last act' of that person's 'official life'. Thus none of the voyages in *The Shadow-Line* demonstrates that ordered (and shared) sequence of beginning, middle, and unambiguous end that characterized *The Nigger of the 'Narcissus'*. They wind around, stop before they should, continue when the

[25] Mégroz, *Joseph Conrad's Mind and Method*, 202.

reader expects them to end, intersect with other travellers heading in a different direction, and generally exhibit that untidiness that is associated with life rather than with art.

If both works invite the reader to draw a parallel between the literal sea-voyage and the symbolic voyage of life, the later work suggests that Conrad's art and vision now recognized greater complexities in life and fiction. Indeed *The Shadow-Line* displays that more general modernist suspicion of the neat plots (in life and in art) that are mocked by Virginia Woolf in essays such as 'Modern Fiction'. Our lives do not begin at a convenient starting point, proceed along well-signposted paths to a destination, or finish with a sense of inevitable and satisfying closure. My plot does not run parallel to your plot: while I am starting my first command, you are entering a new stage of frustrated hopes; while you are buried at sea, I sail back to port. And even if I sign off my ship unexpectedly just as you did a few short weeks earlier, the significance of these two apparently identical acts is utterly different; they are events within two quite dissimilar plots.[26]

However the unexpected in life can form part of the symmetrical plot of fiction, and if *The Shadow-Line* is modernist in its sudden moves forward and backwards (like *The Nigger of the 'Narcissus'* the novella recounts experiences of literal becalming and storm), this does not mean that it is a carelessly or randomly structured work. On the contrary, it is characterized by intricate patterns of reference, echoes, and repetitions. Conrad's comment in the 'Author's Note' that it is 'in its brevity a fairly complex piece of work' is fully justified. To give one small example: references to bottles of medicine form a small but significant recurrent motif in the work. The dyspeptic Chief Engineer's trust in 'a certain patent medicine in which his own belief was absolute' of which he promises the captain two bottles (p. 6) is echoed both in 'them little bottles' in the steward's room that Captain Giles later mentions to the captain, and also in the bottles of quinine in

[26] Conrad's suspicion of the traditional plot did not begin with *The Shadow-Line*: in a letter to R. B. Cunninghame Graham of 7 Jan. 1898 he commented bitterly: 'You must have a *plot*! If you haven't, every fool reviewer will kick you because there can't be literature without plot' (*Letters*, ii. 5–6).

which the captain himself believes, to which 'I pinned my faith' (p. 72).

In a letter written to Richard Curle in 1923—the year before his own death—Conrad commented on a critic of his work:

My own impression is that what he really meant was that my manner of telling, perfectly devoid of familiarity as between author and reader, aimed essentially at the imtimacy [*sic*] of a personal communication, without any thought for other effects. As a matter of fact, the thought for effects is there all the same (often at the cost of mere directness of narrative) and can be detected in my unconventional grouping and perspective, which are purely temperamental and wherein almost all my 'art' consists. That, I suspect, has been the difficulty the critics felt in classifying it as romantic or realistic. Whereas, as a matter of fact, it is fluid, depending upon grouping (sequence) which shifts, and on the changing lights giving varied effects of perspective.[27]

Although such a *post facto* statement cannot be granted automatic authority, especially from an author notoriously unreliable in comments about his own work, the passage is suggestive, for *The Shadow-Line* does indeed offer the intimacy of a 'personal communication' without 'familiarity'. While the reader may feel very close to the narrator the work does not seem to have, in Keats's phrase, 'a palpable design on us'.

The text is not characterized as a written or spoken narrative,[28] and unlike the 'Marlow' narratives no occasion for its delivery is indicated and no addressees within the fictional world are specified. The framed narratives of 'Youth' and 'Heart of Darkness' encourage the reader to feel part of a community of listeners, listening rather than reading, and listening to an Englishman rather than reading the words of a 'foreigner'. But the way that these earlier works are narrated carries with it a certain

[27] Richard Curle (ed.), *Conrad to a Friend: 150 Selected Letters from Joseph Conrad to Richard Curle* (London: Sampson Low, Marston & Company, 1928), 191, dated 14 July 1923.

[28] Although, as F. R. Leavis points out, the tale is written in prose that 'with all its poetic resourcefulness and its finish, keeps closely in touch with speech'. F. R. Leavis, 'The Shadow-Line', in *Anna Karenina and Other Essays* (London: Chatto & Windus, 1967), 100. The two diary excerpts are, of course, presented as written accounts.

artificiality as well. The narrator speaks for an unnaturally long time, and the narration of inner experiences presents problems (especially when these experiences are only half-conscious or do not involve verbalization). Some variation and flexibility can be provided by means of a retrospective shift from the younger Marlow to the elder Marlow, and from Marlow to the unnamed frame narrator (as in 'Youth', 'Heart of Darkness', and *Chance*) or to the 'privileged man' who receives Marlow's concluding written narrative in *Lord Jim*. Such shifts have to be handled very carefully if they are not to appear artificial or confusing. The lack of an equally precise narrative anchoring in *The Shadow-Line*, however, allows Conrad greater flexibility. There is for example no foundational written source for the narrative (apart from the brief extracts from the diary) such as caused him difficulty in *Under Western Eyes*. As a result, although in both the Marlow narratives and *The Shadow-Line* the reader moves between *observing* and *observing with* the narrator, in the later work this movement is more subtle. It is as if at this stage in his writing career Conrad is able to dispense with the narrative scaffolding he used earlier and to make use of a more free-floating narrative voice. In a technical sense the narrative *represents* events, experiences, states of mind, without making use of a narrator who *expresses* this information within the world of the fiction.[29] This is not, of course, to claim that *The Shadow-Line* is a greater work than, say, 'Heart of Darkness'—it is by common consent a more minor one. But the narrative method employed in each work is thematically appropriate, and the more flexible narrative technique of *The Shadow-Line* suits its more introspective and confessional concern with issues of maturing and memory.

The Shadow-Line was filmed in 1976 by the Polish director Andrzej Wajda, with the part of the narrator (who is portrayed as Conrad himself) played by Marek Kondrat, and that of Ransome by Tom Wilkinson. The film has its defenders, and sequences are undoubtedly powerful—and visually stunning. But many

[29] The distinction between depiction and expression in fictional narratives is discussed at length in Ann Banfield, *Unspeakable Sentences: Narration and Depiction in the Language of Fiction* (London: Routledge, 1982).

commentators—including Wajda himself[30]—have expressed dissatisfaction with the film. One reason for the film's comparative failure may well be that the fluidity of the novella's narrative is lost in Wajda's more or less realist adaptation. Conrad's literary narrative technique is ideally suited to the presentation of those inner experiences undergone by the young captain, while Wajda's filmic narrative is not.[31]

The Shadow-Line is the masterpiece of Conrad's final period. The influential view of Conrad's work suggested by Thomas Moser's *Joseph Conrad: Achievement and Decline*[32] (the decline starting after *Under Western Eyes*) has much to recommend it, for it can be argued that the novels that follow *Under Western Eyes* fail to match the achievement of the earlier great works from *Lord Jim* onwards. It is also the case that the best of Conrad's shorter fiction is written before 1910—with one signal exception: *The Shadow-Line*. If this were Conrad's sole work of fiction it would still be read today.

[30] Wajda has commented: 'When I think about adaptation I recall what Hamlet said to his mother: "I must be cruel, only to be kind". I wasn't cruel enough to *The Shadow-Line*, I pursued the mood, the understatement, the elusive nature of words. And so I created an inarticulate, elusive and uncommunicative film.' The comment is cited in http://www.wajda.pl/en/filmy/film19.html, accessed 26 Apr. 2002.

[31] A more extended discussion of the relationship between Conrad's novella and Wajda's film can be found in Jakob Lothe, *Narrative in Fiction and Film: An Introduction* (Oxford: Oxford University Press, 2000).

[32] Thomas C. Moser, *Joseph Conrad: Achievement and Decline* (Cambridge, Mass.: Harvard University Press, 1957).

NOTE ON THE TEXT

In his 'Author's Note' to *The Shadow-Line* (written in 1920) Conrad reports that he had had the tale 'for a long time in my mind', and he alludes to an earlier, alternative title: *First Command*. As the Introduction points out, a letter dating from 1899 confirms that Conrad is reporting the work's history accurately (see p. xiii). *First Command* is mentioned again in letters written in May and September of 1900 to David Meldrum of Blackwood's publishing house; in the first of these letters (22 May 1900) Conrad says: 'It will turn out to be a record of personal experience purely. Just as well—maybe!' (*Letters*, ii. 273). The next extant mention of the work comes on 3 February 1915 when Conrad comments to his agent J. B. Pinker that he proposes to write a story for the 'Met.'—i.e. the New York *Metropolitan Magazine*:

> It's an old subject something in [the] style of Youth. I've carried it in my head for years under the name of First Command. Whether it will be a 300 pounder or a 500 pounder I cant say. Probably it will run to some length. An early personal experience thing. (*Letters*, v. 441)

In a letter tentatively dated 18 March 1915 by the editors of the *Collected Letters*, Conrad again writes to Pinker saying that he will shortly send 'the first half of the story' to him, and noting 'By the way the title will be: *The Shadow-line* it having a sort of spiritual meaning' (*Letters*, v. 458). Given Conrad's comment in his 'Author's Note' that 'no suggestion of the Supernatural' would have been found in the tale had it been published under the title of *First Command*, the comment is interesting.

Conrad followed his normal path of considerable optimism over the completion date coupled with (again a typical) process of steady upward revision of the work's estimated length. Thus although a letter to Pinker in early May 1915 reports confidently that 'The Shadow-line is nearly finished' (*Letters*, v. 474), it is followed by a succession of others making similar claims, while the date at the end of Conrad's manuscript of the work is actually 15 December 1915.

The first draft of the work was mostly written by hand, but as Conrad explained to John Quinn in a letter dated 24 December 1915:

> The next production is a sort of autobiography—a personal experience—dramatised in the telling—the MS of which amounts to about 200 pp of pen and ink and a few (about 30) or so of type. That was when I could not hold the pen and tried to get on dictating to an operator who came from town for 3 days. From a literary point of view it will be curious for critics to compare my dictated to my written manner of expressing myself. (*Letters*, v. 543)

This MS is the property of The Beinecke Rare Book and Manuscript Library, Yale University, and consists of the following sections.

1. Handwritten sheets numbered 1 to 187. The numbering excludes number 71, and includes duplicate numbers 106, 117, 126, 140 and 146. This gives an actual total of 191 sheets.
2. A single sheet of typescript, numbered 103 and heavily corrected, that appears to be 'genuine typescript', i.e. a sheet typed from corrected MS. This sheet is marked 'End Part Ist'. It appears to be what Conrad called 'rough' (rather than 'clean') typed copy.
3. Typed sheets numbered 1 to 19, 19a, 20 to 23, 23a, 24 to 43, 43a, 44 to 51, two unnumbered sheets, sheets numbered 2a to 19a, and a final unnumbered sheet. The sheet numbered 1 is headed 'Part II'.
4. Handwritten sheets numbered A to Z, AA to SS, and a final sheet labelled 'The Last', a total of 46 sheets.

The MS thus consists of 236 handwritten sheets and 76 typed sheets. The first section of handwritten text immediately prior to the typescript concludes with the words 'I left him to his immobility' (p. 61). The typescript section ends with 'for the rest she must take her chance' (p. 90).

Conrad's normal practice was to have his initial longhand draft 'rough' typed with generous line-spacing to facilitate additions and corrections, and then to have this retyped to produce a 'clean' copy for the printer. In the case of *The Shadow-Line*, Conrad wrote to Quinn: 'The typewritten (first state) copy of that story does not exist. The printers have a *clean*, typed copy which cannot be of any interest to you or anybody else, either from the collector's or the literary point of view' (27 February 1916; *Letters*, v. 559). In a further letter to Quinn dated 10 August 1916 he wrote: 'If you like to have the *corr*^{d} *typed copy* of *Shadow Line* to put in your collection with the MS, I will send it to you' (*Letters*, v. 633), and in a subsequent letter to Eugene F. Saxton (dated 31 August 1916) he commented: 'As to the type-copies of the last 2 stories (Shadow-line & A Warrior's Soul) I can't send them to you because the printers both in Eng^{d} and in US have got them' (*Letters*, v. 648). The two typed versions of the work remain unlocated.

The work was published in the New York *Metropolitan Magazine* in two instalments in September and October 1916. The first of these instalments ends in cliffhanger fashion with the captain watching Mr Burns holding 'a very shining pair of scissors, which he tried before my very eyes to jab at his throat', a sentence which occurs, in slightly modified form, in the English first edition (E1) four paragraphs before the end of Section IV. Thus the two parts of the *Metropolitan* serial do not correspond to the two parts of the MS.

After his negotiations with *Land and Water* ended with a rejection, Pinker placed the work with the *English Review*, in which it appeared in seven instalments running from September 1916 to March 1917. Conrad told Pinker that the editor Austin Harrison's proceedings 'have been exasperating me all along', and that Harrison 'has been doling it out in drops, as if it were poison. No wonder he spoiled its taste altogether'.[1] Nevertheless E1 almost duplicates Harrison's 'poisonous drops': its six sections correspond to the instalments of the *English Review*, with the one difference that E1's section six is divided into two in the periodical, with a seventh section beginning with the words 'Yes. It was a relief' (p. 99).

[1] Letter to Pinker: dated by G. Jean-Aubry to 'early 1917', *Joseph Conrad: Life and Letters*: ii. 181.

Although the work was, as Conrad commented to Pinker, written for the New York *Metropolitan Magazine*, the version published in this journal is very heavily cut; it excludes, for example, the whole important early sequence involving the duplicity of the steward of the Sailor's Home. The cuts may have been made with Conrad's tacit assent for in a letter to Pinker of 18 December 1915 he wrote:

> Now my dear Pinker should L[and] & W[ater] or the Met[ropolitan] raise any question as to its length pray have no hesitation in telling me.
>
> I shan't like to do it—but I can reduce Part I to three pages if necessary. And the full length will always remain for book-form which is the only form that counts—for me. (*Letters*, v. 541)

Book publication in the UK was by J. M. Dent in March 1917, and in the USA by Doubleday-Page in April 1917.

While Pinker was still trying to place the work with an English periodical, Conrad wrote to him about the two 'clean' typed copies: 'As to the copy: of the 2 *clean* sets you may of course show one to Land & Water at once. The other set (for america) please send first to me for a couple of days for another look over. I never get Am*can* proofs as you know' (?17 December 1915; *Letters*, v. 538). Even so, there are relatively few differences between E1 and the American first edition, and generally it can be said that the textual transmission and publication history of *The Shadow-Line* are relatively unproblematic compared to some of Conrad's other works.

The proof corrections to the 1921 Heinemann Collected Edition of the work are not likely to have been made by Conrad. Both the 1921 Heinemann edition and the 1920 American Sun-Dial edition (the basis of the later 1924 Dent Uniform edition, reissued in the late 1940s and early 1950s as the Dent Collected Edition), for example, correct Captain Ellis's comment about the steward from 'he might have taken an overdose out of one of them little bottles he keeps in his room' (p. 32) to 'one of those little bottles'. This is very much in line with the consistent post-authorial gentrification of Conrad's texts practised by the Heinemann copy-editors in particular. But Conrad's version is clearly to be preferred, fixing Captain Ellis's character more memorably through his colloquial use of English. I am indebted to John Stape who kindly examined the corrected page proofs of the Heinemann Collected Edition in the Rosenbach Museum and Library for me. He reports that these are date-stamped from 28 February 1921 to 3 March 1921 and read by 'EG'. The proofs were produced while Conrad was in Corsica and so were almost certainly not read by him.

The present edition reproduces the text of the first English edition, to which a total of only seventeen changes have been made (see below). Where changes to E1 have seemed necessary, readings from Conrad's MS and the *English Review* have been preferred, as these editions have greater authority than either the American first edition or periodical. In the second paragraph, for example, the American serial reads 'One knows well enough that all mankind has streamed that way', which is certainly more idiomatic than E1's 'had streamed that way'. But the version in E1 reflects Conrad's difficulty with English tenses, and the fact that this is also the reading in both the English serial and the American first book edition suggests very strongly that the American serial reading is an unauthorized correction by the American serial copy-editor. (Marlow's comment in 'Heart of Darkness' that women 'live in a world of their own, and there had never been anything like it, and never can be', displays the same characteristically unidiomatic 'had' where normal English usage would require 'has'.)

This does not mean that it can be assumed that variants in the American serial and book editions are always the responsibility of a copy-editor or typesetter, and are always without any authorial status, but it does mean that such variants have to be carefully scrutinized before being adopted. A total of just three minor variants from these editions are incorporated in the present edition. Of these, one is a reading from the American serial. On p. 76, in the one-sentence paragraph reading 'Mr. Burns glared spectrally, but otherwise was wonderfully composed', the word 'was' is missing from all other versions of the text with authorial status. Even though the American serial reading may well not be authorial, the sentence in E1 is clearly unsatisfactory and the American serial provides the only satisfactory reading that might reflect Conrad's wishes. The two variants adopted from the first American book edition are both minor and involve the hyphenation of adjectival compounds.

The base-text for Conrad's 'Author's Note' is the 1921 Heinemann Collected Edition. The first draft of this Note consists of a heavily corrected typescript now in the Beinecke Rare Book and Manuscript Library, Yale University, which concludes with Conrad's handwritten comment: 'The original first draft text, dictated to the machine. One copy (and carbon) embodying corr^{ns} made for printers in Eng^{d} and U.S.'. It is signed with Conrad's initials and dated 'May 1920'. The 'machine' is almost certainly a typewriter rather than a recording device; Conrad regularly refers to the typewriter as 'the machine' in his letters. For example in letters to J. B. Pinker dated 2 January 1908 and 9 February 1916 he writes: 'Please have it run through the machine 1 copy only' (*Letters*, iv. 7), and 'Please have the enclosed 20 pp of the story run through the machine' (*Letters*, v. 552). A comparison of the published version against this typescript has revealed only small variations which may represent Conrad's proof corrections, and accordingly no changes have been made to the published version.

Emendations to the English first edition are listed below with the E1 reading following the square bracket. Where an editorial decision has been made, the precedent is normally the earliest one, except that where a variant occurs in both the English and American periodicals the English is cited since Conrad did not receive proofs for the American publication.

In certain cases E1 is inconsistent with regard to the use of capitals and hyphens, and such inconsistencies have been removed. E1's 'Bankok' has also been altered to 'Bangkok': see the explanatory note for p. 26.

The following symbols are used editorially:

Ed. Editor
MS Beinecke manuscript

Eser	*English Review* serial
Aser	*Metropolitan* serial
A1	first American book edition.

3: 2	*D'autres* Ed.] *D'autre*
3: 2	*miroir* Ed.] *mirroir*
3: 3	*désespoir* Ed.] *déséspoir*
4: 31	love; MS] love,
7: 10	a hotel MS] an hotel
8: 29	of oriental MS] or Oriental
19: 16	world; MS] world:
20: 30	philistinish MS] Philistinish
20: 31	hunted-animal A1] hunted animal
23: 2	that no doubt MS] that, no doubt,
40: 8	temples gorgeous MS] temples, gorgeous
69: 23	fast-ebbing A1] fast ebbing
71: 14	find . . . Eser] find / .
76: 28	was wonderfully Aser] wonderfully
77: 23	North-East Ed.] Nord-East *see also explanatory note*
91: 3	fever-wasted Ed.] fever - wasted
99: 23	sir? Ed.] sir.

SELECT BIBLIOGRAPHY

Biographies and Letters

Baines, Jocelyn, *Joseph Conrad: A Critical Biography* (London: Weidenfeld & Nicolson, 1960).

Batchelor, John, *The Life of Joseph Conrad* (Oxford: Blackwell, 1994).

Ford, Ford Madox, *Joseph Conrad: A Personal Remembrance* (Boston: Little, Brown, 1924; New York: Ecco, 1989).

Jean-Aubry, G., *Joseph Conrad: Life and Letters*, 2 vols. (London: Heinemann, 1927).

Karl, Frederick R., *Joseph Conrad: The Three Lives* (London: Faber, 1979).

—— and Davies, Laurence (eds.), *The Collected Letters of Joseph Conrad* (Cambridge: Cambridge University Press, 1983–).

Knowles, Owen, *A Conrad Chronology* (Basingstoke: Macmillan, 1989).

Najder, Zdzisław, *Conrad's Polish Background* (Oxford: Oxford University Press, 1964).

—— *Joseph Conrad: A Chronicle* (Cambridge: Cambridge University Press, 1983).

Ray, Martin (ed.), *Joseph Conrad: Interviews and Recollections* (Basingstoke: Macmillan, 1990).

Sherry, Norman, *Conrad's Eastern World* (London: Cambridge University Press, 1966).

—— *Conrad's Western World* (London: Cambridge University Press, 1971).

—— *Conrad and His World* (London: Thames & Hudson, 1972).

Stape, J. H., and Knowles, Owen (eds.), *A Portrait in Letters: Correspondence to and about Conrad* (Amsterdam: Rodopi, 1996).

Watts, Cedric, *Joseph Conrad: A Literary Life* (Basingstoke: Macmillan, 1989).

Criticism

Berthoud, Jacques, *Joseph Conrad: The Major Phase* (Cambridge: Cambridge University Press, 1978).

Bradbrook, Muriel, *Joseph Conrad: Poland's English Genius* (Cambridge: Cambridge University Press, 1941).

Daleski, Hillel M., *Joseph Conrad: The Way of Dispossession* (London: Faber, 1977).

Erdinast-Vulcan, Daphna, *Joseph Conrad and the Modern Temper* (Oxford: Oxford University Press, 1991).

Fogel, Aaron, *Coercion to Speak: Conrad's Poetics of Dialogue* (Cambridge, Mass.: Harvard University Press, 1985).

Gordon, John Dozier, *Joseph Conrad: The Making of a Novelist* (Cambridge, Mass.: Harvard University Press, 1940).

Guerard, Albert J., *Conrad the Novelist* (Cambridge, Mass.: Harvard University Press, 1958).

Hampson, Robert, *Joseph Conrad: Betrayal and Identity* (Basingstoke: Macmillan, 1992).

Hawthorn, Jeremy, *Joseph Conrad: Language and Fictional Self-Consciousness* (London: Edward Arnold, 1979).

—— *Joseph Conrad: Narrative Technique and Ideological Commitment* (London: Edward Arnold, 1990).

Knowles, Owen, and Moore, Gene, *The Oxford Reader's Companion to Conrad* (Oxford: Oxford University Press, 2000).

Lothe, Jakob, *Conrad's Narrative Method* (Oxford: Oxford University Press, 1989).

Morf, Gustav, *The Polish Shades and Ghosts of Joseph Conrad* (New York: Astra, 1976).

Moser, Thomas, *Joseph Conrad: Achievement and Decline* (Cambridge, Mass.: Harvard University Press, 1957).

Murfin, Ross (ed.), *Conrad Revisited: Essays for the Eighties* (Tuscaloosa, Ala.: University of Alabama Press, 1985).

Said, Edward, *Joseph Conrad and the Fiction of Autobiography* (Cambridge, Mass.: Harvard University Press, 1966).

Sherry, Norman (ed.), *Conrad: The Critical Heritage* (London: Routledge & Kegan Paul, 1973).

Spittles, Brian, *Joseph Conrad* (Basingstoke: Macmillan, 1992).

Stape, J. H. (ed.), *The Cambridge Companion to Joseph Conrad* (Cambridge: Cambridge University Press, 1996).

Watt, Ian, *Conrad in the Nineteenth Century* (London: Chatto & Windus, 1980).

—— *Essays on Conrad* (Cambridge: Cambridge University Press, 2000).

Watts, Cedric, *A Preface to Conrad* (London: Longman, 1982, 1993).

—— *The Deceptive Text: An Introduction to Covert Plots* (Brighton: Harvester, 1984).

Chapters on Conrad in Critical Texts

Armstrong, Paul B., *The Challenge of Bewilderment: Understanding and Representation in James, Conrad and Ford* (Ithaca, NY: Cornell University Press, 1987).

Graham, Kenneth, *Indirections of the Novel: James, Conrad and Ford* (Cambridge: Cambridge University Press, 1988).

Leavis, F. R., *The Great Tradition: George Eliot, Henry James, Joseph Conrad* (London: Chatto & Windus, 1948).

Levenson, Michael, *A Genealogy of Modernism* (Cambridge: Cambridge University Press, 1984).

—— *Modernism and the Fate of Individuality* (Cambridge: Cambridge University Press, 1991).

White, Allon, *The Uses of Obscurity: The Fiction of Early Modernism* (London: Routledge & Kegan Paul, 1981).

Whiteley, Patrick J., *Knowledge and Experimental Realism in Conrad, Lawrence and Woolf* (Baton Rouge: Louisiana State University Press, 1987).

Periodicals and Bibliographies

There are two important journals devoted to Conrad—*The Conradian* and *Conradiana*—and several scholarly critical bibliographies, though to date no single comprehensive bibliography of Conrad's entire oeuvre. The most helpful selective guide for the student and general reader is Owen Knowles's *An Annotated Critical Bibliography of Joseph Conrad* (Hemel Hempstead: Harvester Wheatsheaf, 1992). Further details of recent scholarship can be found in the *MLA International Bibliography* which is also available on CD-Rom and on-line.

Useful Web Sites

http://lang.nagoya-u.ac.jp/~matsuoka/Conrad.html [offers a large number of hyperlinks to many other specialized Conrad web sites or relevant parts of other web sites]

http://www.library.utoronto.ca/utel/authors/conradj.html [a sound academic complement to the above]

http://members.tripod.com/~JTKNK/ [focuses mainly on the activities of the Joseph Conrad Foundation but also provides access to a number of e-texts]

On The Shadow-Line

Billy, Ted, *A Wilderness of Words: Closure and Disclosure in Conrad's Short Fiction* (Lubbock: Texas Tech University Press, 1997).

Geddes, Gary, *Conrad's Later Novels* (Montreal: McGill-Queen's University Press, 1980).

Kerr, Douglas, 'Conrad and the "Three Ages of Man": *Youth*, *The Shadow-Line*, *The End of the Tether*', *The Conradian* 23/2 (1998), 27–44.

Land, Stephen K., *Conrad and the Paradox of Plot* (London: Macmillan Press, 1984).

Leavis, F. R., 'The Shadow-Line', in *Anna Karenina and Other Essays* (London: Chatto & Windus, 1967).

Thomas, Mark Ellis, 'Doubling and Difference in Conrad: *The Secret Sharer*, *Lord Jim*, and *The Shadow-Line*', *Conradiana* 27/3 (1995), 222–34.

Watt, Ian, 'Story and Idea in Conrad's "The Shadow-Line"', *Critical Quarterly*, 2 (Summer 1960), 133–48.

Further Reading in Oxford World's Classics

Conrad, Joseph, *Chance*, ed. Martin Ray.

—— *Heart of Darkness and Other Tales*, ed. Cedric Watts.

—— *The Lagoon and Other Stories*, ed. William Atkinson.

—— *Lord Jim*, ed. Jacques Berthoud.

—— *Nostromo*, ed. Keith Carabine.

—— *An Outcast of the Islands*, ed. J. H. Stape and Hans van Marle.

—— *The Secret Agent*, ed. Roger Tennant.

—— *Typhoon and Other Tales*, ed. Cedric Watts.

—— *Under Western Eyes*, ed. Jeremy Hawthorn.

—— *Victory*, ed. John Batchelor.

A CHRONOLOGY OF JOSEPH CONRAD

	Life	*Historical and Cultural Background*
The Polish Years: 1857–1873		
1857	3 December: Józef Teodor Konrad Korzeniowski born to Apollo Korzeniowski and Ewa (née Bobrowska) Korzeniowska in Berdyczów (Berdichev), Polish Ukraine	Indian Mutiny; Flaubert, *Madame Bovary* 1859: Darwin, *On the Origin of Species* 1860: Turgenev, *On the Eve*
1861	October: Conrad's father arrested and imprisoned in Warsaw by the Russian authorities for anti-Russian conspiracy	American Civil War begins; emancipation of the serfs in Russia; Dickens, *Great Expectations*
1862	May: Conrad's parents convicted of 'political activities' and exiled to Vologda, Russia; Conrad goes with them	Rise of Bismarck in Prussia; Turgenev, *Fathers and Sons*; Victor Hugo, *Les Misérables*
1863	Exile continues in Chernikhov	Polish insurrection; death of Thackeray
1865	18 April: death of Ewa Korzeniowska	American Civil War ends; Tolstoy, *War and Peace* (1865–72) 1866: Dostoevsky, *Crime and Punishment* 1867: Karl Marx, *Das Kapital*
1868	Korzeniowski permitted to leave Russia; settles with his son in Lwów, Austrian Poland	Dostoevsky, *The Idiot*
1869	February: Conrad and his father move to Cracow; 23 May: death of Apollo Korzeniowski; Conrad's uncle Tadeusz Bobrowski becomes his unofficial guardian	Suez Canal opens; Flaubert, *L'Éducation sentimentale*; Matthew Arnold, *Culture and Anarchy*; J. S. Mill, *The Subjection of Women*
1870–3	Lives in Cracow with his maternal grandmother, Teofila Bobrowska; studies with his tutor, Adam Pulman	Franco-Prussian War; Education Act; death of Dickens 1871: Darwin, *The Descent of Man* 1872: George Eliot, *Middlemarch*
1873	Goes to school in Lwów; May–June: tours Switzerland and N. Italy with his tutor	Death of J. S. Mill, publication of his *Autobiography*

	Life	*Historical and Cultural Background*
The Years at Sea: 1874–1893		
1874	September: leaves for Marseille and takes a position with Delestang et Fils, bankers and shippers; December: Conrad's sea-life begins; sails as passenger in the *Mont-Blanc* to Martinique	First Impressionist Exhibition in Paris; Britain extends influence in Malaya
1875	June–December: sails across the Atlantic as apprentice in the *Mont-Blanc*	Tolstoy, *Anna Karenina* (1875–6)
1876–7	July–February: steward in the *Saint-Antoine* sailing from Marseille to South America	Alexander Graham Bell demonstrates the telephone; Wagner's 'The Ring Cycle' performed in Bayreuth; death of George Sand
1877	March–December: possibly involved in Carlist arms smuggling to Spain	Russia declares war on Turkey; Britain annexes Transvaal
1878	March: apparent suicide attempt; April: sails in British steamer *Mavis*; June: lands in England for first time; July: joins British coastal ship *Skimmer of the Sea* as ordinary seaman; October: departs from London in the *Duke of Sutherland* bound for Australia	The Congress of Berlin; James, *The Europeans*
1879–80	October: arrives back in London; December–January: sails in the *Europa* bound for Australia	British Zulu War; Ibsen, *A Doll's House*; James, *Daisy Miller*; Meredith, *The Egoist*
1880	Takes lodgings in London; May: passes second-mate's examination; August: joins the *Loch Etive* bound for Australia as third mate	Edison develops electric lighting; deaths of George Eliot and Flaubert; Dostoevsky, *The Brothers Karamazov*
1881	September: signs on as second mate in the *Palestine* bound for Bangkok	Tsar Alexander II assassinated; deaths of Dostoevsky and Carlyle

	Life	*Historical and Cultural Background*
1882–3	The *Palestine* repaired in Falmouth but sinks off Sumatra	Married Women's Property Act in Britain; deaths of Darwin and Garibaldi
1883	July: reunited with his uncle Tadeusz Bobrowski at Marienbad; September: signs on as second mate in the *Riversdale* bound for South Africa and Madras, India	Nietzsche, *Also Sprach Zarathustra*; deaths of Turgenev, Wagner, and Marx
1884	June: sails in the *Narcissus* from Bombay, India, to Dunkirk as second mate; December: passes examination as first mate	Berlin Conference (14 nations), 'The Scramble for Africa'; the Fabian Society founded; Mark Twain, *Huckleberry Finn*
1885	April: sails for Calcutta and Singapore aboard the *Tilkhurst* as second mate	Death of General Gordon at Khartoum; Zola, *Germinal*
1886	August: becomes a naturalized British subject; November: gains his Master's Certificate; briefly signs on as second mate in the *Falconhurst*	Stevenson, *Dr. Jekyll and Mr. Hyde*; Nietzsche, *Beyond Good and Evil*
1887–8	Makes four voyages to the Malay Archipelago as first mate; February (1887): sails for Java in the *Highland Forest* but is injured and hospitalized in Singapore; August: joins the *Vidar* in Singapore bound for Borneo; January (1888): appointed Master of the *Otago* at Bangkok and sails for Australia	Queen Victoria's Golden Jubilee; Verdi, *Otello* 1888: Wilhelm II becomes Kaiser; British 'protectorate' over Matabeleland, Sarawak, North Borneo, and Brunei; death of Matthew Arnold
1889	Resigns from the *Otago*; March: released from his status as a Russian subject; June: settles briefly in London and in the autumn begins writing *Almayer's Folly*	London Dock Strike; Cecil Rhodes founds the British South Africa Co.; death of Robert Browning

	Life	*Historical and Cultural Background*
1890	February: returns to Polish Ukraine for the first time in 16 years and visits his uncle Tadeusz Bobrowski; April: in Brussels; appointed by the Société Anonyme Belge pour le Commerce du Haut-Congo; Mid-May: sails for the Congo; August–September: commands the *Roi des Belges* from Stanley Falls to Kinshasa but falls ill with dysentery and malaria; sails for Europe in November	The Partition of Africa; Ibsen, *Hedda Gabler*; William Morris, *News from Nowhere*; J. G. Frazer, *The Golden Bough* (1890–1914)
1891–3	January (1891): back in England; February–March: hospitalized in London; April–May: travels to Champel-les-Bains near Geneva for a cure and returns to London in June, to be temporarily employed by Barr, Moering & Co.; November: joins the *Torrens*, his last sailing ship, and makes four voyages as first mate; meets John Galsworthy and Edward (Ted) Sanderson on one return passage; July (1893): resigns from the *Torrens* but remains on the payroll till mid-October; August–September: visits his uncle in Ukraine; November: briefly joins the *Adowa* at Rouen, France	1891: Hardy, *Tess of the D'Urbervilles*; Wilde, *The Picture of Dorian Gray* 1892: Death of Tennyson 1893: Dvořák, 'New World' Symphony, Verdi, *Falstaff*

	Life	*Historical and Cultural Background*
Conrad the Writer: 1894–1924		
1894	January: leaves the *Adowa* and returns to London; 10 February: Tadeusz Bobrowski dies; April–May: finishes and revises *Almayer's Folly*; August: again at Champel-les-Bains for hydrotherapy; October: meets Edward Garnett; November: meets Jessie George, his future wife	Nicholas II becomes Tsar; 'Dreyfus case' in France; death of Robert Louis Stevenson
1895	April: *Almayer's Folly* published	Crane, *The Red Badge of Courage*; H. G. Wells, *The Time Machine*; death of Engels, Hardy, *Jude the Obscure*
1896	March: *An Outcast of the Islands*; marries Jessie George; they live in Stanford-le-Hope, Essex	Puccini, *La Bohème*; death of William Morris
1897	Meets R. B. Cunninghame Graham, Henry James, and Stephen Crane; March: moves to Ivy Walls, Essex; December: *The Nigger of the 'Narcissus'*	Queen Victoria's Diamond Jubilee; H. G. Wells, *The Invisible Man*
1898	Meets Ford Madox (Hueffer) Ford and H. G. Wells; 15 January: Alfred Borys Conrad born; April: *Tales of Unrest*; October: leases Pent Farm, Postling, Kent	Curies discover radium; Wilde, *The Ballad of Reading Gaol*; H. G. Wells, *The War of the Worlds*
1899	February: finishes 'Heart of Darkness'	Boer War begins
1900	September: J. B. Pinker becomes Conrad's literary agent; October: *Lord Jim*	Russia occupies Manchuria; Freud, *The Interpretation of Dreams*; deaths of Oscar Wilde, Ruskin, Nietzsche, Crane
1901	June: *The Inheritors* (with Ford)	Death of Queen Victoria; Marconi transmits first transatlantic Morse Code signal; Kipling, *Kim*

	Life	*Historical and Cultural Background*
1902	November: *Youth: A Narrative and Two Other Stories* ('Heart of Darkness' and 'The End of the Tether')	Balfour's Education Act; death of Zola; Gorky, *The Lower Depths*
1903	April: *Typhoon and Other Stories* October: *Romance* (with Ford)	Wright brothers' first flight; Shaw, *Man and Superman*; James, *The Ambassadors*; Butler, *The Way of All Flesh*
1904	October: *Nostromo*	Russo-Japanese War; Anglo-French *Entente Cordiale*; Chekhov, *The Cherry Orchard*; James, *The Golden Bowl*; death of Chekhov
1905	January–May: resides in Capri, Italy; June: *One Day More* staged in London	Abortive revolution in Russia; beginning of the Women's Suffrage Movement; Freud, *Three Essays on the Theory of Sexuality*; Debussy, *La Mer*
1906	Meets Arthur Marwood, who becomes a close friend; 2 August: John Conrad born; October: *The Mirror of the Sea: Memories and Impressions*	Anglo-Russian Entente; death of Ibsen; Galsworthy, *The Man of Property*
1907	May–August: at Champel-les-Bains for the children's health; September: *The Secret Agent*; moves to Someries, Luton Hoo, Bedfordshire	Cubist Exhibition in Paris; Shaw, *Major Barbara*
1908	August: *A Set of Six*	Bennett, *The Old Wives' Tale*
1909	February: moves to rented rooms in Aldington, near Hythe, Kent; July: deteriorating relations with Ford culminate in a break	Peary reaches the North Pole; Blériot flies across the Channel; Marinetti launches the Futurist movement
1910	January: quarrels with Pinker; physical and mental breakdown for three months; June: moves to new home, Capel House, Orlestone, Kent	The Union of South Africa created; death of Tolstoy; Post-Impressionist Exhibition, London; E. M. Forster, *Howards End*; Yeats, *The Green Helmet*
1911	October: *Under Western Eyes*	Amundsen reaches the South Pole; the *Blaue Reiter* group formed, Munich
1912	January: *Some Reminiscences* (later retitled *A Personal Record*); October: *'Twixt Land and Sea*	*Titanic* sinks; Schoenberg, *Pierrot Lunaire*; Pound, *Ripostes*; Mann, *Death in Venice*

	Life	*Historical and Cultural Background*
1913	March: meets F. N. Doubleday to discuss a collected edition of his work; September: first meets Bertrand Russell	D. H. Lawrence, *Sons and Lovers*; Proust, *A la recherche du temps perdu* (1913–27); Stravinsky, *The Rite of Spring*
1914	January: *Chance*; July–November: visits Poland with his family and is detained for several weeks by the outbreak of the war	Outbreak of First World War; Polish Legion fights Russians; Joyce, *Dubliners*
1915	February: *Within the Tides*; March: *Victory* (USA; September in UK)	Germans sink the *Lusitania*; Einstein, *General Theory of Relativity*; Pound, *Cathay*; D. H. Lawrence, *The Rainbow*; Ford, *The Good Soldier*
1916	March: sits for a bust by the sculptor Jo Davidson; August: visits Foreign Office and Admiralty to discuss propaganda articles	Battles of Verdun and Somme; Joyce, *A Portrait of the Artist as a Young Man*; death of Henry James
1917	March: *The Shadow-Line*; November: London for a three-month stay	The Russian Revolution; USA enters war; Jung, *The Psychology of the Unconscious*; T. S. Eliot, *Prufrock and Other Observations*; Shaw, *Heartbreak House*
1918	May: first meets G. Jean-Aubry; October: his son Borys hospitalized in Rouen, suffering from shell-shock	Spengler, *The Decline of the West*; death of Wilfred Owen; November, Armistice signed; Polish Republic restored
1919	March: stage version of *Victory* in London; April: *The Arrow of Gold*; May: sells film rights to four of his novels; October: moves to his last home—Oswalds, Bishopsbourne, near Canterbury, Kent	Treaty of Versailles; Keynes, *The Economic Consequences of the Peace*; Walter Gropius founds the *Bauhaus*
1920	May: *The Rescue* (USA; June in UK)	League of Nations founded; Poles rout Russian invaders; D. H. Lawrence, *Women in Love*
1921	February: *Notes on Life and Letters*; The Collected Edition begins publication in England (Heinemann) and the USA (Doubleday)	Irish Free State created; Rutherford and Chadwick work on splitting the atom

	Life	*Historical and Cultural Background*
1922	November: stage version of *The Secret Agent*, London	Mussolini forms fascist government in Italy; BBC founded; T. S. Eliot, *The Waste Land*; Joyce, *Ulysses*; Woolf, *Jacob's Room*
1923	May–June: visits USA; December: *The Rover*	Yeats wins Nobel Prize for Literature
1924	11 January: birth of first grandson, Philip James; March: sits for sculptor Jacob Epstein; May: declines knighthood; 3 August: dies of a heart attack; buried in Canterbury Cemetery; September: *The Nature of a Crime* (with Ford); October: *Laughing Anne & One Day More: Two Plays*; November: Ford, *Joseph Conrad: A Personal Remembrance*	Death of Lenin; E. M. Forster, *A Passage to India*; Mann, *The Magic Mountain*; Shaw, *St. Joan*
1925	January: *Tales of Hearsay*; September: *Suspense* (unfinished)	Fall of Trotsky, rise of Stalin; Shaw wins the Nobel Prize for Literature; Hitler, *Mein Kampf*; Woolf, *Mrs. Dalloway*
1926	March: *Last Essays*	General Strike; Kafka, *The Castle*
1928	June: *The Sisters*	Death of Thomas Hardy; D. H. Lawrence, *Lady Chatterley's Lover*

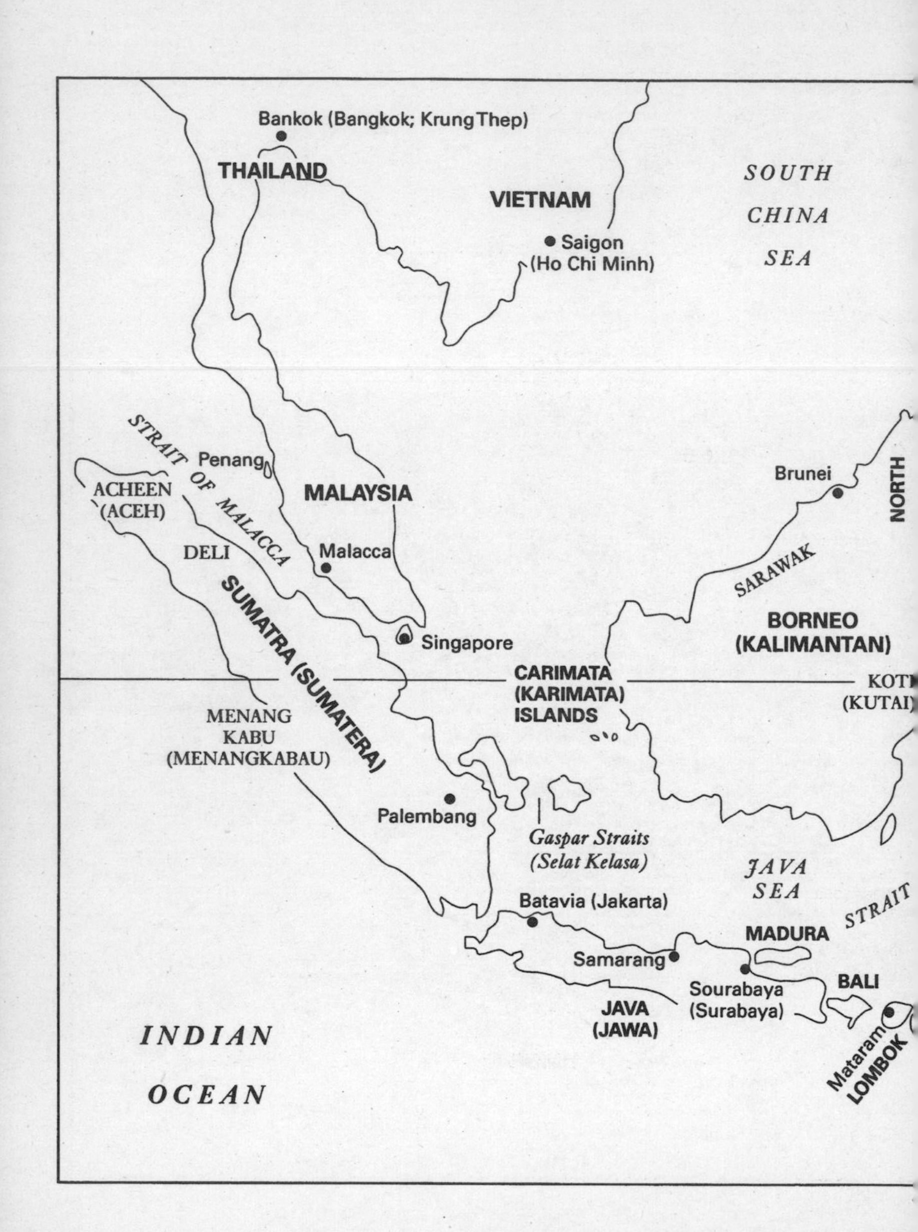
Bankok (Bangkok; Krung Thep)
THAILAND
VIETNAM
Saigon
(Ho Chi Minh)
SOUTH
CHINA
SEA
STRAIT OF MALACCA
Penang
ACHEEN
(ACEH)
MALAYSIA
Brunei
NORTH
DELI
Malacca
SARAWAK
SUMATRA (SUMATERA)
Singapore
BORNEO
(KALIMANTAN)
CARIMATA
(KARIMATA)
ISLANDS
KOTI
(KUTAI)
MENANG
KABU
(MENANGKABAU)
Palembang
Gaspar Straits
(Selat Kelasa)
JAVA
SEA
Batavia (Jakarta)
STRAIT
MADURA
Samarang
Sourabaya
(Surabaya)
BALI
JAVA
(JAWA)
INDIAN
OCEAN
Mataram
LOMBOK

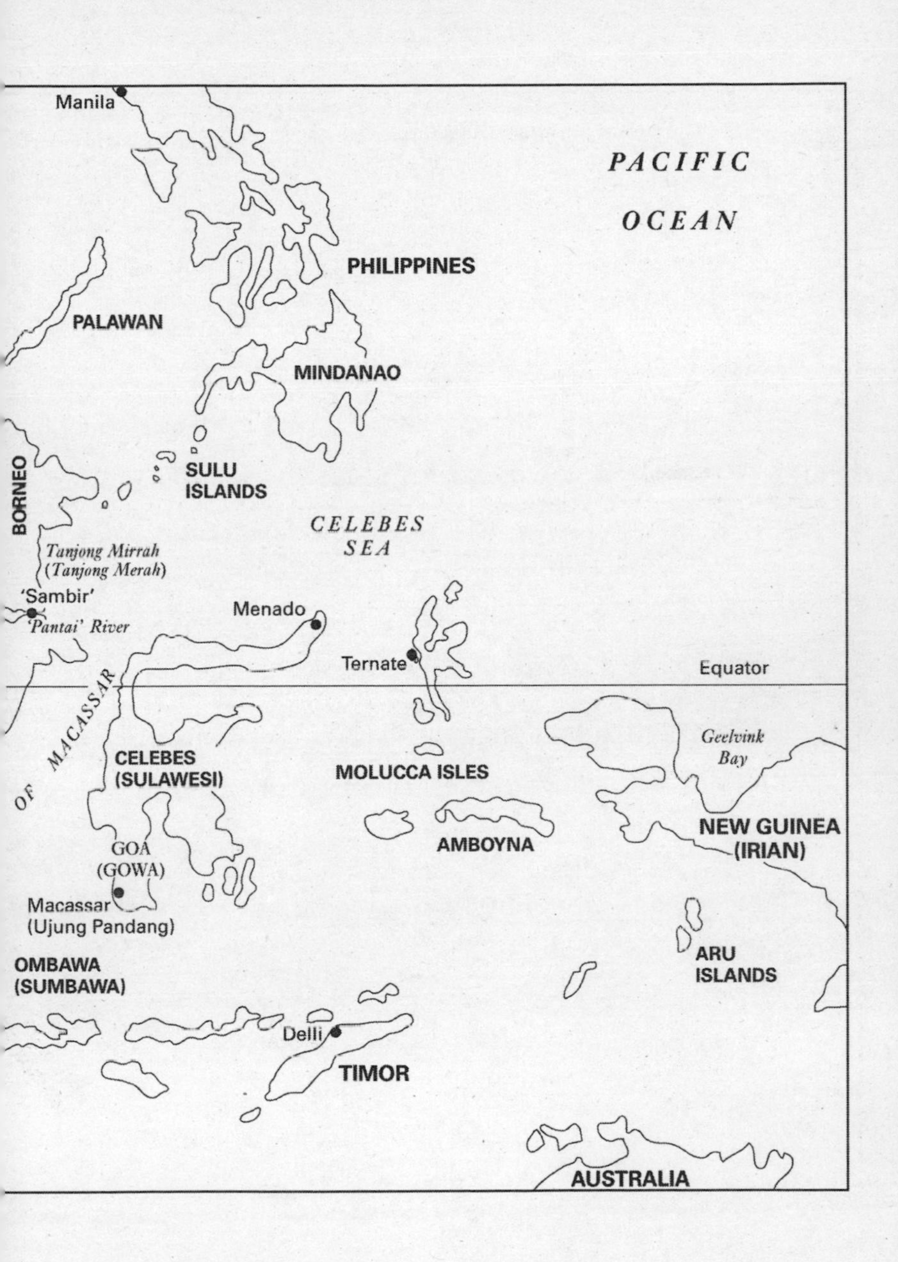
Manila
PACIFIC
OCEAN
PHILIPPINES
PALAWAN
MINDANAO
BORNEO
SULU
ISLANDS
CELEBES
SEA
Tanjong Mirrah
(Tanjong Merah)
'Sambir'
'Pantai' River
Menado
Ternate
Equator
OF MACASSAR
CELEBES
(SULAWESI)
MOLUCCA ISLES
Geelvink
Bay
NEW GUINEA
(IRIAN)
AMBOYNA
GOA
(GOWA)
Macassar
(Ujung Pandang)
ARU
ISLANDS
OMBAWA
(SUMBAWA)
Delli
TIMOR
AUSTRALIA

THE SHADOW-LINE

A Confession

"Worthy of my undying regard"*

TO

BORYS AND ALL OTHERS

WHO LIKE HIMSELF HAVE CROSSED

IN EARLY YOUTH THE SHADOW-LINE

OF THEIR GENERATION

WITH LOVE*

THE SHADOW-LINE

. . . —D'autres fois, calme plat, grand miroir
*De mon désespoir.**

BAUDELAIRE.

I

ONLY the young have such moments. I don't mean the very young. No. The very young have, properly speaking, no moments. It is the privilege of early youth to live in advance of its days in all the beautiful continuity of hope which knows no pauses and no introspection.

One closes behind one the little gate of mere boyishness—and enters an enchanted garden. Its very shades glow with promise. Every turn of the path has its seduction. And it isn't because it is an undiscovered country.* One knows well enough that all mankind had streamed that way. It is the charm of universal experience from which one expects an uncommon or personal sensation—a bit of one's own.

One goes on recognising the landmarks of the predecessors, excited, amused, taking the hard luck and the good luck together—the kicks and the halfpence,* as the saying is—the picturesque common lot that holds so many possibilities for the deserving or perhaps for the lucky. Yes. One goes on. And the time, too, goes on—till one perceives ahead a shadow-line warning one that the region of early youth, too, must be left behind.

This is the period of life in which such moments of which I have spoken are likely to come. What moments? Why, the moments of boredom, of weariness, of dissatisfaction. Rash moments. I mean moments when the still young are inclined to commit rash actions, such as getting married suddenly or else throwing up a job for no reason.

This is not a marriage story. It wasn't so bad as that with me.

My action, rash as it was, had more the character of divorce—almost of desertion. For no reason on which a sensible person could put a finger I threw up my job—chucked my berth—left the ship of which the worst that could be said was that she was a steamship and therefore, perhaps, not entitled to that blind loyalty* which. . . . However, it's no use trying to put a gloss on what even at the time I myself half suspected to be a caprice.

It was in an Eastern port.* She was an Eastern ship, inasmuch as then she belonged to that port. She traded among dark islands on a blue reef-scarred sea, with the Red Ensign over the taffrail and at her masthead a house-flag, also red, but with a green border and with a white crescent* in it. For an Arab owned her, and a Syed at that.* Hence the green border on the flag. He was the head of a great House of Straits Arabs, but as loyal a subject of the complex British Empire as you could find east of the Suez Canal. World politics did not trouble him at all, but he had a great occult power amongst his own people.

It was all one to us who owned the ship. He had to employ white men in the shipping part of his business, and many of those he so employed had never set eyes on him from the first to the last day. I myself saw him but once, quite accidentally on a wharf—an old, dark little man blind in one eye, in a snowy robe and yellow slippers. He was having his hand severely kissed by a crowd of Malay pilgrims to whom he had done some favour, in the way of food and money. His alms-giving, I have heard, was most extensive, covering almost the whole Archipelago.* For isn't it said that "The charitable man is the friend of Allah"?

Excellent (and picturesque) Arab owner, about whom one needed not to trouble one's head, a most excellent Scottish ship—for she was that from the keel up—excellent sea-boat, easy to keep clean, most handy in every way, and if it had not been for her internal propulsion, worthy of any man's love; I cherish to this day a profound respect for her memory. As to the kind of trade she was engaged in and the character of my shipmates, I could not have been happier if I had had the life and the men made to my order by a benevolent Enchanter.

And suddenly I left all this. I left it in that, to us, inconsequential manner in which a bird flies away from a comfortable branch. It was as though all unknowing I had heard a whisper or seen something. Well—perhaps! One day I was perfectly right and the next everything was gone—glamour, flavour, interest, contentment—everything. It was one of these moments, you know. The green sickness of late youth* descended on me and carried me off. Carried me off that ship, I mean.

We were only four white men on board, with a large crew of Kalashes* and two Malay petty officers. The Captain* stared hard as if wondering what ailed me. But he was a sailor, and he, too, had been young at one time. Presently a smile came to lurk under his thick iron-grey moustache, and he observed that, of course, if I felt I must go he couldn't keep me by main force. And it was arranged that I should be paid off the next morning. As I was going out of the chart-room he added suddenly, in a peculiar wistful tone, that he hoped I would find what I was so anxious to go and look for. A soft, cryptic utterance which seemed to reach deeper than any diamond-hard tool could have done. I do believe he understood my case.

But the second engineer* attacked me differently. He was a sturdy young Scot, with a smooth face and light eyes. His honest red countenance emerged out of the engine-room companion and then the whole robust man, with shirt sleeves turned up, wiping slowly the massive fore-arms with a lump of cotton-waste. And his light eyes expressed bitter distaste, as though our friendship had turned to ashes. He said weightily: "Oh! Aye! I've been thinking it was about time for you to run away home and get married to some silly girl."

It was tacitly understood in the port that John Nieven* was a fierce mysogynist; and the absurd character of the sally convinced me that he meant to be nasty—very nasty—had meant to say the most crushing thing he could think of. My laugh sounded deprecatory. Nobody but a friend could be so angry as that. I became a little crestfallen. Our chief engineer also took a characteristic view of my action, but in a kindlier spirit.

He was young, too, but very thin, and with a mist of fluffy brown beard all round his haggard face. All day long, at sea or in harbour, he could be seen walking hastily up and down the after-deck, wearing an intense, spiritually rapt expression, which was caused by a perpetual consciousness of unpleasant physical sensations in his internal economy. For he was a confirmed dyspeptic. His view of my case was very simple. He said it was nothing but deranged liver. Of course! He suggested I should stay for another trip and meantime dose myself with a certain patent medicine in which his own belief was absolute. "I'll tell you what I'll do. I'll buy you two bottles, out of my own pocket. There. I can't say fairer than that, can I?"

I believe he would* have perpetrated the atrocity (or generosity) at the merest sign of weakening on my part. By that time, however, I was more discontented, disgusted, and dogged than ever. The past eighteen months, so full of new and varied experience, appeared a dreary, prosaic waste of days. I felt—how shall I express it?—that there was no truth to be got out of them.

What truth? I should have been hard put to it to explain. Probably, if pressed, I would have burst into tears simply. I was young enough for that.

Next day the Captain and I transacted our business in the Harbour Office. It was a lofty, big, cool, white room, where the screened light of day glowed serenely. Everybody in it—the officials, the public—were in white. Only the heavy polished desks gleamed darkly in a central avenue, and some papers lying on them were blue. Enormous punkahs sent from on high a gentle draught through that immaculate interior and upon our perspiring heads.

The official behind the desk we approached grinned amiably and kept it up till, in answer to his perfunctory question, "Sign off and on again?" my Captain answered, "No! Signing off for good." And then his grin vanished in sudden solemnity. He did not look at me again till he handed me my papers with a sorrowful expression, as if they had been my passports for Hades.

While I was putting them away he murmured some question to the Captain, and I heard the latter answer good-humouredly:

"No. He leaves us to go home."

"Oh!" the other exclaimed, nodding mournfully over my sad condition.

I didn't know him outside the official building, but he leaned forward over the desk to shake hands with me, compassionately, as one would with some poor devil going out to be hanged; and I am afraid I performed my part ungraciously, in the hardened manner of an impenitent criminal.

No homeward-bound mail-boat was due for three or four days. Being now a man without a ship, and having for a time broken my connection with the sea—become, in fact, a mere potential passenger—it would have been more appropriate perhaps if I had gone to stay at a hotel. There it was, too, within a stone's throw of the Harbour Office, low, but somehow palatial, displaying its white, pillared pavilions surrounded by trim grass plots. I would have felt a passenger indeed in there! I gave it a hostile glance and directed my steps towards the Officers' Sailors' Home.*

I walked in the sunshine, disregarding it, and in the shade of the big trees on the esplanade without enjoying it. The heat of the tropical East descended through the leafy boughs, enveloping my thinly-clad body, clinging to my rebellious discontent, as if to rob it of its freedom.

The Officers' Home was a large bungalow with a wide verandah and a curiously suburban-looking little garden of bushes and a few trees between it and the street. That institution partook somewhat of the character of a residential club, but with a slightly Governmental flavour about it, because it was administered by the Harbour Office. Its manager was officially styled Chief Steward.* He was an unhappy, wizened little man, who if put into a jockey's rig would have looked the part to perfection. But it was obvious that at some time or other in his life, in some capacity or other, he had been connected with the sea. Possibly in the comprehensive capacity of a failure.

I should have thought his employment a very easy one, but he used to affirm for some reason or other that his job would be the death of him some day. It was rather mysterious. Perhaps everything naturally was too much trouble for him. He certainly seemed to hate having people in the house.

On entering it I thought he must be feeling pleased. It was as still as a tomb. I could see no one in the living rooms; and the verandah, too, was empty, except for a man at the far end dozing prone in a long chair. At the noise of my footsteps he opened one horribly fish-like eye. He was a stranger to me. I retreated from there, and, crossing the dining-room—a very bare apartment with a motionless punkah hanging over the centre table—I knocked at a door labelled in black letters: "Chief Steward."

The answer to my knock being a vexed and doleful plaint: "Oh, dear! Oh, dear! What is it now?" I went in at once.

It was a strange room to find in the tropics. Twilight and stuffiness reigned in there. The fellow had hung enormously ample, dusty, cheap lace curtains over his windows, which were shut. Piles of cardboard boxes, such as milliners and dressmakers use in Europe, cumbered the corners; and by some means he had procured for himself the sort of furniture that might have come out of a respectable parlour in the East End of London*—a horsehair sofa, arm-chairs of the same. I glimpsed grimy antimacassars scattered over that horrid upholstery, which was awe-inspiring, insomuch that one could not guess what mysterious accident, need, or fancy had collected it there. Its owner had taken off his tunic, and in white trousers and a thin short-sleeved singlet prowled behind the chair-backs nursing his meagre elbows.

An exclamation of dismay escaped him when he heard that I had come for a stay; but he could not deny that there were plenty of vacant rooms.

"Very well. Can you give me the one I had before?"

He emitted a faint moan from behind a pile of cardboard boxes on the table, which might have contained gloves or handkerchiefs or neckties. I wonder what the fellow did keep in them? There was a smell of decaying coral, of oriental dust, of zoological specimens in that den of his. I could only see the top of his head and his unhappy eyes levelled at me over the barrier.

"It's only for a couple of days," I said, intending to cheer him up.

"Perhaps you would like to pay in advance?" he suggested eagerly.

"Certainly not!" I burst out directly I could speak. "Never heard of such a thing! This is the most infernal cheek. . . ."

He had seized his head in both hands—a gesture of despair which checked my indignation.

"Oh, dear! Oh, dear! Don't fly out like this. I am asking everybody."

"I don't believe it," I said bluntly.

"Well, I am going to. And if you gentlemen all agreed to pay in advance I could make Hamilton* pay up too. He's always turning up ashore dead broke, and even when he has some money he won't settle his bills. I don't know what to do with him. He swears at me and tells me I can't chuck a white man out into the street here. So if you only would. . . ."

I was amazed. Incredulous too. I suspected the fellow of gratuitous impertinence. I told him with marked emphasis that I would see him and Hamilton hanged first, and requested him to conduct me to my room with no more of his nonsense. He produced then a key from somewhere and led the way out of his lair, giving me a vicious sidelong look in passing.

"Any one I know staying here?" I asked him before he left my room.

He had recovered his usual pained impatient tone, and said that Captain Giles* was there, back from a Solo Sea trip. Two other guests were staying also. He paused. And, of course, Hamilton, he added.

"Oh, yes! Hamilton," I said, and the miserable creature took himself off with a final groan.

His impudence still rankled when I came into the dining-room at tiffin time. He was there on duty overlooking the Chinamen servants. The tiffin was laid on one end only of the long table, and the punkah was stirring the hot air lazily—mostly above a barren waste of polished wood.

We were four around the cloth. The dozing stranger from the chair was one. Both his eyes were partly opened now, but they did not seem to see anything. He was supine. The dignified person next him, with short side whiskers and a carefully scraped chin, was, of course, Hamilton. I have never seen any one so full of dignity for the station in life Providence had been pleased to place him in. I had been told that he regarded me as a rank outsider.* He raised not only his eyes, but his eyebrows as well, at the sound I made pulling back my chair.

Captain Giles was at the head of the table. I exchanged a few words of greeting with him and sat down on his left. Stout and pale, with a great shiny dome of a bald forehead and prominent brown eyes, he might have been anything but a seaman. You would not have been surprised to learn that he was an architect. To me (I know how absurd it is) to me he looked like a church-warden. He had the appearance of a man from whom you would expect sound advice, moral sentiments, with perhaps a platitude or two thrown in on occasion, not from a desire to dazzle, but from honest conviction.

Though very well known and appreciated in the shipping world, he had no regular employment. He did not want it. He had his own peculiar position. He was an expert. An expert in—how shall I say it?—in intricate navigation. He was supposed to know more about remote and imperfectly charted parts of the Archipelago than any man living. His brain must have been a perfect warehouse of reefs, positions, bearings, images of headlands, shapes of obscure coasts, aspects of innumerable islands, desert and otherwise. Any ship, for instance, bound on a trip to Palawan or somewhere that way would have Captain Giles on board, either in temporary command or "to assist the master."* It was said that he had a retaining fee from a wealthy firm of Chinese steamship owners, in view of such services. Besides, he was always ready to relieve any man who wished to take a spell ashore for a time. No owner was ever known to object to an arrangement of that sort. For it seemed to be the established opinion at the port that Captain Giles was as good as the best, if not a little better. But in Hamilton's view he was an "outsider." I believe that for Hamilton the generalisation "outsider" covered the whole lot of us; though I suppose that he made some distinctions in his mind.

I didn't try to make conversation with Captain Giles, whom I had not seen more than twice in my life. But, of course, he knew who I was. After a while, inclining his big shiny head my way, he addressed me first in his friendly fashion. He presumed from seeing me there, he said, that I had come ashore for a couple of days' leave.

He was a low-voiced man. I spoke a little louder, saying that: No—I had left the ship for good.

"A free man for a bit," was his comment.

"I suppose I may call myself that—since eleven o'clock," I said.

Hamilton had stopped eating at the sound of our voices. He laid down his knife and fork gently, got up, and muttering something about "this infernal heat cutting one's appetite," went out of the room. Almost immediately we heard him leave the house down the verandah steps.

On this Captain Giles remarked easily that the fellow had no doubt gone off to look after my old job. The Chief Steward, who had been leaning against the wall, brought his face of an unhappy goat nearer to the table and addressed us dolefully. His object was to unburden himself of his eternal grievance against Hamilton. The man kept him in hot water with the Harbour Office as to the state of his accounts. He wished to goodness he would get my job, though in truth what would it be? Temporary relief at best.

I said: "You needn't worry. He won't get my job. My successor is on board already."

He was surprised, and I believe his face fell a little at the news. Captain Giles gave a soft laugh. We got up and went out on the verandah, leaving the supine stranger to be dealt with by the Chinamen. The last thing I saw they had put a plate with a slice of pine-apple on it before him and stood back to watch what would happen. But the experiment seemed a failure. He sat insensible.

It was imparted to me in a low voice by Captain Giles that this was an officer of some Rajah's yacht* which had come into our port to be dry-docked. Must have been "seeing life" last night, he added, wrinkling his nose in an intimate, confidential way which pleased me vastly. For Captain Giles had prestige. He was credited with wonderful adventures and with some mysterious tragedy in his life. And no man had a word to say against him. He continued:

"I remember him first coming ashore here some years ago. Seems only the other day. He was a nice boy. Oh! these nice boys!"

I could not help laughing aloud. He looked startled, then joined in the laugh. "No! No! I didn't mean that,"* he cried. "What I meant is that some of them do go soft mighty quick out here."

Jocularly I suggested the beastly heat as the first cause. But Captain Giles disclosed himself possessed of a deeper philosophy. Things out East were made easy for white men. That was all right. The difficulty was to go on keeping white, and some of these nice boys did not know how. He gave me a searching look, and in a benevolent, heavy-uncle manner asked point blank:

"Why did you throw up your berth?"

I became angry all of a sudden; for you can understand how exasperating such a question was to a man who didn't know. I said to myself that I ought to shut up that moralist; and to him aloud I said with challenging politeness:

"Why . . . ? Do you disapprove?"

He was too disconcerted to do more than mutter confusedly: "I! . . . In a general way . . ." and then gave me up. But he retired in good order, under the cover of a heavily humorous remark that he, too, was getting soft, and that this was his time for taking his little siesta—when he was on shore. "Very bad habit. Very bad habit."

The simplicity of the man would have disarmed a touchiness even more youthful than mine. So when next day at tiffin he bent his head towards me and said that he had met my late Captain last evening, adding in an undertone: "He's very sorry you left. He had never had a mate that suited him so well," I answered him earnestly, without any affectation, that I certainly hadn't been so comfortable in any ship or with any commander in all my sea-going days.

"Well—then," he murmured.

"Haven't you heard, Captain Giles, that I intend to go home?"

"Yes," he said benevolently. "I have heard that sort of thing so often before."

"What of that?" I cried. I thought he was the most dull, unimaginative man I had ever met. I don't know what more I would have said, but the much-belated Hamilton came in just then and took his usual seat. So I dropped into a mumble.

"Anyhow, you shall see it done this time."

Hamilton, beautifully shaved, gave Captain Giles a curt nod, but didn't even condescend to raise his eyebrows at me; and when he spoke it was only to tell the Chief Steward that the food on his plate wasn't fit to be set before a gentleman. The individual addressed seemed much too unhappy to groan. He only cast his eyes up to the punkah and that was all.

Captain Giles and I got up from the table, and the stranger next to Hamilton followed our example, manœuvring himself to his feet with difficulty. He, poor fellow, not because he was hungry but I verily believe only to recover his self-respect, had tried to put some of that unworthy food into his mouth. But after dropping his fork twice and generally making a failure of it, he had sat still with an air of intense mortification combined with a ghastly glazed stare. Both Giles and I had avoided looking his way at table.

On the verandah he stopped short on purpose to address to us anxiously a long remark which I failed to understand completely. It sounded like some horrible unknown language. But when Captain Giles, after only an instant for reflection, answered him with homely friendliness, "Aye, to be sure. You are right there," he appeared very much gratified indeed, and went away (pretty straight too) to seek a distant long chair.

"What was he trying to say?" I asked with disgust.

"I don't know. Mustn't be down too much on a fellow. He's feeling pretty wretched, you may be sure; and tomorrow he'll feel worse yet."

Judging by the man's appearance it seemed impossible. I wondered what sort of complicated debauch had reduced him to that unspeakable condition. Captain Giles' benevolence was spoiled by a curious air of complacency which I disliked. I said with a little laugh:

"Well, he will have you to look after him."

He made a deprecatory gesture, sat down, and took up a paper. I did the same. The papers were old and uninteresting, filled up mostly with dreary stereotyped descriptions of Queen Victoria's first jubilee celebrations.* Probably we should have quickly fallen into a tropical afternoon doze if it had not been for Hamilton's voice raised in the dining-room. He was finishing his tiffin there. The big double doors stood wide open permanently, and he could not have had any idea how near to the doorway our chairs were placed. He was heard in a loud, supercilious tone answering some statement ventured by the Chief Steward.

"I am not going to be rushed into anything. They will be glad enough to get a gentleman I imagine. There is no hurry."

A loud whispering from the steward succeeded and then again Hamilton was heard with even intenser scorn.

"What? That young ass who fancies himself for having been chief mate with Kent so long? . . . Preposterous."

Giles and I looked at each other. Kent being the name of my late commander, Captain Giles' whisper, "He's talking of you," seemed to me sheer waste of breath. The Chief Steward must have stuck to his point whatever it was, because Hamilton was heard again more supercilious, if possible, and also very emphatic:

"Rubbish, my good man! One doesn't *compete* with a rank outsider like that. There's plenty of time."

Then there was pushing of chairs, footsteps in the next room, and plaintive expostulations from the Steward, who was pursuing Hamilton, even out of doors through the main entrance.

"That's a very insulting sort of man," remarked Captain Giles—superfluously, I thought. "Very insulting. You haven't offended him in some way, have you?"

"Never spoke to him in my life," I said grumpily. "Can't imagine what he means by competing. He has been trying for my job after I left—and didn't get it. But that isn't exactly competition."

Captain Giles balanced his big benevolent head thoughtfully. "He didn't get it," he repeated very slowly. "No, not likely either, with Kent. Kent is no end sorry you left him. He gives you the name of a good seaman too."

I flung away the paper I was still holding. I sat up, I slapped the table with my open palm. I wanted to know why he would keep harping on that, my absolutely private affair. It was exasperating, really.

Captain Giles silenced me by the perfect equanimity of his gaze. "Nothing to be annoyed about," he murmured reasonably, with an evident desire to soothe the childish irritation he had aroused. And he was really a man of an appearance so inoffensive that I tried to explain myself as much as I could. I told him that I did not want to hear any more about what was past and gone. It had been very nice while it lasted, but now it was done with I preferred not to talk about it or even think about it. I had made up my mind to go home.

He listened to the whole tirade in a particular, lending-the-ear attitude, as if trying to detect a false note in it somewhere; then straightened himself up and appeared to ponder sagaciously over the matter.

"Yes. You told me you meant to go home. Anything in view there?"

Instead of telling him that it was none of his business I said sullenly:

"Nothing that I know of."

I had indeed considered that rather blank side of the situation I had created for myself by leaving suddenly my very satisfactory employment. And I was not very pleased with it. I had it on the tip of my tongue to say that common sense had nothing to do with my action, and that therefore it didn't deserve the interest Captain Giles seemed to be taking in it. But he was puffing at a short wooden pipe now, and looked so guileless, dense, and commonplace, that it seemed hardly worth while to puzzle him either with truth or sarcasm.

He blew a cloud of smoke, then surprised me by a very abrupt: "Paid your passage money yet?"

Overcome by the shameless pertinacity of a man to whom it was rather difficult to be rude, I replied with exaggerated meekness that I had not done so yet. I thought there would be plenty of time to do that tomorrow.

And I was about to turn away, withdrawing my privacy from his fatuous, objectless attempts to test what sort of stuff it was made of, when he laid down his pipe in an extremely significant manner, you know, as if a critical moment had come, and leaned sideways over the table between us.

"Oh! You haven't yet!" He dropped his voice mysteriously. "Well, then I think you ought to know that there's something going on here."

I had never in my life felt more detached from all earthly goings on. Freed from the sea for a time, I preserved the sailor's consciousness of complete independence from all land affairs. How could they concern me? I gazed at Captain Giles' animation with scorn rather than with curiosity.

To his obviously preparatory question whether our steward had spoken to me that day I said he hadn't. And what's more he would have had precious little encouragement if he had tried to. I didn't want the fellow to speak to me at all.

Unrebuked by my petulance, Captain Giles, with an air of immense sagacity, began to tell me a minute tale about a Harbour Office peon. It was absolutely pointless. A peon was seen walking that morning on the verandah with a letter in his hand. It was in an official envelope. As the habit of these fellows is, he had shown it to the first white man he came across. That man was our friend in the arm-chair. He, as I knew, was not in a state to interest himself in any sublunary matters. He could only wave the peon away. The peon then wandered on along the verandah and came upon Captain Giles, who was there by an extraordinary chance. . . .

At this point he stopped with a profound look. The letter, he continued, was addressed to the Chief Steward. Now what could Captain Ellis, the Master Attendant, want to write to the Steward for? The fellow went every morning, anyhow, to the Harbour Office with his report, for orders or what not. He hadn't been back more than an hour before there was an office peon chasing him with a note. Now what was that for?

And he began to speculate. It was not for this—and it could not be for that. As to that other thing it was unthinkable.

The fatuousness of all this made me stare. If the man had not been somehow a sympathetic personality I would have resented it like an insult. As it was, I felt only sorry for him. Something remarkably earnest in his gaze prevented me from laughing in his face. Neither did I yawn at him. I just stared.

His tone became a shade more mysterious. Directly the fellow (meaning the Steward) got that note he rushed for his hat and bolted out of the house. But it wasn't because the note called him to the Harbour Office. He didn't go there. He was not absent long enough for that. He came darting back in no time, flung his hat away, and raced about the dining-room moaning and slapping his forehead. All these exciting facts and manifestations had been observed by Captain Giles. He had, it seems, been meditating upon them ever since.

I began to pity him profoundly. And in a tone which I tried to make as little sarcastic as possible I said that I was glad he had found something to occupy his morning hours.

With his disarming simplicity he made me observe, as if it were a matter of some consequence, how strange it was that he should have spent the morning indoors at all. He generally was out before tiffin, visiting various offices, seeing his friends in the harbour, and so on. He had felt out of sorts somewhat on rising. Nothing much. Just enough to make him feel lazy.

All this with a sustained, holding stare which, in conjunction with the general inanity of the discourse, conveyed the impression of mild, dreary lunacy.* And when he hitched his chair a little and dropped his voice to the low note of mystery, it flashed upon me that high professional reputation was not necessarily a guarantee of sound mind.

It never occurred to me then that I didn't know in what soundness of mind exactly consisted and what a delicate and, upon the whole, unimportant matter it was. With some idea of not hurting his feelings I blinked at him in an interested manner. But when he proceeded to ask me mysteriously whether I remembered what had passed just now between that Steward of ours and "that man Hamilton," I only grunted sour assent and turned away my head.

"Aye. But do you remember every word?" he insisted tactfully.

"I don't know. It's none of my business," I snapped out, consigning, moreover, the Steward and Hamilton aloud to eternal perdition.

I meant to be very energetic and final, but Captain Giles continued to gaze at me thoughtfully. Nothing could stop him. He went on to point out that my personality was involved in that conversation. When I tried to preserve the semblance of unconcern he became positively cruel. I heard what the man had said? Yes? What did I think of it then?—he wanted to know.

Captain Giles' appearance excluding the suspicion of mere sly malice, I came to the conclusion that he was simply the most tactless idiot on earth. I almost despised myself for the weakness of attempting to enlighten his common understanding. I started to explain that I did not think anything whatever. Hamilton was not worth a thought. What such an offensive loafer . . .—"Aye! that he is," interjected Captain Giles—. . . thought or said was below any decent man's contempt, and I did not propose to take the slightest notice of it.

This attitude seemed to me so simple and obvious that I was really astonished at Giles giving no sign of assent. Such perfect stupidity was almost interesting.

"What would you like me to do?" I asked laughing. "I can't start a row with him because of the opinion he has formed of me. Of course, I've heard of the contemptuous way he alludes to me. But he doesn't intrude his contempt on my notice. He has never expressed it in my hearing. For even just now he didn't know we could hear him. I should only make myself ridiculous."

That hopeless Giles went on puffing at his pipe moodily. All at once his face cleared, and he spoke.

"You missed my point."

"Have I? I am very glad to hear it," I said.

With increasing animation he stated again that I had missed his point. Entirely. And in a tone of growing self-conscious complacency he told me that few things escaped his attention, and he was rather used to think them out, and generally from his experience of life and men arrived at the right conclusion.

This bit of self-praise, of course, fitted excellently the laborious inanity of the whole conversation. The whole thing strengthened in me that obscure feeling of life being but a waste of days, which, half-unconsciously, had driven me out of a comfortable berth, away from men I liked, to flee from the menace of emptiness . . . and to find inanity at the first turn. Here was a man of recognised character and achievement disclosed as an absurd and dreary chatterer. And it was probably like this everywhere—from east to west, from the bottom to the top of the social scale.

A great discouragement fell on me. A spiritual drowsiness. Giles' voice was going on complacently; the very voice of the universal hollow conceit. And I was no longer angry with it. There was nothing original, nothing new, startling, informing to expect from the world; no opportunities to find out something about oneself, no wisdom to acquire, no fun to enjoy. Everything was stupid and overrated, even as Captain Giles was. So be it.

The name of Hamilton suddenly caught my ear and roused me up.

"I thought we had done with him," I said, with the greatest possible distaste.

"Yes. But considering what we happened to hear just now I think you ought to do it."

"Ought to do it?" I sat up bewildered. "Do what?"

Captain Giles confronted me very much surprised.

"Why! Do what I have been advising you to try. You go and ask the Steward what was there in that letter from the Harbour Office. Ask him straight out."

I remained speechless for a time. Here was something unexpected and original enough to be altogether incomprehensible. I murmured, astounded.

"But I thought it was Hamilton that you . . ."

"Exactly. Don't you let him. You do what I tell you. You tackle that Steward. You'll make him jump, I bet," insisted Captain Giles, waving his smouldering pipe impressively at me. Then he took three rapid puffs at it.

His aspect of triumphant acuteness was indescribable. Yet the man remained a strangely sympathetic creature. Benevolence radiated from him ridiculously, mildly, impressively. It was irritating, too. But I pointed out coldly, as one who deals with the incomprehensible, that I didn't see any reason to expose myself to a snub from the fellow. He was a very unsatisfactory steward and a miserable wretch besides, but I would just as soon think of tweaking his nose.

"Tweaking his nose," said Captain Giles in a scandalised tone. "Much use it would be to you."

That remark was so irrelevant that one could make no answer to it. But the sense of the absurdity was beginning at last to exercise its well-known fascination. I felt I must not let the man talk to me any more. I got up, observing curtly that he was too much for me—that I couldn't make him out.

Before I had time to move away he spoke again in a changed tone of obstinacy and puffing nervously at his pipe.

"Well—he's a—no account cuss—anyhow. You just—ask him. That's all."

That new manner impressed me—or rather made me pause. But sanity asserting its sway at once I left the verandah after giving him a mirthless smile. In a few strides I found myself in the dining-room, now cleared and empty. But during that short time various thoughts occurred to me, such as: that Giles had been making fun of me, expecting some amusement at my expense; that I probably looked silly and gullible; that I knew very little of life. . . .

The door facing me across the dining-room flew open to my extreme surprise. It was the door inscribed with the word "Steward" and the man himself ran out of his stuffy philistinish lair* in his absurd hunted-animal manner, making for the garden door.

To this day I don't know what made me call after him: "I say! Wait a minute." Perhaps it was the sidelong glance he gave me; or possibly I was yet under the influence of Captain Giles' mysterious earnestness. Well, it was an impulse of some sort; an effect of that force somewhere within our lives which shapes them this way or that.* For if these words had not escaped from my lips (my will had nothing to do with that) my existence would, to be sure, have been still a seaman's existence, but directed on now to me utterly inconceivable lines.

No. My will had nothing to do with it. Indeed, no sooner had I made that fateful noise than I became extremely sorry for it. Had the man stopped and faced me I would have had to retire in disorder. For I had no notion to carry out Captain Giles' idiotic joke, either at my own expense or at the expense of the Steward.

But here the old human instinct of the chase came into play. He pretended to be deaf, and I, without thinking a second about it, dashed along my own side of the dining table and cut him off at the very door.

"Why can't you answer when you are spoken to?" I asked roughly.

He leaned against the lintel of the door.* He looked extremely wretched. Human nature is, I fear, not very nice right through. There are ugly spots in it. I found myself growing angry, and that, I believe, only because my quarry looked so woe-begone. Miserable beggar!

I went for him without more ado. "I understand there was an official communication to the Home from the Harbour Office this morning. Is that so?"

Instead of telling me to mind my own business, as he might have done, he began to whine with an undertone of impudence. He couldn't see me anywhere this morning. He couldn't be expected to run all over the town after me.

"Who wants you to?" I cried. And then my eyes became opened to the inwardness of things and speeches the triviality of which had been so baffling and tiresome.

I told him I wanted to know what was in that letter. My sternness of tone and behaviour was only half assumed. Curiosity can be a very fierce sentiment—at times.

He took refuge in a silly, muttering sulkiness. It was nothing to me, he mumbled. I had told him I was going home. And since I was going home he didn't see why he should. . .

That was the line of his argument, and it was irrelevant enough to be almost insulting. Insulting to one's intelligence, I mean.

In that twilight region between youth and maturity, in which I had my being then, one is peculiarly sensitive to that kind of insult. I am afraid my behaviour to the Steward became very rough indeed. But it wasn't in him to face out anything or anybody. Drug habit or solitary tippling, perhaps. And when I forgot myself so far as to swear at him he broke down and began to shriek.

I don't mean to say that he made a great outcry. It was a cynical shrieking confession, only faint—piteously faint. It wasn't very coherent either, but sufficiently so to strike me dumb at first. I turned my eyes from him in righteous indignation, and perceived Captain Giles in the verandah doorway surveying quietly the scene, his own handiwork, if I may express it in that way. His smouldering black pipe was very noticeable in his big, paternal fist. So, too, was the glitter of his heavy gold watch-chain across the breast of his white tunic. He exhaled an atmosphere of virtuous sagacity thick enough for any innocent soul to fly to confidently. I flew to him.

"You would never believe it," I cried. "It was a notification that a master is wanted for some ship. There's a command apparently going about and this fellow puts the thing in his pocket."

The Steward screamed out in accents of loud despair, "You will be the death of me!"

The mighty slap he gave his wretched forehead was very loud, too. But when I turned to look at him he was no longer there. He had rushed away somewhere out of sight. This sudden disappearance made me laugh.

This was the end of the incident—for me. Captain Giles, however, staring at the place where the Steward had been, began to haul at his gorgeous gold chain till at last the watch came up from the deep pocket like solid truth from a well.* Solemnly he lowered it down again and only then said:

"Just three o'clock. You will be in time—if you don't lose any, that is."

"In time for what?" I asked.

"Good Lord! For the Harbour Office. This must be looked into."

Strictly speaking, he was right. But I've never had much taste for investigation, for showing people up and all that no doubt ethically meritorious kind of work. And my view of the episode was purely ethical. If any one had to be the death of the Steward I didn't see why it shouldn't be Captain Giles himself, a man of age and standing, and a permanent resident. Whereas I, in comparison, felt myself a mere bird of passage in that port. In fact, it might have been said that I had already broken off my connection. I muttered that I didn't think—it was nothing to me. . . .

"Nothing!" repeated Captain Giles, giving some signs of quiet, deliberate indignation. "Kent warned me you were a peculiar young fellow. You will tell me next that a command is nothing to you—and after all the trouble I've taken, too!"

"The trouble!" I murmured, uncomprehending. What trouble? All I could remember was being mystified and bored by his conversation for a solid hour after tiffin. And he called that taking a lot of trouble.

He was looking at me with a self-complacency which would have been odious in any other man. All at once, as if a page of a book had been turned over disclosing a word which made plain all that had gone before, I perceived that this matter had also another than an ethical aspect.

And still I did not move. Captain Giles lost his patience a little. With an angry puff at his pipe he turned his back on my hesitation.

But it was not hesitation on my part. I had been, if I may express myself so, put out of gear mentally. But as soon as I had convinced myself that this stale, unprofitable world of my discontent* contained such a thing as a command to be seized, I recovered my powers of locomotion.

It's a good step from the Officers' Home to the Harbour Office; but with the magic word "Command" in my head I found myself suddenly on the quay as if transported there in the twinkling of an eye, before a portal of dressed white stone above a flight of shallow white steps.

All this seemed to glide towards me swiftly. The whole great roadstead to the right was just a mere flicker of blue, and the dim cool hall swallowed me up out of the heat and glare of which I had not been aware till the very moment I passed in from it.

The broad inner staircase insinuated itself under my feet somehow. Command is a strong magic. The first human beings I perceived distinctly since I had parted with the indignant back of Captain Giles was the crew of the harbour steam-launch lounging on the spacious landing about the curtained archway of the shipping office.

It was there that my buoyancy abandoned me. The atmosphere of officialdom would kill anything that breathes the air of human endeavour, would extinguish hope and fear alike in the supremacy of paper and ink. I passed heavily under the curtain which the Malay coxswain of the harbour launch raised for me. There was nobody in the office except the clerks, writing in two industrious rows. But the head Shipping-Master hopped down from his elevation and hurried along on the thick mats to meet me in the broad central passage.

He had a Scottish name, but his complexion was of a rich olive hue, his short beard was jet black, and his eyes, also black, had a languishing expression.* He asked confidentially:

"You want to see Him?"

All lightness of spirit and body having departed from me at the touch of officialdom, I looked at the scribe without animation and asked in my turn wearily:

"What do you think? Is it any use?"

"My goodness! He has asked for you twice today."

This emphatic He was the supreme authority, the Marine Superintendent, the Harbour-Master—a very great person in the eyes of every single quill-driver* in the room. But that was nothing to the opinion he had of his own greatness.

Captain Ellis looked upon himself as a sort of divine (pagan) emanation, the deputy-Neptune* for the circumambient seas. If he did not actually rule the waves,* he pretended* to rule the fate of the mortals whose lives were cast upon the waters.*

This uplifting illusion made him inquisitorial and peremptory. And as his temperament was choleric* there were fellows who were actually afraid of him. He was redoubtable, not in virtue of his office, but because of his unwarrantable assumptions. I had never had anything to do with him before.

I said: "Oh! He has asked for me twice. Then perhaps I had better go in."

"You must! You must!"

The Shipping-Master led the way with a mincing gait round the whole system of desks to a tall and important-looking door, which he opened with a deferential action of the arm.

He stepped right in (but without letting go of the handle) and, after gazing reverently down the room for a while, beckoned me in by a silent jerk of the head. Then he slipped out at once and shut the door after me most delicately.

Three lofty windows gave on the harbour. There was nothing in them but the dark-blue sparkling sea and the paler luminous blue of the sky. My eye caught in the depths and distances of these blue tones the white speck of some big ship just arrived and about to anchor in the outer roadstead. A ship from home—after perhaps ninety days at sea. There is something touching about a ship coming in from sea and folding her white wings* for a rest.

The next thing I saw was the top-knot of silver hair surmounting Captain Ellis' smooth red face, which would have been apoplectic if it hadn't had such a fresh appearance.

Our deputy-Neptune had no beard on his chin, and there was no trident to be seen standing in a corner anywhere, like an umbrella. But his hand was holding a pen—the official pen, far mightier than the sword* in making or marring the fortune of simple toiling men. He was looking over his shoulder at my advance.

When I had come well within range he saluted me by a nerve-shattering: "Where have you been all this time?"

As it was no concern of his I did not take the slightest notice of the shot. I said simply that I had heard there was a master needed for some vessel, and being a sailing-ship man* I thought I would apply. . . .

He interrupted me. "Why! Hang it! *You* are the right man for that job—if there had been twenty others after it. But no fear of that. They are all afraid to catch hold. That's what's the matter."

He was very irritated. I said innocently: "Are they, sir. I wonder why?"

"Why!" he fumed. "Afraid of the sails. Afraid of a white crew. Too much trouble. Too much work. Too long out here. Easy life and deck-chairs more their mark. Here I sit with the Consul-General's cable before me, and the only man fit for the job not to be found anywhere. I began to think you were funking it too. . . ."

"I haven't been long getting to the office,"* I remarked calmly.

"You have a good name out here, though," he growled savagely without looking at me.

"I am very glad to hear it from you, sir," I said.

"Yes. But you are not on the spot when you are wanted. You know you weren't. That steward of yours wouldn't dare to neglect a message from this office. Where the devil did you hide yourself for the best part of the day?"

I only smiled kindly down on him, and he seemed to recollect himself, and asked me to take a seat. He explained that the master of a British ship having died in Bangkok* the Consul-General had cabled to him a request for a competent man to be sent out to take command.

Apparently, in his mind, I was the man from the first, though for the looks of the thing the notification addressed to the Sailors' Home was general. An agreement had already been prepared. He gave it to me to read, and when I handed it back to him with the remark that I accepted its terms, the deputy-Neptune signed it, stamped it with his own exalted hand, folded it in four (it was a sheet of blue foolscap), and presented it to me—a gift of extraordinary potency, for, as I put it in my pocket, my head swam a little.

"This is your appointment to the command," he said with a certain gravity. "An official appointment binding the owners to conditions which you have accepted. Now—when will you be ready to go?"

I said I would be ready that very day if necessary. He caught me at my word with great readiness. The steamer *Melita** was leaving for Bangkok that evening about seven. He would request her captain officially to give me a passage and wait for me till ten o'clock.

Then he rose from his office chair, and I got up too. My head swam, there was no doubt about it, and I felt a heaviness of limbs as if they had grown bigger since I had sat down on that chair. I made my bow.

A subtle change in Captain Ellis' manner became perceptible as though he had laid aside the trident of deputy-Neptune. In reality, it was only his official pen that he had dropped on getting up.*

II

HE shook hands with me: "Well, there you are, on your own, appointed officially under my responsibility."

He was actually walking with me to the door. What a distance off it seemed! I moved like a man in bonds. But we reached it at last. I opened it with the sensation of dealing with mere dream-stuff,* and then at the last moment the fellowship of seamen asserted itself, stronger than the difference of age and station. It asserted itself in Captain Ellis' voice.

"Goodbye—and good luck to you," he said so heartily that I could only give him a grateful glance. Then I turned and went out, never to see him again in my life. I had not made three steps into the outer office when I heard behind my back a gruff, loud, authoritative voice, the voice of our deputy-Neptune.

It was addressing the head Shipping-Master, who, having let me in, had, apparently, remained hovering in the middle distance ever since.

"Mr. R., let the harbour launch have steam up to take the captain here on board the *Melita* at half-past nine tonight."

I was amazed at the startled assent of R.'s "Yes, sir." He ran before me out on the landing. My new dignity sat yet so lightly on me that I was not aware that it was I, the Captain, the object of this last graciousness. It seemed as if all of a sudden a pair of wings had grown on my shoulders. I merely skimmed along the polished floor.

But R. was impressed.

"I say!" he exclaimed on the landing, while the Malay crew of the steam-launch standing by looked stonily at the man for whom they were going to be kept on duty so late, away from their gambling, from their girls, or their pure domestic joys. "I say! His own launch. What have you done to him?"

His stare was full of respectful curiosity. I was quite confounded.

"Was it for me? I hadn't the slightest notion," I stammered out.

He nodded many times. "Yes. And the last person who had it before you was a Duke. So, there!"

I think he expected me to faint on the spot. But I was in too much of a hurry for emotional displays. My feelings were already in such a whirl that this staggering information did not seem to make the slightest difference. It fell into the seething cauldron of my brain, and I carried it off with me after a short but effusive passage of leave-taking with R.

The favour of the great throws an aureole round the fortunate object of its selection. That excellent man inquired whether he could do anything for me. He had known me only by sight, and he was well aware he would never see me again; I was, in common with the other seamen of the port, merely a subject for official writing, filling up of forms with all the artificial superiority of a man of pen and ink to the men who grapple with realities outside the consecrated walls of official buildings. What ghosts we must have been to him! Mere symbols to juggle with in books and heavy registers, without brains and muscles and perplexities; something hardly useful and decidedly inferior.

And he—the office hours being over—wanted to know if he could be of any use to me!

I ought, properly speaking—I ought to have been moved to tears. But I did not even think of it. It was only another miraculous manifestation of that day of miracles. I parted from him as if he had been a mere symbol. I floated down the staircase. I floated out of the official and imposing portal. I went on floating along.

I use that word rather than the word "flew," because I have a distinct impression that, though uplifted by my aroused youth, my movements were deliberate enough. To that mixed white, brown, and yellow portion of mankind, out abroad on their own affairs, I presented the appearance of a man walking rather sedately. And nothing in the way of abstraction could have equalled my deep detachment from the forms and colours of this world.* It was, as it were, absolute.

And yet, suddenly, I recognised Hamilton. I recognised him without effort, without a shock, without a start. There he was, strolling towards the Harbour Office with his stiff, arrogant dignity. His red face made him noticeable at a distance. It flamed, over there, on the shady side of the street.

He had perceived me too. Something (unconscious exuberance of spirits perhaps) moved me to wave my hand to him elaborately. This lapse from good taste happened before I was aware that I was capable of it.

The impact of my impudence stopped him short, much as a bullet might have done. I verily believe he staggered, though as far as I could see he didn't actually fall. I had gone past in a moment and did not turn my head. I had forgotten his existence.

The next ten minutes might have been ten seconds or ten centuries for all my consciousness had to do with it. People might have been falling dead around me, houses crumbling, guns firing, I wouldn't have known. I was thinking: "By Jove! I have got it." *It* being the command. It had come about in a way utterly unforeseen in my modest day-dreams.

I perceived that my imagination had been running in conventional channels and that my hopes had always been drab stuff. I had envisaged a command as a result of a slow course of promotion in the employ of some highly respectable firm. The reward of faithful service. Well, faithful service was all right. One would naturally give that for one's own sake, for the sake of the ship, for the love of the life of one's choice; not for the sake of the reward.

There is something distasteful in the notion of a reward.

And now here I had my command, absolutely in my pocket, in a way undeniable indeed, but most unexpected; beyond my imaginings, outside all reasonable expectations, and even notwithstanding the existence of some sort of obscure intrigue to keep it away from me. It is true that the intrigue was feeble, but it helped the feeling of wonder—as if I had been specially destined for that ship I did not know, by some power higher than the prosaic agencies of the commercial world.

A strange sense of exultation began to creep into me. If I had worked for that command ten years or more there would have been nothing of the kind. I was a little frightened.

"Let us be calm," I said to myself.

Outside the door of the Officers' Home the wretched Steward

seemed to be waiting for me. There was a broad flight of a few steps, and he ran to and fro on the top of it as if chained there. A distressed cur. He looked as though his throat were too dry for him to bark.

I regret to say I stopped before going in. There had been a revolution in my moral nature. He waited open-mouthed, breathless, while I looked at him for half a minute.

"And you thought you could keep me out of it," I said scathingly.

"You said you were going home," he squeaked miserably. "You said so. You said so."

"I wonder what Captain Ellis will have to say to that excuse," I uttered slowly with a sinister meaning.

His lower jaw had been trembling all the time and his voice was like the bleating of a sick goat.

"You have given me away? You have done for me?"

Neither his distress nor yet the sheer absurdity of it was able to disarm me. It was the first instance of harm being attempted to be done to me—at any rate, the first I had ever found out. And I was still young enough, still too much on this side of the shadow-line, not to be surprised* and indignant at such things.

I gazed at him inflexibly. Let the beggar suffer. He slapped his forehead and I passed in, pursued, into the dining-room, by his screech: "I always said you'd be the death of me."

This clamour not only overtook me, but went ahead as it were on to the verandah and brought out Captain Giles.

He stood before me in the doorway in all the commonplace solidity of his wisdom. The gold chain glittered on his breast. He clutched a smouldering pipe.

I extended my hand to him warmly and he seemed surprised, but did respond heartily enough in the end, with a faint smile of superior knowledge which cut my thanks short as if with a knife. I don't think that more than one word came out. And even for that one, judging by the temperature of my face, I had blushed as if for a bad action. Assuming a detached tone, I wondered how on earth he had managed to spot the little underhand game that had been going on.

He murmured complacently that there were but few things done in the town that he could not see the inside of. And as to this house, he had been using it off and on for nearly ten years. Nothing that went on in it could escape his great experience. It had been no trouble to him. No trouble at all.

Then in his quiet thick tone he wanted to know if I had complained formally of the Steward's action.

I said that I hadn't—though, indeed, it was not for want of opportunity. Captain Ellis had gone for me bald-headed* in a most ridiculous fashion for being out of the way when wanted.

"Funny old gentleman," interjected Captain Giles. "What did you say to that?"

"I said simply that I came along the very moment I heard of his message. Nothing more. I didn't want to hurt the Steward. I would scorn to harm such an object. No. I made no complaint, but I believe he thinks I've done so. Let him think. He's got a fright that he won't forget in a hurry, for Captain Ellis would kick him out into the middle of Asia. . . ."

"Wait a moment," said Captain Giles, leaving me suddenly. I sat down feeling very tired, mostly in my head. Before I could start a train of thought he stood again before me, murmuring the excuse that he had to go and put the fellow's mind at ease.

I looked up with surprise. But in reality I was indifferent. He explained that he had found the Steward lying face downwards on the horsehair sofa. He was all right now.

"He would not have died of fright," I said contemptuously.

"No. But he might have taken an overdose out of one of them little bottles he keeps in his room," Captain Giles argued seriously. "The confounded fool has tried to poison himself once—a couple of years ago."

"Really," I said without emotion. "He doesn't seem very fit to live, anyhow."

"As to that, it may be said of a good many."

"Don't exaggerate like this!" I protested, laughing irritably. "But I wonder what this part of the world would do if you were to leave off looking after it, Captain Giles? Here you have got me a command and saved the Steward's life in one afternoon. Though why you should have taken all that interest in either of us is more than I can understand."

Captain Giles remained silent for a minute. Then gravely:

"He's not a bad steward really. He can find a good cook, at any rate. And, what's more, he can keep him when found. I remember the cooks we had here before his time. . . ."

I must have made a movement of impatience, because he interrupted himself with an apology for keeping me yarning there, while no doubt I needed all my time to get ready.

What I really needed was to be alone for a bit. I seized this opening hastily. My bedroom was a quiet refuge in an apparently uninhabited wing of the building. Having absolutely nothing to do (for I had not unpacked my things), I sat down on the bed and abandoned myself to the influences of the hour. To the unexpected influences. . . .

And first I wondered at my state of mind. Why was I not more surprised? Why? Here I was, invested with a command in the twinkling of an eye, not in the common course of human affairs, but more as if by enchantment. I ought to have been lost in astonishment. But I wasn't. I was very much like people in fairy tales. Nothing ever astonishes them. When a fully appointed gala coach is produced out of a pumpkin to take her to a ball Cinderella does not exclaim. She gets in quietly and drives away to her high fortune.

Captain Ellis (a fierce sort of fairy) had produced a command out of a drawer almost as unexpectedly as in a fairy tale. But a command is an abstract idea, and it seemed a sort of "lesser marvel" till it flashed upon me that it involved the concrete existence of a ship.

A ship! My ship! She was mine, more absolutely mine for possession and care than anything in the world; an object of responsibility and devotion. She was there waiting for me, spellbound, unable to move, to live, to get out into the world (till I came), like an enchanted princess. Her call had come to me as if from the clouds. I had never suspected her existence. I didn't know how she looked, I had barely heard her name, and yet we were indissolubly united for a certain portion of our future, to sink or swim together!*

A sudden passion of anxious impatience rushed through my veins and gave me such a sense of the intensity of existence as I have never felt before or since. I discovered how much of a seaman I was, in heart, in mind, and, as it were, physically—a man exclusively of sea and ships; the sea the only world that counted, and the ships the test of manliness, of temperament, of courage and fidelity—and of love.

I had an exquisite moment. It was unique also. Jumping up from my seat, I paced up and down my room for a long time. But when I came into the dining-room I behaved with sufficient composure. I only couldn't eat anything at dinner.

Having declared my intention not to drive but to walk down to the quay, I must render the wretched Steward justice that he bestirred himself to find me some coolies for the luggage. They departed, carrying all my worldly possessions (except a little money I had in my pocket) slung from a long pole. Captain Giles volunteered to walk down with me.

We followed the sombre, shaded alley across the Esplanade. It was moderately cool there under the trees. Captain Giles remarked, with a sudden laugh: "I know who's jolly thankful at having seen the last of you."

I guessed that he meant the Steward. The fellow had borne himself to me in a sulkily frightened manner at the last. I expressed my wonder that he should have tried to do me a bad turn for no reason at all.

"Don't you see that what he wanted was to get rid of our friend Hamilton by dodging him in front of you for that job? That would have removed him for good, see?"

"Heavens!" I exclaimed, feeling humiliated somehow. "Can it be possible? What a fool he must be! That overbearing, impudent loafer! Why! He couldn't . . . And yet he's nearly done it,* I believe; for the Harbour Office was bound to send somebody."

"Aye. A fool like our Steward can be dangerous sometimes," declared Captain Giles sententiously. "Just because he is a fool," he added, imparting further instruction in his complacent low tones. "For," he continued in the manner of a set demonstration, "no sensible person would risk being kicked out of the only berth between himself and starvation just to get rid of a simple annoyance—a small worry. Would he now?"

"Well, no," I conceded, restraining a desire to laugh at that something mysteriously earnest in delivering the conclusions of his wisdom as though they were the product of prohibited operations. "But that fellow looks as if he were rather crazy. He must be."

"As to that, I believe everybody in the world is a little mad,"* he announced quietly.

"You make no exceptions?" I inquired, just to hear his answer.

He kept silent for a little while, then got home in an effective manner.

"Why! Kent says that even of you."

"Does he?" I retorted, extremely embittered all at once against my former captain. "There's nothing of that in the written character* from him which I've got in my pocket. Has he given you any instances of my lunacy?"

Captain Giles explained in a conciliating tone that it had been only a friendly remark in reference to my abrupt leaving the ship for no apparent reason.

I muttered grumpily: "Oh! leaving his ship," and mended my pace. He kept up by my side in the deep gloom of the avenue as if it were his conscientious duty to see me out of the colony as an undesirable character. He panted a little, which was rather pathetic in a way. But I was not moved. On the contrary. His discomfort gave me a sort of malicious pleasure.

Presently I relented, slowed down, and said:

"What I really wanted was to get a fresh grip. I felt it was time. Is that so very mad?"

He made no answer. We were issuing from the avenue. On the bridge over the canal a dark, irresolute figure seemed to be awaiting something or somebody.

It was a Malay policeman, barefooted, in his blue uniform. The silver band on his little round cap shone dimly in the light of the street lamp. He peered in our direction timidly.

Before we could come up to him he turned about and walked in front of us in the direction of the jetty. The distance was some hundred yards; and then I found my coolies squatting on their heels. They had kept the pole on their shoulders, and all my worldly goods, still tied to the pole, were resting on the ground between them. As far as the eye could reach along the quay there was not another soul abroad except the police peon, who saluted us.

It seems he had detained the coolies as suspicious characters, and had forbidden them the jetty. But at a sign from me he took off the embargo with alacrity. The two patient fellows, rising together with a faint grunt, trotted off along the planks, and I prepared to take my leave of Captain Giles, who stood there with an air as though his mission were drawing to a close. It could not be denied that he had done it all. And while I hesitated about an appropriate sentence he made himself heard:

"I expect you'll have your hands pretty full of tangled up business."

I asked him what made him think so; and he answered that it was his general experience of the world. Ship a long time away from her port, owners inaccessible by cable, and the only man who could explain matters dead and buried.

"And you yourself new to the business in a way," he concluded in a sort of unanswerable tone.

"Don't insist," I said. "I know it only too well. I only wish you could impart to me some small portion of your experience before I go. As it can't be done in ten minutes I had better not begin to ask you. There's that harbour launch waiting for me too. But I won't feel really at peace till I have that ship of mine out in the Indian Ocean."

He remarked casually that from Bangkok to the Indian Ocean was a pretty long step. And this murmur, like a dim flash from a dark lantern, showed me for a moment the broad belt of islands and reefs between that unknown ship, which was mine, and the freedom of the great waters of the globe.

But I felt no apprehension. I was familiar enough with the Archipelago by that time. Extreme patience and extreme care would see me through the region of broken land, of faint airs and of dead water to where I would feel at last my command swing on the great swell and list over to the great breath of regular winds, that would give her the feeling of a large, more intense life. The road would be long. All roads are long that lead towards one's heart's desire. But this road my mind's eye could see on a chart, professionally, with all its complications and difficulties, yet simple enough in a way. One is a seaman or one is not. And I had no doubt of being one.

The only part I was a stranger to was the Gulf of Siam. And I mentioned this to Captain Giles. Not that I was concerned very much. It belonged to the same region the nature of which I knew, into whose very soul I seemed to have looked during the last months of that existence with which I had broken now, suddenly, as one parts with some enchanting company.

"The gulf . . . Ay! A funny piece of water—that," said Captain Giles.

Funny, in this connection, was a vague word. The whole thing sounded like an opinion uttered by a cautious person mindful of actions for slander.

I didn't inquire as to the nature of that funniness. There was really no time. But at the very last he volunteered a warning.

"Whatever you do keep to the east side of it. The west side is dangerous at this time of the year. Don't let anything tempt you over. You'll find nothing but trouble there."

Though I could hardly imagine what could tempt me to involve my ship amongst the currents and reefs of the Malay shore, I thanked him for the advice.

He gripped my extended arm warmly, and the end of our acquaintance came suddenly in the words: "Goodnight."

That was all he said: "Goodnight." Nothing more. I don't know what I intended to say, but surprise made me swallow it, whatever it was. I choked slightly, and then exclaimed with a sort of nervous haste: "Oh! Goodnight, Captain Giles, goodnight."

His movements were always deliberate, but his back had receded some distance along the deserted quay before I collected myself enough to follow his example and made a half turn in the direction of the jetty.

Only my movements were not deliberate. I hurried down to the steps and leaped into the launch. Before I had fairly landed in her stern-sheets the slim little craft darted away from the jetty with a sudden swirl of her propeller and the hard rapid puffing of the exhaust in her vaguely gleaming brass funnel amidships.

The misty churning at her stern was the only sound in the world. The shore lay plunged in the silence of the deepest slumber.* I watched the town recede still and soundless in the hot night, till the abrupt hail, "Steam-launch, ahoy!" made me spin round face forward. We were close to a white, ghostly steamer. Lights shone on her decks, in her portholes. And the same voice shouted from her: "Is that our passenger?"

"It is," I yelled.

Her crew had been obviously on the jump. I could hear them running about. The modern spirit of haste was loudly vocal in the orders to "Heave away on the cable"—to "Lower the side-ladder," and in urgent requests to me to "Come along, sir! We have been delayed three hours for you. . . . Our time is seven o'clock, you know!"

I stepped on the deck. I said "No! I don't know." The spirit of modern hurry was embodied in a thin, long-armed, long-legged man, with a closely-clipped grey beard. His meagre hand* was hot and dry. He declared feverishly:

"I am hanged if I would have waited another five minutes—harbour-master or no harbour-master."

"That's your own business," I said. "I didn't ask you to wait for me."

"I hope you don't expect any supper," he burst out. "This isn't a boarding-house afloat. You are the first passenger I ever had in my life and I hope to goodness you will be the last."

I made no answer to this hospitable communication; and, indeed, he didn't wait for any, bolting away on to his bridge to get his ship under way.

For the four days he had me on board he did not depart from that half-hostile attitude. His ship having been delayed three hours on my account he couldn't forgive me for not being a more distinguished person. He was not exactly outspoken about it, but that feeling of annoyed wonder was peeping out perpetually in his talk.

He was absurd.

He was also a man of much experience, which he liked to trot out; but no greater contrast with Captain Giles could have been imagined. He would have amused me if I had wanted to be amused. But I did not want to be amused. I was like a lover looking forward to a meeting. Human hostility was nothing to me. I thought of my unknown ship. It was amusement enough, torment enough, occupation enough.

He perceived my state, for his wits were sufficiently sharp for that, and he poked sly fun at my preoccupation in the manner some nasty, cynical old men assume towards the dreams and illusions of youth. I, on my side, refrained from questioning him as to the appearance of my ship, though I knew that being in Bangkok every month or so he must have known her by sight. I was not going to expose the ship, my ship! to some slighting reference.

He was the first really unsympathetic man I had ever come in contact with. My education was far from being finished, though I didn't know it. No! I didn't know it.

All I knew was that he disliked me and had some contempt for my person. Why? Apparently because his ship had been delayed three hours on my account. Who was I to have such a thing done for me? Such a thing had never been done for him. It was a sort of jealous indignation.

My expectation, mingled with fear, was wrought to its highest pitch. How slow had been the days of the passage and how soon they were over. One morning, early, we crossed the bar, and while the sun was rising splendidly over the flat spaces of the land we steamed up the innumerable bends, passed under the shadow of the great gilt pagoda,* and reached the outskirts of the town.

There it was, spread largely on both banks, the Oriental capital which had as yet suffered no white conqueror; an expanse of brown houses of bamboo, of mats, of leaves, of a vegetable-matter style of architecture, sprung out of the brown soil on the banks of the muddy river. It was amazing to think that in those miles of human habitations there was not probably half a dozen pounds of nails. Some of those houses of sticks and grass, like the nests of an aquatic race, clung to the low shores. Others seemed to grow out of the water; others again floated in long anchored rows in the very middle of the stream. Here and there in the distance, above the crowded mob of low, brown roof ridges, towered great piles of masonry, King's Palace,* temples gorgeous and dilapidated, crumbling under the vertical sunlight, tremendous, overpowering, almost palpable, which seemed to enter one's breast with the breath of one's nostrils and soak into one's limbs through every pore of one's skin.

The ridiculous victim of jealousy had for some reason or other to stop his engines just then. The steamer drifted slowly up with the tide. Oblivious of my new surroundings I walked the deck, in anxious, deadened abstraction, a commingling of romantic reverie with a very practical survey of my qualifications. For the time was approaching for me to behold my command and to prove my worth in the ultimate test of my profession.

Suddenly I heard myself called by that imbecile. He was beckoning me to come up on his bridge.

I didn't care very much for that, but as it seemed that he had something particular to say I went up the ladder.

He laid his hand on my shoulder and gave me a slight turn, pointing with his other arm at the same time.

"There! That's your ship, Captain," he said.

I felt a thump in my breast—only one, as if my heart had then ceased to beat. There were ten or more ships moored along the bank, and the one he meant was partly hidden from my sight by her next astern. He said: "We'll drift abreast her in a moment."

What was his tone? Mocking? Threatening? Or only indifferent? I could not tell. I suspected some malice in this unexpected manifestation of interest.

He left me, and I leaned over the rail of the bridge looking over the side. I dared not raise my eyes. Yet it had to be done—and, indeed, I could not have helped myself. I believe I trembled.

But directly my eyes had rested on my ship all my fear

vanished. It went off swiftly, like a bad dream. Only that a dream leaves no shame behind it, and that I felt a momentary shame at my unworthy suspicions.

Yes, there she was. Her hull, her rigging filled my eye with a great content. That feeling of life-emptiness which had made me so restless for the last few months lost its bitter plausibility, its evil influence, dissolved in a flow of joyous emotion.

At the first glance I saw that she was a high-class vessel, a harmonious creature in the lines of her fine body, in the proportioned tallness of her spars. Whatever her age and her history, she had preserved the stamp of her origin. She was one of those craft that, in virtue of their design and complete finish, will never look old. Amongst her companions moored to the bank, and all bigger than herself, she looked like a creature of high breed—an Arab steed in a string of cart-horses.

A voice behind me said in a nasty equivocal tone: "I hope you are satisfied with her, Captain." I did not even turn my head. It was the master of the steamer, and whatever he meant, whatever he thought of her, I knew that, like some rare women, she was one of those creatures whose mere existence is enough to awaken an unselfish delight. One feels that it is good to be in the world in which she has her being.

That illusion of life and character which charms one in men's finest handiwork radiated from her. An enormous baulk of teakwood timber swung over her hatchway; lifeless matter, looking heavier and bigger than anything aboard of her. When they started lowering it the surge of the tackle sent a quiver through her from water-line to the trucks up the fine nerves of her rigging, as though she had shuddered at the weight. It seemed cruel to load her so. . . .

Half-an-hour later, putting my foot on her deck for the first time, I received the feeling of deep physical satisfaction. Nothing could equal the fullness of that moment, the ideal completeness of that emotional experience which had come to me without the preliminary toil and disenchantments of an obscure career.

My rapid glance ran over her, enveloped, appropriated the form concreting the abstract sentiment of my command. A lot of details perceptible to a seaman struck my eye vividly in that instant. For the rest, I saw her disengaged from the material conditions of her being. The shore to which she was moored was as if it did not exist. What were to me all the countries of the globe? In all the parts of the world washed by navigable waters our relation to each other would be the same—and more intimate than there are words to express in the language. Apart from that, every scene and episode would be a mere passing show. The very gang of yellow coolies busy about the main hatch was less substantial than the stuff dreams are made of.* For who on earth would dream of Chinamen? . . .

I went aft, ascended the poop, where, under the awning, gleamed the brasses of the yacht-like fittings, the polished surfaces of the rails,* the glass of the skylights. Right aft two seamen, busy cleaning the steering gear, with the reflected ripples of light running playfully up their bent backs, went on with their work, unaware of me and of the almost affectionate glance I threw at them in passing towards the companion-way of the cabin.

The doors stood wide open, the slide was pushed right back. The half-turn of the staircase cut off the view of the lobby.* A low humming ascended from below, but it stopped abruptly at the sound of my descending footsteps.

III

THE first thing I saw down there was the upper part of a man's body projecting backwards, as it were, from one of the doors at the foot of the stairs. His eyes looked at me very wide and still. In one hand he held a dinner plate, in the other a cloth.

"I am your new Captain," I said quietly.

In a moment, in the twinkling of an eye, he had got rid of the plate and the cloth and jumped to open the cabin door. As soon as I passed into the saloon he vanished, but only to reappear instantly, buttoning up a jacket he had put on with the swiftness of a "quick-change" artist.*

"Where's the chief mate?" I asked.

"In the hold, I think, sir. I saw him go down the after-hatch ten minutes ago."

"Tell him I am on board."

The mahogany table under the skylight shone in the twilight like a dark pool of water. The sideboard, surmounted by a wide looking-glass in an ormolu frame, had a marble top. It bore a pair of silver-plated lamps and some other pieces—obviously a harbour display. The saloon itself was panelled in two kinds of wood in the excellent, simple taste prevailing when the ship was built.

I sat down in the arm-chair at the head of the table—the captain's chair, with a small tell-tale compass swung above it—a mute reminder of unremitting vigilance.

A succession of men had sat in that chair. I became aware of that thought suddenly, vividly, as though each had left a little of himself between the four walls of these ornate bulkheads; as if a sort of composite soul, the soul of command, had whispered suddenly to mine of long days at sea and of anxious moments.

"You, too!" it seemed to say, "you, too, shall taste of that peace and that unrest in a searching intimacy with your own self—obscure as we were and as supreme in the face of all the winds and all the seas, in an immensity that receives no impress, preserves no memories, and keeps no reckoning of lives."

Deep within the tarnished ormolu frame, in the hot half-light sifted through the awning, I saw my own face propped between my hands. And I stared back at myself with the perfect detachment of distance, rather with curiosity than with any other feeling, except of some sympathy for this latest representative of what for all intents and purposes was a dynasty; continuous not in blood, indeed, but in its experience, in its training, in its conception of duty, and in the blessed simplicity of its traditional point of view on life.

It struck me that this quietly staring man whom I was watching, both as if he were myself and somebody else, was not exactly a lonely figure. He had his place in a line of men whom he did not know, of whom he had never heard; but who were fashioned by the same influences, whose souls in relation to their humble life's work had no secrets for him.

Suddenly I perceived that there was another man in the saloon, standing a little on one side and looking intently at me. The chief mate. His long, red moustache determined the character of his physiognomy, which struck me as pugnacious in (strange to say) a ghastly sort of way.

How long had he been there looking at me, appraising me in my unguarded day-dreaming state? I would have been more disconcerted if, having the clock set in the top of the mirror-frame right in front of me, I had not noticed that its long hand had hardly moved at all.

I could not have been in that cabin more than two minutes altogether. Say three. . . . So he could not have been watching me more than a mere fraction of a minute, luckily. Still, I regretted the occurrence.

But I showed nothing of it as I rose leisurely (it had to be leisurely) and greeted him with perfect friendliness.

There was something reluctant and at the same time attentive in his bearing. His name was Burns.* We left the cabin and went round the ship together. His face in the full light of day appeared very worn, meagre, even haggard. Somehow I had a delicacy as to looking too often at him; his eyes, on the contrary, remained fairly glued on my face. They were greenish and had an expectant expression.

He answered all my questions readily enough, but my ear seemed to catch a tone of unwillingness. The second officer, with three or four hands, was busy forward. The mate mentioned his name and I nodded to him in passing. He was very young. He struck me as rather a cub.*

When we returned below I sat down on one end of a deep, semi-circular, or, rather, semi-oval settee, upholstered in red plush. It extended right across the whole after-end of the cabin. Mr. Burns, motioned to sit down, dropped into one of the swivel-chairs round the table, and kept his eyes on me as persistently as ever, and with that strange air as if all this were make-believe and he expected me to get up, burst into a laugh, slap him on the back, and vanish from the cabin.

There was an odd stress in the situation which began to make me uncomfortable. I tried to react against this vague feeling.

"It's only my inexperience," I thought.

In the face of that man, several years, I judged, older than myself, I became aware of what I had left already behind me—my youth. And that was indeed poor comfort. Youth is a fine thing, a mighty power—as long as one does not think of it. I felt I was becoming self-conscious. Almost against my will I assumed a moody gravity. I said: "I see you have kept her in very good order, Mr. Burns."

Directly I had uttered these words I asked myself angrily why the deuce did I want to say that? Mr. Burns in answer had only blinked at me. What on earth did he mean?

I fell back on a question which had been in my thoughts for a long time—the most natural question on the lips of any seaman whatever joining a ship. I voiced it (confound this self-consciousness) in a *dégagé* cheerful tone: "I suppose she can travel—what?"

Now a question like this might have been answered normally, either in accents of apologetic sorrow or with a visibly suppressed pride, in a "I don't want to boast, but you shall see" sort of tone.

There are sailors, too, who would have been roughly outspoken: "Lazy brute," or openly delighted: "She's a flyer." Two ways, if four manners.

But Mr. Burns found another way, a way of his own which had, at all events, the merit of saving his breath, if no other.

Again he did not say anything. He only frowned. And it was an angry frown. I waited. Nothing more came.

"What's the matter? . . . Can't you tell after being nearly two years in the ship?" I addressed him sharply.

He looked as startled for a moment as though he had discovered my presence only that very moment. But this passed off almost at once. He put on an air of indifference. But I suppose he thought it better to say something. He said that a ship needed, just like a man, the chance to show the best she could do, and that this ship had never had a chance since he had been on board of her. Not that he could remember. The last captain* . . . He paused.

"Has he been so very unlucky?" I asked with frank incredulity. Mr. Burns turned his eyes away from me. No, the late captain was not an unlucky man. One couldn't say that. But he had not seemed to want to make use of his luck.

Mr. Burns—man of enigmatic moods—made this statement with an inanimate face and staring wilfully at the rudder-casing. The statement itself was obscurely suggestive. I asked quietly:

"Where did he die?"

"In this saloon. Just where you are sitting now," answered Mr. Burns.

I repressed a silly impulse to jump up; but upon the whole I was relieved to hear that he had not died in the bed which was now to be mine. I pointed out to the chief mate that what I really wanted to know was where he had buried his late captain.

Mr. Burns said that it was at the entrance to the gulf. A roomy grave; a sufficient answer. But the mate, overcoming visibly something within him—something like a curious reluctance to believe in my advent (as an irrevocable fact, at any rate), did not stop at that—though, indeed, he may have wished to do so.

As a compromise with his feelings, I believe, he addressed himself persistently to the rudder-casing, so that to me he had the appearance of a man talking in solitude, a little unconsciously, however.

His tale was that at seven bells in the forenoon watch* he had all hands mustered on the quarter-deck and told them that they had better go down to say goodbye to the captain.

Those words, as if grudged to an intruding personage, were enough for me to evoke vividly that strange ceremony: The bare-footed, bare-headed seamen crowding shyly into that cabin, a small mob pressed against that sideboard, uncomfortable rather than moved, shirts open on sunburnt chests, weather-beaten faces, and all staring at the dying man with the same grave and expectant expression.

"Was he conscious?" I asked.

"He didn't speak, but he moved his eyes to look at them," said the mate.

After waiting a moment Mr. Burns motioned the crew to leave the cabin, but he detained the two eldest men to stay with the captain while he went on deck with his sextant to "take the sun." It was getting towards noon and he was anxious to obtain a good observation for latitude. When he returned below to put his sextant away he found that the two men had retreated out into the lobby. Through the open door he had a view of the captain lying easy against the pillows. He had "passed away" while Mr. Burns was taking his observation. As near noon as possible. He had hardly changed his position.

Mr. Burns sighed, glanced at me inquisitively, as much as to say, "Aren't you going yet?" and then turned his thoughts from his new captain back to the old, who, being dead, had no authority, was not in anybody's way, and was much easier to deal with.

Mr. Burns dealt with him at some length. He was a peculiar man—of sixty-five about—iron grey, hard-faced, obstinate, and uncommunicative. He used to keep the ship loafing at sea for inscrutable reasons. Would come on deck at night sometimes, take some sail off her, God only knows why or wherefore, then go below, shut himself up in his cabin, and play on the violin for hours—till daybreak perhaps. In fact, he spent most of his time day or night playing the violin. That was when the fit took him.* Very loud, too.

It came to this, that Mr. Burns mustered his courage one day and remonstrated earnestly with the captain. Neither he nor the second mate could get a wink of sleep in their watches below for the noise. . . . And how could they be expected to keep awake while on duty? he pleaded. The answer of that stern man was that if he and the second mate didn't like the noise, they were welcome to pack up their traps and walk over the side. When this alternative was offered the ship happened to be 600 miles from the nearest land.

Mr. Burns at this point looked at me with an air of curiosity. I began to think that my predecessor was a remarkably peculiar old man.

But I had to hear stranger things yet. It came out that this stern, grim, wind-tanned, rough, sea-salted, taciturn sailor of sixty-five was not only an artist, but a lover as well. In Haiphong, when they got there after a course of most unprofitable peregrinations (during which the ship was nearly lost twice), he got himself, in Mr. Burns' own words, "mixed up" with some woman. Mr. Burns had had no personal knowledge of that affair, but positive evidence of it existed in the shape of a photograph* taken in Haiphong. Mr. Burns found it in one of the drawers in the captain's room.

In due course I, too, saw that amazing human document (I even threw it overboard later). There he sat, with his hands reposing on his knees, bald, squat, grey, bristly, recalling a wild boar somehow; and by his side towered an awful, mature, white female with rapacious nostrils and a cheaply ill-omened stare in her enormous eyes. She was disguised in some semi-oriental, vulgar, fancy costume. She resembled a low-class medium or one of those women who tell fortunes by cards for half-a-crown.* And yet she was striking. A professional sorceress from the slums. It was incomprehensible. There was something awful in the thought that she was the last reflection of the world of passion for the fierce soul which seemed to look at one out of the sardonically savage face of that old seaman. However, I noticed that she was holding some musical instrument—guitar or mandoline—in her hand. Perhaps that was the secret of her sortilege.*

For Mr. Burns that photograph explained why the unloaded ship was kept sweltering at anchor for three weeks in a pestilential hot harbour without air. They lay there and gasped. The captain, appearing now and then on short visits, mumbled to Mr. Burns unlikely tales about some letters he was waiting for.

Suddenly, after vanishing for a week, he came on board in the middle of the night and took the ship out to sea with the first break of dawn. Daylight showed him looking wild and ill. The mere getting clear of the land took two days, and somehow or other they bumped slightly on a reef. However, no leak developed, and the captain, growling "no matter," informed Mr. Burns that he had made up his mind to take the ship to Hong-Kong and dry-dock her there.

At this Mr. Burns was plunged into despair. For indeed, to beat up to Hong-Kong against a fierce monsoon, with a ship not sufficiently ballasted and with her supply of water not completed, was an insane project.

But the captain growled peremptorily, "Stick her at it," and Mr. Burns, dismayed and enraged, stuck her at it, and kept her at it, blowing away sails, straining the spars, exhausting the crew—nearly maddened by the absolute conviction that the attempt was impossible and was bound to end in some catastrophe.

Meantime the captain, shut up in his cabin and wedged in a corner of his settee against the crazy bounding of the ship, played the violin—or, at any rate, made continuous noise on it.

When he appeared on deck he would not speak and not always answer when spoken to. It was obvious that he was ill in some mysterious manner, and beginning to break up.

As the days went by the sounds of the violin became less and less loud, till at last only a feeble scratching would meet Mr. Burns' ear as he stood in the saloon listening outside the door of the captain's state-room.

One afternoon in perfect desperation he burst into that room and made such a scene, tearing his hair and shouting such horrid imprecations that he cowed the contemptuous spirit of the sick man. The water-tanks were low, they had not gained 50 miles in a fortnight. She would never reach Hong-Kong.

It was like fighting desperately towards destruction for the ship and the men. This was evident without argument. Mr. Burns, losing all restraint, put his face close to his Captain's and fairly yelled: "You, sir, are going out of the world. But I can't wait till you are dead before I put the helm up. You must do it yourself. You must do it now!"

The man on the couch snarled in contempt: "So I am going out of the world—am I?"

"Yes, sir—you haven't many days left in it," said Mr. Burns calming down. "One can see it by your face."

"My face, eh? . . . Well, put the helm up and be damned to you."

Burns flew on deck, got the ship before the wind, then came down again, composed but resolute.

"I've shaped a course for Pulo Condor,* sir," he said. "When we make it, if you are still with us, you'll tell me into what port you wish me to take the ship and I'll do it."

The old man gave him a look of savage spite, and said those atrocious words in deadly, slow tones:

"If I had my wish, neither the ship nor any of you would ever reach a port. And I hope you won't."

Mr. Burns was profoundly shocked. I believe he was positively frightened at the time. It seems, however, that he managed to produce such an effective laugh* that it was the old man's turn to be frightened. He shrank within himself and turned his back on him.

"And his head was not gone then," Mr. Burns assured me excitedly. "He meant every word of it."

Such was practically the late captain's last speech. No connected sentence passed his lips afterwards. That night he used the last of his strength to throw his fiddle over the side. No one had actually seen him in the act, but after his death Mr. Burns couldn't find the thing anywhere. The empty case was very much in evidence, but the fiddle was clearly not in the ship. And where else could it have gone to but overboard?

"Threw his violin overboard!" I exclaimed.

"He did," cried Mr. Burns excitedly. "And it's my belief he would have tried to take the ship down with him if it had been in human power. He never meant her to see home again. He wouldn't write to his owners, he never wrote to his old wife either—he wasn't going to. He had made up his mind to cut adrift from everything.* That's what it was. He didn't care for business, or freights, or for making a passage—or anything. He meant to have gone wandering about the world till he lost her with all hands."*

Mr. Burns looked like a man who had escaped great danger. For a little he would have exclaimed: "If it hadn't been for me!" And the transparent innocence of his indignant eyes was underlined quaintly by the arrogant pair of moustaches which he proceeded to twist, and as if extend, horizontally.

I might have smiled if I had not been busy with my own sensations, which were not those of Mr. Burns. I was already the man in command. My sensations could not be like those of any other man on board. In that community I stood, like a king in his country, in a class all by myself. I mean an hereditary king, not a mere elected head of a state. I was brought there to rule by an agency as remote from the people and as inscrutable almost to them as the Grace of God.

And like a member of a dynasty, feeling a semi-mystical bond with the dead, I was profoundly shocked by my immediate predecessor.

That man had been in all essentials but his age just such another man as myself. Yet the end of his life was a complete act of treason, the betrayal of a tradition which seemed to me as imperative as any guide on earth could be. It appeared that even at sea a man could become the victim of evil spirits. I felt on my face the breath of unknown powers that shape our destinies.*

Not to let the silence last too long I asked Mr. Burns if he had written to his captain's wife. He shook his head. He had written to nobody.*

In a moment he became sombre. He never thought of writing. It took him all his time to watch incessantly the loading of the ship by a rascally Chinese stevedore. In this Mr. Burns gave me the first glimpse of the real chief mate's soul which dwelt uneasily in his body.

He mused, then hastened on with gloomy force.

"Yes! The captain died as near noon as possible. I looked through his papers in the afternoon. I read the service over him at sunset and then I stuck the ship's head north and brought her in here. I—brought—her—in."

He struck the table with his fist.

"She would hardly have come in by herself," I observed. "But why didn't you make for Singapore instead?"

His eyes wavered. "The nearest port," he muttered sullenly.

I had framed the question in perfect innocence, but this answer (the difference in distance was insignificant) and his manner offered me a clue to the simple truth. He took the ship to a port where he expected to be confirmed in his temporary command from lack of a qualified master to put over his head. Whereas Singapore, he surmised justly, would be full of qualified men. But his naïve reasoning forgot to take into account the telegraph cable reposing on the bottom of the very Gulf up which he had turned that ship which he imagined himself to have saved from destruction. Hence the bitter flavour of our interview. I tasted it more and more distinctly—and it was less and less to my taste.

"Look here, Mr. Burns," I began, very firmly. "You may as well understand that I did not run after this command. It was pushed in my way. I've accepted it. I am here to take the ship home first of all, and you may be sure that I shall see to it that every one of you on board here does his duty to that end. This is all I have to say—for the present."

He was on his feet by this time, but instead of taking his dismissal he remained with trembling, indignant lips, and looking at me hard as though, really, after this, there was nothing for me to do in common decency but to vanish from his outraged sight. Like all very simple emotional states this was moving. I felt sorry for him—almost sympathetic, till (seeing that I did not vanish) he spoke in a tone of forced restraint.

"If I hadn't a wife and a child at home you may be sure, sir, I would have asked you to let me go the very minute you came on board."

I answered him with a matter-of-course calmness as though some remote third person were in question.

"And I, Mr. Burns, would not have let you go. You have signed the ship's articles as chief officer, and till they are terminated at the final port of discharge I shall expect you to attend to your duty and give me the benefit of your experience to the best of your ability."

Stony incredulity lingered in his eyes; but it broke down before my friendly attitude. With a slight upward toss of his arms (I got to know that gesture well afterwards) he bolted out of the cabin.

We might have saved ourselves that little passage of harmless sparring. Before many days had elapsed it was Mr. Burns who was pleading with me anxiously not to leave him behind; while I could only return him but doubtful answers. The whole thing took on a somewhat tragic complexion.

And this horrible problem was only an extraneous episode, a mere complication in the general problem of how to get that ship—which was mine with her appurtenances and her men, with her body and her spirit now slumbering in that pestilential river—how to get her out to sea.

Mr. Burns, while still acting captain, had hastened to sign a charter-party which in an ideal world without guile would have been an excellent document. Directly I ran my eye over it I foresaw trouble ahead unless the people of the other part were quite exceptionally fair-minded and open to argument.

Mr. Burns, to whom I imparted my fears, chose to take great umbrage at them. He looked at me with that usual incredulous stare, and said bitterly:

"I suppose, sir, you want to make out I've acted like a fool?"

I told him, with my systematic kindliness which always seemed to augment his surprise, that I did not want to make out anything. I would leave that to the future.

And, sure enough, the future brought in a lot of trouble. There were days when I used to remember Captain Giles with nothing short of abhorrence. His confounded acuteness had let me in for this job; while his prophecy that I "would have my hands full" coming true, made it appear as if done on purpose to play an evil joke on my young innocence.

Yes. I had my hands full of complications which were most valuable as "experience." People have a great opinion of the advantages of experience. But in that connection experience means always something disagreeable as opposed to the charm and innocence of illusions.

I must say I was losing mine rapidly. But on these instructive complications I must not enlarge more than to say that they could all be resumed in the one word: Delay.*

A mankind which has invented the proverb, "Time is money," will understand my vexation. The word "Delay" entered the secret chamber of my brain, resounded there like a tolling bell which maddens the ear, affected all my senses, took on a black colouring, a bitter taste, a deadly meaning.

"I am really sorry to see you worried like this. Indeed, I am . . ."

It was the only humane speech I used to hear at that time. And it came from a doctor,* appropriately enough.

A doctor is humane by definition. But that man was so in reality. His speech was not professional. I was not ill. But other people were, and that was the reason of his visiting the ship.

He was the doctor of our Legation and, of course, of the Consulate too. He looked after the ship's health, which generally was poor, and trembling, as it were, on the verge of a break-up. Yes. The men ailed. And thus time was not only money, but life as well.

I had never seen such a steady ship's company. As the doctor remarked to me: "You seem to have a most respectable lot of seamen." Not only were they consistently sober, but they did not even want to go ashore. Care was taken to expose them as little as possible to the sun. They were employed on light work under the awnings. And the humane doctor commended me.

"Your arrangements appear to me to be very judicious, my dear Captain."

It is difficult to express how much that pronouncement

comforted me. The Doctor's round full face framed in a light-coloured whisker was the perfection of a dignified amenity. He was the only human being in the world who seemed to take the slightest interest in me. He would generally sit in the cabin for half-an-hour or so at every visit.

I said to him one day:

"I suppose the only thing now is to take care of them as you are doing, till I can get the ship to sea?"

He inclined his head, shutting his eyes under the large spectacles, and murmured:

"The sea . . . undoubtedly."

The first member of the crew fairly knocked over was the Steward—the first man to whom I had spoken on board. He was taken ashore (with choleraic symptoms*) and died there at the end of a week. Then, while I was still under the startling impression of this first home-thrust of the climate, Mr. Burns gave up and went to bed in a raging fever without saying a word to anybody.

I believe he had partly fretted himself into that illness; the climate did the rest with the swiftness of an invisible monster ambushed in the air, in the water, in the mud of the river-bank. Mr. Burns was a predestined victim.

I discovered him lying on his back, glaring sullenly and radiating heat on one like a small furnace. He would hardly answer my questions, and only grumbled: Couldn't a man take an afternoon off duty with a bad headache—for once?

That evening, as I sat in the saloon after dinner, I could hear him muttering continuously in his room. Ransome, who was clearing the table, said to me:

"I am afraid, sir, I won't be able to give the mate all the attention he's likely to need. I will have to be forward in the galley a great part of my time."

Ransome was the cook. The mate had pointed him out to me the first day, standing on the deck, his arms crossed on his broad chest, gazing on the river.

Even at a distance his well-proportioned figure, something thoroughly sailor-like in his poise, made him noticeable. On nearer view the intelligent, quiet eyes, a well-bred face, the disciplined independence of his manner made up an attractive personality. When, in addition, Mr. Burns told me that he was the best seaman in the ship, I expressed my surprise that in his earliest prime and of such appearance he should sign on as cook on board a ship.

"It's his heart," Mr. Burns had said. "There's something wrong with it. He mustn't exert himself too much or he may drop dead suddenly."

And he was the only one the climate had not touched—perhaps because, carrying a deadly enemy in his breast, he had schooled himself into a systematic control of feelings and movements. When one was in the secret this was apparent in his manner. After the poor Steward died, and as he could not be replaced by a white man in this Oriental port, Ransome had volunteered to do the double work.

"I can do it all right, sir, as long as I go about it quietly," he had assured me.

But obviously he couldn't be expected to take up sick-nursing in addition. Moreover, the doctor peremptorily ordered Mr. Burns ashore.

With a seaman on each side holding him up under the arms, the mate went over the gangway more sullen than ever. We built him up with pillows in the gharry, and he made an effort to say brokenly:

"Now—you've got—what you wanted—got me out of—the ship."

"You were never more mistaken in your life, Mr. Burns," I said quietly, duly smiling at him; and the trap drove off to a sort of sanatorium, a pavilion of bricks which the doctor had in the grounds of his residence.

I visited Mr. Burns regularly. After the first few days, when he didn't know anybody, he received me as if I had come either to gloat over a crushed enemy or else to curry favour with a deeply-wronged person. It was either one or the other, just as it happened according to his fantastic sick-room moods. Whichever it was, he managed to convey it to me even during the period when he appeared almost too weak to talk. I treated him to my invariable kindliness.

Then one day, suddenly, a surge of downright panic burst through all this craziness.

If I left him behind in this deadly place he would die. He felt it, he was certain of it. But I wouldn't have the heart to leave him ashore. He had a wife and child in Sydney.

He produced his wasted fore-arms from under the sheet which covered him and clasped his fleshless claws. He would die! He would die here. . . .

He absolutely managed to sit up, but only for a moment, and when he fell back I really thought that he would die there and then. I called to the Bengali dispenser, and hastened away from the room.

Next day he upset me thoroughly by renewing his entreaties. I returned an evasive answer, and left him the picture of ghastly despair. The day after I went in with reluctance, and he attacked me at once in a much stronger voice and with an abundance of argument which was quite startling. He presented his case with a sort of crazy vigour, and asked me finally how would I like to have a man's death on my conscience? He wanted me to promise that I would not sail without him.

I said that I really must consult the doctor first. He cried out at that. The doctor! Never! That would be a death sentence.

The effort had exhausted him. He closed his eyes, but went on rambling in a low voice. I had hated him from the start. The late captain had hated him too. Had wished him dead. Had wished all hands dead. . . .

"What do you want to stand in with that wicked corpse for, sir? He'll have you too," he ended, blinking his glazed eyes vacantly.

"Mr. Burns," I cried, very much discomposed, "what on earth are you talking about?"

He seemed to come to himself, though he was too weak to start.

"I don't know," he said languidly. "But don't ask that doctor, sir. You and I are sailors. Don't ask him, sir. Some day perhaps you will have a wife and child yourself."

And again he pleaded for the promise that I would not leave

him behind. I had the firmness of mind not to give it to him. Afterwards this sternness seemed criminal; for my mind was made up. That prostrated man, with hardly strength enough to breathe and ravaged by a passion of fear, was irresistible. And, besides, he had happened to hit on the right words. He and I were sailors. That was a claim, for I had no other family. As to the wife-and-child (some day) argument it had no force. It sounded merely bizarre.

I could imagine no claim that would be stronger and more absorbing than the claim of that ship, of these men snared in the river by silly commercial complications, as if in some poisonous trap.

However, I had nearly fought my way out. Out to sea. The sea—which was pure, safe, and friendly. Three days more.

That thought sustained and carried me on my way back to the ship. In the saloon the doctor's voice greeted me, and his large form followed his voice, issuing out of the starboard spare cabin where the ship's medicine chest was kept securely lashed in the bed-place.

Finding that I was not on board he had gone in there, he said, to inspect the supply of drugs, bandages, and so on. Everything was completed and in order.

I thanked him; I had just been thinking of asking him to do that very thing, as in a couple of days, as he knew, we were going to sea, where all our troubles of every sort would be over at last.

He listened gravely and made no answer. But when I opened to him my mind as to Mr. Burns he sat down by my side, and, laying his hand on my knee amicably, begged me to think what it was I was exposing myself to.

The man was just strong enough to bear being moved and no more. But he couldn't stand a return of the fever. I had before me a passage of sixty days perhaps, beginning with intricate navigation and ending probably with a lot of bad weather. Could I run the risk of having to go through it single-handed, with no chief officer and with a second quite a youth? . . .

He might have added that it was my first command too. He did probably think of that fact, for he checked himself. It was very present to my mind.

He advised me earnestly to cable to Singapore for a chief officer, even if I had to delay my sailing for a week.

"Not a day," I said. The very thought gave me the shivers. The hands seemed fairly fit, all of them, and this was the time to get them away. Once at sea I was not afraid of facing anything. The sea was now the only remedy for all my troubles.

The doctor's glasses were directed at me like two lamps searching the genuineness of my resolution. He opened his lips as if to argue further, but shut them again without saying anything. I had a vision of poor Burns so vivid in his exhaustion, helplessness, and anguish, that it moved me more than the reality I had come away from only an hour before. It was purged from the drawbacks of his personality, and I could not resist it.

"Look here," I said. "Unless you tell me officially that the man must not be moved I'll make arrangements to have him brought on board tomorrow, and shall take the ship out of the river next morning, even if I have to anchor outside the bar for a couple of days to get her ready for sea."

"Oh! I'll make all the arrangements myself," said the doctor at once. "I spoke as I did only as a friend—as a well-wisher, and that sort of thing."

He rose in his dignified simplicity and gave me a warm handshake, rather solemnly, I thought. But he was as good as his word. When Mr. Burns appeared at the gangway carried on a stretcher, the doctor himself walked by its side. The programme had been altered in so far that this transportation had been left to the last moment, on the very morning of our departure.

It was barely an hour after sunrise. The doctor waved his big arm to me from the shore and walked back at once to his trap, which had followed him empty to the river-side. Mr. Burns, carried across the quarter-deck, had the appearance of being absolutely lifeless. Ransome went down to settle him in his cabin. I had to remain on deck to look after the ship, for the tug had got hold of our tow-rope already.

The splash of our shore-fasts falling in the water produced a complete change of feeling in me. It was like the imperfect relief of awakening from a nightmare. But when the ship's head swung down the river away from that town, Oriental and squalid, I missed the expected elation of that striven-for moment. What there was, undoubtedly, was a relaxation of tension which translated itself into a sense of weariness after an inglorious fight.

About midday we anchored a mile outside the bar. The afternoon was busy for all hands. Watching the work from the poop, where I remained all the time, I detected in it some of the languor of the six weeks spent in the steaming heat of the river. The first breeze would blow that away. Now the calm was complete. I judged that the second officer—a callow youth with an unpromising face—was not, to put it mildly, of that invaluable stuff from which a commander's right hand is made. But I was glad to catch along the main deck a few smiles on those seamen's faces at which I had hardly had time to have a good look as yet. Having thrown off the mortal coil of shore affairs,* I felt myself familiar with them and yet a little strange, like a long-lost wanderer among his kin.

Ransome flitted continually to and fro between the galley and the cabin. It was a pleasure to look at him. The man positively had grace. He alone of all the crew had not had a day's illness in port. But with the knowledge of that uneasy heart within his breast I could detect the restraint he put on the natural sailor-like agility of his movements. It was as though he had something very fragile or very explosive to carry about his person and was all the time aware of it.

I had occasion to address him once or twice. He answered me in his pleasant quiet voice and with a faint, slightly wistful smile. Mr. Burns appeared to be resting. He seemed fairly comfortable.

After sunset I came out on deck again to meet only a still void. The thin, featureless crust of the coast could not be distinguished. The darkness had risen around the ship like a mysterious emanation from the dumb and lonely waters. I leaned on the rail and turned my ear to the shadows of the night. Not a sound. My command might have been a planet* flying vertiginously on its appointed path in a space of infinite silence. I clung to the rail as if my sense of balance were leaving me for good. How absurd. I hailed nervously.

"On deck there!"

The immediate answer, "Yes, sir," broke the spell. The anchor-watch man ran up the poop ladder smartly. I told him to report at once the slightest sign of a breeze coming.

Going below I looked in on Mr. Burns. In fact, I could not avoid seeing him, for his door stood open. The man was so wasted that, in that white cabin, under a white sheet, and with his diminished head sunk in the white pillow, his red moustaches captured one's eyes exclusively, like something artificial—a pair of moustaches from a shop exhibited there in the harsh light of the bulkhead-lamp without a shade.

While I stared with a sort of wonder he asserted himself by opening his eyes and even moving them in my direction. A minute stir.

"Dead calm, Mr. Burns," I said resignedly.

In an unexpectedly distinct voice Mr. Burns began a rambling speech. Its tone was very strange, not as if affected by his illness, but as if of a different nature. It sounded unearthly. As to the matter, I seemed to make out that it was the fault of the "old man"—the late captain—ambushed down there* under the sea with some evil intention. It was a weird story.

I listened to the end; then stepping into the cabin I laid my hand on the mate's forehead. It was cool. He was light-headed only from extreme weakness. Suddenly he seemed to become aware of me, and in his own voice—of course, very feeble—he asked regretfully:

"Is there no chance at all to get under way, sir?"

"What's the good of letting go our hold of the ground only to drift, Mr. Burns?"* I answered.

He sighed, and I left him to his immobility. His hold on life was as slender as his hold on sanity. I was oppressed by my lonely responsibilities.* I went into my cabin to seek relief in a few hours' sleep, but almost before I closed my eyes the man on deck came down reporting a light breeze. Enough to get under way with, he said.

And it was no more than just enough. I ordered the windlass manned, the sails loosed, and the topsails set. But by the time I had cast the ship I could hardly feel any breath of wind. Nevertheless, I trimmed the yards and put everything on her. I was not going to give up the attempt.

IV

WITH her anchor at the bow and clothed in canvas to her very trucks, my command seemed to stand as motionless as a model ship set on the gleams and shadows of polished marble.* It was impossible to distinguish land from water in the enigmatical tranquillity of the immense forces of the world. A sudden impatience possessed me.

"Won't she answer the helm at all?" I said irritably to the man whose strong brown hands grasping the spokes of the wheel stood out lighted on the darkness; like a symbol of mankind's claim to the direction of its own fate.

He answered me:

"Yes, sir. She's coming-to slowly."

"Let her head come up to south."

"Aye, aye, sir."

I paced the poop. There was not a sound but that of my footsteps, till the man spoke again.

"She is at south now, sir."

I felt a slight tightness of the chest before I gave out the first course of my first command to the silent night, heavy with dew and sparkling with stars. There was a finality in the act committing me to the endless vigilance of my lonely task.

"Steady her head at that," I said at last. "The course is south."

"South, sir," echoed the man.

I sent below the second mate and his watch and remained in charge, walking the deck through the chill, somnolent hours that precede the dawn.

Slight puffs came and went, and whenever they were strong enough to wake up the black water the murmur alongside ran through my very heart in a delicate crescendo of delight and died away swiftly. I was bitterly tired. The very stars seemed weary of waiting for daybreak. It came at last with a mother-of-pearl sheen at the zenith, such as I had never seen before in the tropics, unglowing, almost grey, with a strange reminder of high latitudes.

The voice of the look-out man hailed from forward:

"Land on the port bow, sir."

"All right."

Leaning on the rail I never even raised my eyes. The motion of the ship was imperceptible. Presently Ransome brought me the cup of morning coffee. After I had drunk it I looked ahead, and in the still streak of very bright pale orange light I saw the land profiled flatly as if cut out of black paper and seeming to float on the water as light as cork. But the rising sun turned it into mere dark vapour, a doubtful, massive shadow trembling in the hot glare.

The watch finished washing decks.* I went below and stopped at Mr. Burns' door (he could not bear to have it shut), but hesitated to speak to him till he moved his eyes. I gave him the news.

"Sighted Cape Liant at daylight. About fifteen miles."

He moved his lips then, but I heard no sound till I put my ear down, and caught the peevish comment: "This is crawling. . . . No luck."

"Better luck than standing still, anyhow," I pointed out resignedly, and left him to whatever thoughts or fancies haunted his hopeless prostration.

Later that morning, when relieved by my second officer, I threw myself on my couch and for some three hours or so I really found oblivion. It was so perfect that on waking up I wondered where I was. Then came the immense relief of the thought: on board my ship! At sea! At sea!

Through the port-holes I beheld an unruffled, sun-smitten horizon. The horizon of a windless day. But its spaciousness alone was enough to give me a sense of a fortunate escape, a momentary exultation of freedom.

I stepped out into the saloon with my heart lighter than it had been for days. Ransome was at the sideboard preparing to lay the table for the first sea dinner of the passage. He turned his head, and something in his eyes checked my modest elation.

Instinctively I asked: "What is it now?" not expecting in the least the answer I got. It was given with that sort of contained serenity which was characteristic of the man.

"I am afraid we haven't left all sickness behind us, sir."

"We haven't! What's the matter?"

He told me then that two of our men had been taken bad with fever in the night. One of them was burning and the other was shivering, but he thought that it was pretty much the same thing. I thought so too. I felt shocked by the news. "One burning, the other shivering, you say? No. We haven't left the sickness behind. Do they look very ill?"

"Middling bad, sir." Ransome's eyes gazed steadily into mine. We exchanged smiles. Ransome's a little wistful, as usual, mine no doubt grim enough, to correspond with my secret exasperation.

I asked:

"Was there any wind at all this morning?"

"Can hardly say that, sir. We've moved all the time though. The land ahead seems a little nearer."

That was it. A little nearer. Whereas if we had only had a little more wind, only a very little more, we might, we should, have been abreast of Liant by this time and increasing our distance from that contaminated shore. And it was not only the distance. It seemed to me that a stronger breeze would have blown away the infection which clung to the ship. It obviously did cling to the ship. Two men. One burning, one shivering. I felt a distinct reluctance to go and look at them. What was the good? Poison is poison. Tropical fever is tropical fever. But that it should have stretched its claw after us over the sea seemed to me an extraordinary and unfair licence.* I could hardly believe that it could be anything worse than the last desperate pluck of the evil from which we were escaping into the clean breath of the sea. If only that breath had been a little stronger. However, there was the quinine against the fever. I went into the spare cabin where the medicine chest was kept to prepare two doses. I opened it full of faith as a man opens a miraculous shrine. The upper part was inhabited by a collection of bottles, all square-shouldered and as like each other as peas. Under that orderly array there were two drawers, stuffed as full of things as one could imagine—paper packages, bandages, cardboard boxes officially labelled. The lower of the two, in one of its compartments, contained our provision of quinine.

There were five bottles, all round and all of a size. One was about a third full. The other four remained still wrapped up in paper and sealed. But I did not expect to see an envelope lying on top of them. A square envelope, belonging, in fact, to the ship's stationery.

It lay so that I could see it was not closed down, and on picking it up and turning it over I perceived that it was addressed to myself. It contained a half-sheet of notepaper, which I unfolded with a queer sense of dealing with the uncanny, but without any excitement as people meet and do extraordinary things in a dream.

"My dear Captain," it began, but I ran to the signature. The writer was the doctor. The date was that of the day on which, returning from my visit to Mr. Burns in the hospital, I had found the excellent doctor waiting for me in the cabin; and when he told me that he had been putting in time inspecting the medicine chest for me. How bizarre! While expecting me to come in at any moment he had been amusing himself by writing me a letter, and then as I came in had hastened to stuff it into the medicine-chest drawer. A rather incredible proceeding. I turned to the text in wonder.

In a large, hurried, but legible hand the good, sympathetic man for some reason, either of kindness or more likely impelled by the irresistible desire to express his opinion, with which he didn't want to damp my hopes before, was warning me not to put my trust in the beneficial effects of a change from land to sea. "I didn't want to add to your worries by discouraging your hopes," he wrote. "I am afraid that, medically speaking, the end of your troubles is not yet." In short, he expected me to have to fight a probable return of tropical illness. Fortunately I had a good provision of quinine. I should put my trust in that, and administer it steadily, when the ship's health would certainly improve.

I crumpled up the letter and rammed it into my pocket. Ransome carried off two big doses to the men forward. As to myself, I did not go on deck as yet. I went instead to the door of Mr. Burns' room, and gave him that news too.

It was impossible to say the effect it had on him. At first I thought that he was speechless. His head lay sunk in the pillow. He moved his lips enough, however, to assure me that he was getting much stronger; a statement shockingly untrue on the face of it.

That afternoon I took my watch as a matter of course. A great over-heated stillness enveloped the ship and seemed to hold her motionless in a flaming ambience composed in two shades of blue. Faint, hot puffs eddied nervelessly from her sails. And yet she moved. She must have. For, as the sun was setting, we had drawn abreast of Cape Liant and dropped it behind us: an ominous retreating shadow in the last gleams of twilight.

In the evening, under the crude glare of his lamp, Mr. Burns seemed to have come more to the surface of his bedding. It was as if a depressing hand had been lifted off him. He answered my few words by a comparatively long, connected speech. He asserted himself strongly. If he escaped being smothered by this stagnant heat, he said, he was confident that in a very few days he would be able to come up on deck and help me.

While he was speaking I trembled lest this effort of energy should leave him lifeless before my eyes. But I cannot deny that there was something comforting in his willingness. I made a suitable reply, but pointed out to him that the only thing that could really help us was wind—a fair wind.

He rolled his head impatiently on the pillow. And it was not comforting in the least to hear him begin to mutter crazily about the late captain, that old man buried in latitude 8° 20′, right in our way—ambushed* at the entrance of the Gulf.

"Are you still thinking of your late Captain, Mr. Burns?" I said. "I imagine the dead feel no animosity against the living. They care nothing for them."

"You don't know that one," he breathed out feebly.

"No. I didn't know him, and he didn't know me. And so he can't have any grievance against me, anyway."

"Yes. But there's all the rest of us on board," he insisted.

I felt the inexpugnable strength of common sense being insidiously menaced by this gruesome, by this insane delusion. And I said:

"You mustn't talk so much. You will tire yourself."

"And there is the ship herself," he persisted in a whisper.

"Now, not a word more," I said, stepping in and laying my hand on his cool forehead. It proved to me that this atrocious absurdity was rooted in the man himself and not in the disease, which, apparently, had emptied him of every power, mental and physical, except that one fixed idea.

I avoided giving Mr. Burns any opening for conversation for the next few days. I merely used to throw him a hasty, cheery word when passing his door. I believe that if he had had the strength he would have called out after me more than once. But he hadn't the strength. Ransome, however, observed to me one afternoon that the mate "seemed to be picking up wonderfully."

"Did he talk any nonsense to you of late?" I asked casually.

"No, sir." Ransome was startled by the direct question; but, after a pause, he added equably: "He told me this morning, sir, that he was sorry he had to bury our late Captain right in the ship's way, as one may say, out of the Gulf."

"Isn't this nonsense enough for you?" I asked, looking confidently at the intelligent, quiet face on which the secret uneasiness in the man's breast had thrown a transparent veil of care.

Ransome didn't know. He had not given a thought to the matter. And with a faint smile he flitted away from me on his never-ending duties, with his usual guarded activity.

Two more days passed. We had advanced a little way—a very little way—into the larger space of the Gulf of Siam. Seizing eagerly upon the elation of the first command thrown into my lap, by the agency of Captain Giles, I had yet an uneasy feeling that such luck as this has got perhaps to be paid for in some way. I had held, professionally, a review of my chances. I was competent enough for that. At least, I thought so. I had a general sense of my preparedness which only a man pursuing a calling he loves can know. That feeling seemed to me the most natural thing in the world. As natural as breathing. I imagined I could not have lived without it.

I don't know what I expected. Perhaps nothing else than that special intensity of existence which is the quintessence of youthful aspirations. Whatever I expected I did not expect to be beset by hurricanes. I knew better than that. In the Gulf of Siam there are no hurricanes. But neither did I expect to find myself bound hand and foot to the hopeless extent which was revealed to me as the days went on.

Not that the evil spell held us always motionless. Mysterious currents drifted us here and there, with a stealthy power made manifest by the changing vistas of the islands fringing the east shore of the Gulf. And there were winds too, fitful and deceitful. They raised hopes only to dash them into the bitterest disappointment, promises of advance ending in lost ground, expiring in sighs, dying into dumb stillness in which the currents had it all their own way—their own inimical way.

The Island of Koh-ring,* a great, black, upheaved ridge amongst a lot of tiny islets, lying upon the glassy water like a triton amongst minnows, seemed to be the centre of the fatal circle. It seemed impossible to get away from it. Day after day it remained in sight. More than once, in a favourable breeze, I would take its bearing in the fast-ebbing twilight, thinking that it was for the last time. Vain hope. A night of fitful airs would undo the gains of temporary favour, and the rising sun would throw out the black relief of Koh-ring, looking more barren, inhospitable, and grim than ever.

"It's like being bewitched, upon my word," I said once to Mr. Burns, from my usual position in the doorway.

He was sitting up in his bed-place. He was progressing towards the world of living men; if he could hardly have been said to have rejoined it yet. He nodded to me his frail and bony head in a wisely mysterious assent.

"Oh, yes, I know what you mean," I said. "But you cannot expect me to believe that a dead man has the power to put out of joint the meteorology of this part of the world.* Though indeed it seems to have gone utterly wrong. The land and sea breezes have got broken up into small pieces. We cannot depend upon them for five minutes together."

"It won't be very long now before I can come up on deck," muttered Mr. Burns, "and then we shall see."

Whether he meant this for a promise to grapple with supernatural evil I couldn't tell. At any rate, it wasn't the kind of assistance I needed. On the other hand, I had been living on deck practically night and day so as to take advantage of every chance to get my ship a little more to the southward. The mate, I could see, was extremely weak yet, and not quite rid of his delusion, which to me appeared but a symptom of his disease. At all events, the hopefulness of an invalid was not to be discouraged. I said:

"You will be most welcome there, I am sure, Mr. Burns. If you go on improving at this rate you'll be presently one of the healthiest men in the ship."

This pleased him, but his extreme emaciation converted his self-satisfied smile into a ghastly exhibition of long teeth under the red moustache.

"Aren't the fellows improving, sir?" he asked soberly, with an extremely sensible expression of anxiety on his face.

I answered him only with a vague gesture and went away from the door. The fact was that disease played with us capriciously very much as the winds did. It would go from one man to another with a lighter or heavier touch, which always left its mark behind, staggering some, knocking others over for a time, leaving this one, returning to another, so that all of them had now an invalidish aspect and a hunted, apprehensive look in their eyes; while Ransome and I, the only two completely untouched, went amongst them assiduously distributing quinine. It was a double fight. The adverse weather held us in front and the disease pressed on our rear. I must say that the men were very good. The constant toil of trimming the yards they faced willingly. But all spring was out of their limbs, and as I looked at them from the poop I could not keep from my mind the dreadful impression that they were moving in poisoned air.

Down below, in his cabin, Mr. Burns had advanced so far as not only to be able to sit up, but even to draw up his legs. Clasping them with bony arms, like an animated skeleton, he emitted deep, impatient sighs.

"The great thing to do, sir," he would tell me on every occasion, when I gave him the chance, "the great thing is to get the ship past 8° 20′ of latitude. Once she's past that we're all right."

At first I used only to smile at him, though, God knows, I had not much heart left for smiles. But at last I lost my patience.

"Oh, yes. The latitude 8° 20′. That's where you buried your late Captain, isn't it?" Then with severity: "Don't you think, Mr. Burns, it's about time you dropped all that nonsense?"

He rolled at me his deep-sunken eyes in a glance of invincible obstinacy. But for the rest, he only muttered, just loud enough for me to hear, something about "Not surprised . . . find . . . play us some beastly trick yet . . ."

Such passages as this were not exactly wholesome for my resolution. The stress of adversity was beginning to tell on me. At the same time I felt a contempt for that obscure weakness of my soul. I said to myself disdainfully that it should take much more than that to affect in the smallest degree my fortitude.

I didn't know then how soon and from what unexpected direction it would be attacked.

It was the very next day. The sun had risen clear of the southern shoulder of Koh-ring, which still hung, like an evil attendant, on our port quarter. It was intensely hateful to my sight. During the night we had been heading all round the compass, trimming the yards again and again, to what I fear must have been for the most part imaginary puffs of air. Then just about sunrise we got for an hour an inexplicable, steady breeze, right in our teeth. There was no sense in it. It fitted neither with the season of the year, nor with the secular experience of seamen as recorded in books, nor with the aspect of the sky. Only purposeful malevolence could account for it. It sent us travelling at a great pace away from our proper course; and if we had been out on pleasure sailing bent it would have been a delightful breeze, with the awakened sparkle of the sea, with the sense of motion and a feeling of unwonted freshness. Then all at once, as if disdaining to carry farther the sorry jest, it dropped and died out completely in less than five minutes. The ship's head swung where it listed;* the stilled sea took on the polish of a steel plate in the calm.

I went below, not because I meant to take some rest, but simply because I couldn't bear to look at it just then. The indefatigable Ransome was busy in the saloon. It had become a regular practice with him to give me an informal health report in the morning. He turned away from the sideboard with his usual pleasant, quiet gaze. No shadow rested on his intelligent forehead.

"There are a good many of them middling bad this morning, sir," he said in a calm tone.

"What? All knocked out?"

"Only two actually in their bunks, sir, but . . ."

"It's the last night that has done for them. We have had to pull and haul all the blessed time."

"I heard, sir. I had a mind to come out and help only, you know. . . ."

"Certainly not. You mustn't. . . . The fellows lie at night about the decks, too. It isn't good for them."

Ransome assented. But men couldn't be looked after like children. Moreover, one could hardly blame them for trying for such coolness and such air as there was to be found on deck. He himself, of course, knew better.

He was, indeed, a reasonable man. Yet it would have been hard to say that the others were not. The last few days had been for us like the ordeal of the fiery furnace.* One really couldn't quarrel with their common, imprudent humanity making the best of the moments of relief, when the night brought in the illusion of coolness and the starlight twinkled through the heavy, dew-laden air. Moreover, most of them were so weakened that hardly anything could be done without everybody that could totter mustering on the braces. No, it was no use remonstrating with them. But I fully believed that quinine was of very great use indeed.

I believed in it. I pinned my faith to it. It would save the men, the ship, break the spell by its medicinal virtue, make time of no account, the weather but a passing worry, and, like a magic powder working against mysterious malefices,* secure the first passage of my first command against the evil powers of calms and pestilence. I looked upon it as more precious than gold, and unlike gold, of which there ever hardly seems to be enough anywhere, the ship had a sufficient store of it. I went in to get it with the purpose of weighing out doses. I stretched my hand with the feeling of a man reaching for an unfailing panacea, took up a fresh bottle and unrolled the wrapper, noticing as I did so that the ends, both top and bottom, had come unsealed. . . .

But why record all the swift steps of the appalling discovery. You have guessed the truth already. There was the wrapper, the bottle, and the white powder inside, some sort of powder! But it wasn't quinine. One look at it was quite enough. I remember that at the very moment of picking up the bottle, before I even dealt with the wrapper, the weight of the object I had in my hand gave me an instant of premonition. Quinine is as light as feathers; and my nerves must have been exasperated into an extraordinary sensibility. I let the bottle smash itself on the floor. The stuff, whatever it was, felt gritty under the sole of my shoe. I snatched up the next bottle and then the next. The weight alone told the tale. One after another they fell, breaking at my feet, not because I threw them down in my dismay, but slipping through my fingers as if this disclosure were too much for my strength.

It is a fact that the very greatness of a mental shock helps one to bear up against it, by producing a sort of temporary insensibility. I came out of the state-room stunned, as if something heavy had dropped on my head. From the other side of the saloon, across the table, Ransome, with a duster in his hand, stared open-mouthed. I don't think that I looked wild. It is quite possible that I appeared to be in a hurry because I was instinctively hastening up on deck. An example this of training become instinct. The difficulties, the dangers, the problems of a ship at sea must be met on deck.

To this fact, as it were of nature, I responded instinctively; which may be taken as a proof that for a moment I must have been robbed of my reason.

I was certainly off my balance, a prey to impulse, for at the bottom of the stairs I turned and flung myself at the doorway of

Mr. Burns' cabin. The wildness of his aspect checked my mental disorder. He was sitting up in his bunk, his body looking immensely long, his head drooping a little sideways, with affected complacency. He flourished, in his trembling hand, on the end of a fore-arm no thicker than a stout walking-stick, a shining pair of scissors which he tried before my very eyes to jab at his throat.

I was to a certain extent horrified; but it was rather a secondary sort of effect, not really strong enough to make me yell at him in some such manner as: "Stop!" . . . "Heavens!" . . . "What are you doing?"

In reality he was simply overtaxing his returning strength in a shaky attempt to clip off the thick growth of his red beard. A large towel was spread over his lap, and a shower of stiff hairs, like bits of copper wire,* was descending on it at every snip of the scissors.

He turned to me his face grotesque beyond the fantasies of mad dreams, one cheek all bushy as if with a swollen flame, the other denuded and sunken, with the untouched long moustache on that side asserting itself, lonely and fierce. And while he stared thunderstruck, with the gaping scissors on his fingers, I shouted my discovery at him fiendishly, in six words, without comment.

V

I HEARD the clatter of the scissors escaping from his hand, noted the perilous heave of his whole person over the edge of the bunk after them, and then, returning to my first purpose, pursued my course on to the deck. The sparkle of the sea filled my eyes. It was gorgeous and barren, monotonous and without hope under the empty curve of the sky. The sails hung motionless and slack, the very folds of their sagging surfaces moved no more than carved granite. The impetuosity of my advent made the man at the helm start slightly. A block aloft squeaked incomprehensibly, for what on earth could have made it do so? It was a whistling note like a bird's. For a long, long time I faced an empty world, steeped in an infinity of silence, through which the sunshine poured and flowed for some mysterious purpose. Then I heard Ransome's voice at my elbow.

"I have put Mr. Burns back to bed, sir."

"You have."

"Well, sir, he got out, all of a sudden, but when he let go of the edge of his bunk he fell down. He isn't light-headed, though, it seems to me."

"No," I said dully, without looking at Ransome. He waited for a moment, then, cautiously as if not to give offence: "I don't think we need lose much of that stuff, sir," he said, "I can sweep it up, every bit of it almost, and then we could sift the glass out. I will go about it at once. It will not make the breakfast late, not ten minutes."

"Oh, yes," I said bitterly. "Let the breakfast wait, sweep up every bit of it, and then throw the damned lot overboard!"

The profound silence returned, and when I looked over my shoulder Ransome—the intelligent, serene Ransome—had vanished from my side. The intense loneliness of the sea acted like poison on my brain. When I turned my eyes to the ship, I had a morbid vision of her as a floating grave. Who hasn't heard of ships found drifting, haphazard, with their crews all dead?* I looked at the seaman at the helm, I had an impulse to speak to him, and, indeed, his face took on an expectant cast as if he had guessed my intention. But in the end I went below, thinking I would be alone with the greatness of my trouble for a little while. But through his open door Mr. Burns saw me come down, and addressed me grumpily: "Well, sir?"

I went in. "It isn't well at all," I said.

Mr. Burns, re-established in his bed-place, was concealing his hirsute cheek in the palm of his hand.

"That confounded fellow has taken away the scissors from me," were the next words he said.

The tension I was suffering from was so great that it was perhaps just as well that Mr. Burns had started on this grievance. He seemed very sore about it and grumbled, "Does he think I am mad, or what?"

"I don't think so, Mr. Burns," I said. I looked upon him at that moment as a model of self-possession. I even conceived on that account a sort of admiration for that man, who had (apart from the intense materiality of what was left of his beard) come as near to being a disembodied spirit as any man can do and live. I noticed the preternatural sharpness of the ridge of his nose, the deep cavities of his temples, and I envied him. He was so reduced that he would probably die very soon. Enviable man! So near extinction—while I had to bear within me a tumult of suffering vitality, doubt, confusion, self-reproach, and an indefinite reluctance to meet the horrid logic of the situation. I could not help muttering: "I feel as if I were going mad myself."

Mr. Burns glared spectrally, but otherwise was wonderfully composed.

"I always thought he would play us some deadly trick," he said, with a peculiar emphasis on the *he*.

It gave me a mental shock, but I had neither the mind, nor the heart, nor the spirit to argue with him. My form of sickness was indifference. The creeping paralysis of a hopeless outlook. So I only gazed at him. Mr. Burns broke into further speech.

"Eh? What? No! You won't believe it? Well, how do you account for this? How do you think it could have happened?"

"Happened?" I repeated dully. "Why, yes, how in the name of the infernal powers did this thing happen?"

Indeed, on thinking it out, it seemed incomprehensible that it should just be like this: the bottles emptied, refilled, rewrapped, and replaced. A sort of plot, a sinister attempt to deceive, a thing resembling sly vengeance—but for what?—or else a fiendish joke. But Mr. Burns was in possession of a theory. It was simple, and he uttered it solemnly in a hollow voice.

"I suppose they have given him about fifteen pounds in Haiphong for that little lot."

"Mr. Burns!" I cried.

He nodded grotesquely over his raised legs, like two broomsticks in the pyjamas, with enormous bare feet at the end.

"Why not? The stuff is pretty expensive in this part of the world, and they were very short of it in Tonkin. And what did he care? You have not known him. I have, and I have defied him. He feared neither God, nor devil, nor man, nor wind, nor sea, nor his own conscience. And I believe he hated everybody and everything. But I think he was afraid to die. I believe I am the only man who ever stood up to him. I faced him in that cabin where you live now, when he was sick, and I cowed him then. He thought I was going to twist his neck for him. If he had had his way we would have been beating up against the North-East monsoon,* as long as he lived and afterwards too, for ages and ages. Acting the Flying Dutchman* in the China Sea! Ha! Ha!"

"But why should he replace the bottles like this?" . . . I began.

"Why shouldn't he? Why should he want to throw the bottles away? They fit the drawer. They belong to the medicine chest."

"And they were wrapped up," I cried.

"Well, the wrappers were there. Did it from habit, I suppose, and as to refilling, there is always a lot of stuff they send in paper parcels that burst after a time. And then, who can tell? I suppose you didn't taste it, sir? But, of course, you are sure . . ."

"No," I said. "I didn't taste it. It is all overboard now."

Behind me, a soft, cultivated voice said: "I have tasted it. It seemed a mixture of all sorts, sweetish, saltish, very horrible."

Ransome, stepping out of the pantry, had been listening for some time, as it was very excusable in him to do.

"A dirty trick," said Mr. Burns. "I always said he would."

The magnitude of my indignation was unbounded. And the kind, sympathetic doctor too. The only sympathetic man I ever knew . . . instead of writing that warning letter, the very refinement of sympathy, why didn't the man make a proper inspection? But, as a matter of fact, it was hardly fair to blame the doctor. The fittings were in order and the medicine chest is an officially arranged affair. There was nothing really to arouse the slightest suspicion. The person I could never forgive was myself. Nothing should ever be taken for granted. The seed of everlasting remorse was sown in my breast.

"I feel it's all my fault," I exclaimed, "mine, and nobody else's. That's how I feel. I shall never forgive myself."

"That's very foolish, sir," said Mr. Burns fiercely.

And after this effort he fell back exhausted on his bed. He closed his eyes, he panted; this affair, this abominable surprise had shaken him up too. As I turned away I perceived Ransome looking at me blankly. He appreciated what it meant, but he managed to produce his pleasant, wistful smile. Then he stepped back into his pantry, and I rushed up on deck again to see whether there was any wind, any breath under the sky, any stir of the air, any sign of hope. The deadly stillness met me again. Nothing was changed except that there was a different man at the wheel. He looked ill. His whole figure drooped, and he seemed rather to cling to the spokes than hold them with a controlling grip. I said to him:

"You are not fit to be here."

"I can manage, sir," he said feebly.

As a matter of fact, there was nothing for him to do. The ship had no steerage way. She lay with her head to the westward, the everlasting Koh-ring visible over the stern, with a few small islets, black spots in the great blaze, swimming before my troubled eyes. And but for those bits of land there was no speck on the sky, no speck on the water, no shape of vapour, no wisp of smoke, no sail, no boat, no stir of humanity, no sign of life, nothing!

The first question was, what to do? What could one do? The first thing to do obviously was to tell the men. I did it that very day. I wasn't going to let the knowledge simply get about. I would face them. They were assembled on the quarter-deck for the purpose. Just before I stepped out to speak to them I discovered that life could hold terrible moments. No confessed criminal had ever been so oppressed by his sense of guilt. This is why, perhaps, my face was set hard and my voice curt and unemotional while I made my declaration that I could do nothing more for the sick, in the way of drugs. As to such care as could be given them they knew they had had it.

I would have held them justified in tearing me limb from limb. The silence which followed upon my words was almost harder to bear than the angriest uproar. I was crushed by the infinite depth of its reproach. But, as a matter of fact, I was mistaken. In a voice which I had great difficulty in keeping firm, I went on: "I suppose, men, you have understood what I said, and you know what it means."

A voice or two were heard: "Yes, sir. . . . We understand."

They had kept silent simply because they thought that they were not called to say anything; and when I told them that I intended to run into Singapore and that the best chance for the ship and the men was in the efforts all of us, sick and well, must make to get her along out of this, I received the encouragement of a low assenting murmur and of a louder voice exclaiming: "Surely there is a way out of this blamed hole."

* * *

Here is an extract from the notes I wrote at the time.*

"We have lost Koh-ring at last. For many days now I don't think I have been two hours below altogether. I remain on deck, of course, night and day, and the nights and the days wheel over us in succession, whether long or short, who can say? All sense of time is lost in the monotony of expectation, of hope, and of desire—which is only one: Get the ship to the southward! Get the ship to the southward! The effect is curiously mechanical; the sun climbs and descends, the night swings over our heads as if somebody below the horizon were turning a crank.* It is the pettiest, the most aimless! . . . and all through that miserable performance I go on, tramping, tramping the deck. How many miles have I walked on the poop of that ship! A stubborn pilgrimage of sheer restlessness, diversified by short excursions below to look upon Mr. Burns. I don't know whether it is an illusion, but he seems to become more substantial from day to day. He doesn't say much, for, indeed, the situation doesn't lend itself to idle remarks. I notice this even with the men as I watch them moving or sitting about the decks. They don't talk to each other. It strikes me that if there exist an invisible ear catching the whispers of the earth, it will find this ship the most silent spot on it. . . .

"No, Mr. Burns has not much to say to me. He sits in his bunk with his beard gone, his moustaches flaming, and with an air of silent determination on his chalky physiognomy. Ransome tells me he devours all the food that is given him to the last scrap, but that, apparently, he sleeps very little. Even at night, when I go below to fill my pipe, I notice that, though dozing flat on his back, he still looks very determined. From the side glance he gives me when awake it seems as though he were annoyed at being interrupted in some arduous mental operation; and as I emerge on deck the ordered arrangement of the stars meets my eye, unclouded, infinitely wearisome. There they are: stars, sun, sea, light, darkness, space, great waters; the formidable Work of the Seven Days,* into which mankind seems to have blundered unbidden. Or else decoyed. Even as I have been decoyed into this awful, this death-haunted command. . . ."

* * *

The only spot of light in the ship at night was that of the compass-lamps, lighting up the faces of the succeeding helmsmen; for the rest we were lost in the darkness, I walking the poop and the men lying about the decks. They were all so reduced by sickness that no watches could be kept. Those who were able to walk remained all the time on duty, lying about in the shadows of the main deck, till my voice raised for an order would bring them to their enfeebled feet, a tottering little group, moving patiently about the ship, with hardly a murmur, a whisper amongst them all. And every time I had to raise my voice it was with a pang of remorse and pity.

Then about four o'clock in the morning a light would gleam forward in the galley. The unfailing Ransome with the uneasy heart, immune, serene, and active, was getting ready the early coffee for the men. Presently he would bring me a cup up on the poop, and it was then that I allowed myself to drop into my deck-chair for a couple of hours of real sleep. No doubt I must have been snatching short dozes when leaning against the rail for a moment in sheer exhaustion; but, honestly, I was not aware of them, except in the painful form of convulsive starts that seemed to come on me even while I walked. From about five, however, until after seven I would sleep openly under the fading stars.

I would say to the helmsman: "Call me at need," and drop into that chair and close my eyes, feeling that there was no more sleep for me on earth. And then I would know nothing till, some time between seven and eight, I would feel a touch on my shoulder and look up at Ransome's face, with its faint, wistful smile and friendly, grey eyes, as though he were tenderly amused at my slumbers. Occasionally the second mate would come up and relieve me at early coffee time. But it didn't really matter. Generally it was a dead calm, or else faint airs so changing and fugitive that it really wasn't worth while to touch a brace for them. If the air steadied at all the seaman at the helm could be trusted for a warning shout: "Ship's all aback, sir!" which like a trumpet-call would make me spring a foot above the deck. Those were the words which it seemed to me would have made me spring up from eternal sleep. But this was not often. I have never met since such breathless sunrises. And if the second mate happened to be there (he had generally one day in three free of fever) I would find him sitting on the skylight half-senseless, as it were, and with an idiotic gaze fastened on some object near by—a rope, a cleat, a belaying pin, a ringbolt.

That young man was rather troublesome. He remained cubbish in his sufferings. He seemed to have become completely imbecile; and when the return of fever drove him to his cabin below the next thing would be that we would miss him from there. The first time it happened Ransome and I were very much alarmed. We started a quiet search and ultimately Ransome discovered him curled up in the sail-locker, which opened into the lobby by a sliding-door. When remonstrated with, he muttered sulkily, "It's cool in there." That wasn't true. It was only dark there.

The fundamental defects of his face were not improved by its uniform livid hue.* It was not so with many of the men. The wastage of ill-health seemed to idealise the general character of the features, bringing out the unsuspected nobility of some, the strength of others, and in one case revealing an essentially comic aspect. He was a short, gingery, active man with a nose and chin of the Punch type,* and whom his shipmates called "Frenchy." I don't know why. He may have been a Frenchman, but I have never heard him utter a single word in French.

To see him coming aft to the wheel comforted one. The blue dungaree trousers turned up the calf, one leg a little higher than the other, the clean check shirt, the white canvas cap, evidently made by himself, made up a whole of peculiar smartness, and the persistent jauntiness of his gait, even, poor fellow, when he couldn't help tottering, told of his invincible spirit. There was also a man called Gambril.* He was the only grizzled person in the ship. His face was of an austere type. But if I remember all their faces, wasting tragically before my eyes, most of their names have vanished from my memory.

The words that passed between us were few and puerile in regard of the situation. I had to force myself to look them in the face. I expected to meet reproachful glances.* There were none. The expression of suffering in their eyes was indeed hard enough to bear. But that they couldn't help. For the rest, I ask myself whether it was the temper of their souls or the sympathy of their imagination that made them so wonderful, so worthy of my undying regard.

For myself, neither my soul was highly tempered, nor my imagination properly under control. There were moments when I felt, not only that I would go mad, but that I had gone mad already; so that I dared not open my lips for fear of betraying myself by some insane shriek. Luckily I had only orders to give, and an order has a steadying influence upon him who has to give it. Moreover, the seaman, the officer of the watch, in me was sufficiently sane. I was like a mad carpenter making a box. Were he ever so convinced that he was King of Jerusalem, the box he would make would be a sane box. What I feared was a shrill note escaping me involuntarily and upsetting my balance. Luckily, again, there was no necessity to raise one's voice. The brooding stillness of the world seemed sensitive to the slightest sound like a whispering gallery. The conversational tone would almost carry a word from one end of the ship to the other. The terrible thing was that the only voice that I ever heard was my own. At night especially it reverberated very lonely amongst the planes of the unstirring sails.

Mr. Burns, still keeping to his bed with that air of secret determination, was moved to grumble at many things. Our interviews were short five-minute affairs, but fairly frequent. I was everlastingly diving down below to get a light, though I did not consume much tobacco at that time. The pipe was always going out; for in truth my mind was not composed enough to enable me to get a decent smoke. Likewise, for most of the time during the twenty-four hours I could have struck matches on deck and held them aloft till the flame burnt my fingers. But I always used to run below. It was a change. It was the only break in the incessant strain; and, of course, Mr. Burns through the open door could see me come in and go out every time.

With his knees gathered up under his chin and staring with his greenish eyes over them, he was a weird figure, and with my knowledge of the crazy notion in his head, not a very attractive one for me. Still, I had to speak to him now and then, and one day he complained that the ship was very silent. For hours and hours, he said, he was lying there, not hearing a sound, till he did not know what to do with himself.

"When Ransome happens to be forward in his galley everything's so still that one might think everybody in the ship was dead," he grumbled. "The only voice I do hear sometimes is yours, sir, and that isn't enough to cheer me up. What's the matter with the men? Isn't there one left that can sing out at the ropes?"*

"Not one, Mr. Burns," I said. "There is no breath to spare on board this ship for that. Are you aware that there are times when I can't muster more than three hands to do anything?"

He asked swiftly but fearfully:

"Nobody dead yet, sir?"

"No."

"It wouldn't do," Mr. Burns declared forcibly. "Mustn't let him. If he gets hold of one he will get them all."

I cried out angrily at this. I believe I even swore at the disturbing effect of these words. They attacked all the self-possession that was left to me. In my endless vigil in the face of the enemy I had been haunted by gruesome images enough. I had had visions of a ship drifting in calms and swinging in light airs, with all her crew dying slowly about her decks. Such things had been known to happen.

Mr. Burns met my outburst by a mysterious silence.

"Look here," I said. "You don't believe yourself what you say. You can't. It's impossible. It isn't the sort of thing I have a right to expect from you. My position's bad enough without being worried with your silly fancies."

He remained unmoved. On account of the way in which the light fell on his head I could not be sure whether he had smiled faintly or not. I changed my tone.

"Listen," I said. "It's getting so desperate that I had thought for a moment, since we can't make our way south, whether I wouldn't try to steer west and make an attempt to reach the mail-boat track.* We could always get some quinine from her, at least. What do you think?"

He cried out: "No, no, no. Don't do that, sir. You mustn't for a moment give up facing that old ruffian. If you do he will get the upper hand of us."

I left him. He was impossible. It was like a case of possession. His protest, however, was essentially quite sound. As a matter of fact, my notion of heading out west on the chance of sighting a problematical steamer could not bear calm examination. On the side where we were we had enough wind, at least from time to time, to struggle on towards the south. Enough, at least, to keep hope alive. But suppose that I had used those capricious gusts of wind to sail away to the westward, into some region where there was not a breath of air for days on end, what then? Perhaps my appalling vision of a ship floating with a dead crew would become a reality for the discovery weeks afterwards by some horror-stricken mariners.

That afternoon Ransome brought me up a cup of tea, and while waiting there, tray in hand, he remarked in the exactly right tone of sympathy:

"You are holding out well, sir."

"Yes," I said. "You and I seem to have been forgotten."

"Forgotten, sir?"

"Yes, by the fever-devil who has got on board this ship," I said.

Ransome gave me one of his attractive, intelligent, quick glances and went away with the tray. It occurred to me that I had been talking somewhat in Mr. Burns' manner. It annoyed me. Yet often in darker moments I forgot myself into an attitude towards our troubles more fit for a contest against a living enemy.

Yes. The fever-devil had not laid his hand yet either on Ransome or on me. But he might at any time. It was one of those thoughts one had to fight down, keep at arm's length at any cost. It was unbearable to contemplate the possibility of Ransome, the housekeeper of the ship, being laid low. And what would happen to my command if I got knocked over, with Mr. Burns too weak to stand without holding on to his bed-place and the second mate reduced to a state of permanent imbecility? It was impossible to imagine, or, rather, it was only too easy to imagine.

I was alone on the poop. The ship having no steerage way, I had sent the helmsman away to sit down or lie down somewhere in the shade. The men's strength was so reduced that all unnecessary calls on it had to be avoided. It was the austere Gambril with the grizzly beard. He went away readily enough, but he was so weakened by repeated bouts of fever, poor fellow, that in order to get down the poop ladder he had to turn sideways and hang on with both hands to the brass rail. It was just simply heart-breaking to watch. Yet he was neither very much worse nor much better than most of the half-dozen miserable victims I could muster up on deck.

It was a terribly lifeless afternoon. For several days in succession low clouds had appeared in the distance, white masses with dark convolutions resting on the water, motionless, almost solid, and yet all the time changing their aspects subtly. Towards evening they vanished as a rule. But this day they awaited the setting sun, which glowed and smouldered sulkily amongst them before it sank down. The punctual and wearisome stars reappeared over our mast-heads, but the air remained stagnant and oppressive.

The unfailing Ransome lighted the binnacle lamps and glided, all shadowy, up to me.

"Will you go down and try to eat something, sir?" he suggested.

His low voice startled me. I had been standing looking out over the rail, saying nothing, feeling nothing, not even the weariness of my limbs, overcome by the evil spell.

"Ransome," I asked abruptly, "how long have I been on deck? I am losing the notion of time."

"Fourteen days, sir," he said. "It was a fortnight last Monday since we left the anchorage."

His equable voice sounded mournful somehow. He waited a bit, then added: "It's the first time that it looks as if we were to have some rain."

I noticed then the broad shadow on the horizon extinguishing the low stars completely, while those overhead, when I looked up, seemed to shine down on us through a veil of smoke.

How it got there, how it had crept up so high, I couldn't say. It had an ominous appearance. The air did not stir. At a renewed invitation from Ransome I did go down into the cabin to—in his words—"try and eat something." I don't know that the trial was very successful. I suppose at that period I did exist on food in the usual way; but the memory is now that in those days life was sustained on invincible anguish, as a sort of infernal stimulant exciting and consuming at the same time.

It's the only period of my life in which I attempted to keep a diary. No, not the only one. Years later, in conditions of moral isolation, I did put down on paper the thoughts and events of a score of days. But this was the first time. I don't remember how it came about or how the pocket-book and the pencil came into my hands. It's inconceivable that I should have looked for them on purpose. I suppose they saved me from the crazy trick of talking to myself.

Strangely enough, in both cases I took to that sort of thing in circumstances in which I did not expect, in colloquial phrase, "to come out of it." Neither could I expect the record to outlast me. This shows that it was purely a personal need for intimate relief and not a call of egotism.

Here I must give another sample of it, a few detached lines, now looking very ghostly to my own eyes, out of the part scribbled that very evening:—*

* * *

"There is something going on in the sky like a decomposition, like a corruption of the air,* which remains as still as ever. After all, mere clouds, which may or may not hold wind or rain. Strange that it should trouble me so. I feel as if all my sins had found me out. But I suppose the trouble is that the ship is still lying motionless, not under command; and that I have nothing to do to keep my imagination from running wild amongst the disastrous images of the worst that may befall us. What's going to happen? Probably nothing. Or anything. It may be a furious squall coming, butt-end foremost.* And on deck there are five men with the vitality and the strength of, say, two. We may have all our sails blown away. Every stitch of canvas has been on her since we broke ground at the mouth of the Mei-nam,* fifteen days ago . . . or fifteen centuries. It seems to me that all my life before that momentous day is infinitely remote, a fading memory of light-hearted youth, something on the other side of a shadow. Yes, sails may very well be blown away. And that would be like a death sentence on the men. We haven't strength enough on board to bend another suit; incredible thought, but it is true. Or we may even get dismasted. Ships have been dismasted in squalls simply because they weren't handled quick enough, and we have no power to whirl the yards around. It's like being bound hand and foot preparatory to having one's throat cut. And what appals me most of all is that I shrink from going on deck to face it. It's due to the ship, it's due to the men who are there on deck—some of them, ready to put out the last remnant of their strength at a word from me. And I am shrinking from it. From the mere vision. My first command. Now I understand that strange sense of insecurity in my past. I always suspected that I might be no good. And here is proof positive. I am shirking it. I am no good."

* * *

At that moment, or, perhaps, the moment after, I became aware of Ransome standing in the cabin. Something in his expression startled me. It had a meaning which I could not make out. I exclaimed:

"Somebody's dead."

It was his turn then to look startled.

"Dead? Not that I know of, sir. I have been in the forecastle only ten minutes ago and there was no dead man there then."

"You did give me a scare," I said.

His voice was extremely pleasant to listen to. He explained that he had come down below to close Mr. Burns' port in case it should come on to rain. He did not know that I was in the cabin, he added.

"How does it look outside?" I asked him.

"Very black indeed, sir. There is something in it for certain."

"In what quarter?"

"All round, sir."

I repeated idly: "All round. For certain," with my elbows on the table.

Ransome lingered in the cabin as if he had something to do there, but hesitated about doing it. I said suddenly:

"You think I ought to be on deck?"

He answered at once but without any particular emphasis or accent: "I do, sir."

I got to my feet briskly, and he made way for me to go out. As I passed through the lobby I heard Mr. Burns' voice saying:

"Shut the door of my room, will you, Steward?" And Ransome's rather surprised: "Certainly, sir."

I thought that all my feelings had been dulled into complete indifference. But I found it as trying as ever to be on deck. The impenetrable blackness beset the ship so close that it seemed that by thrusting one's hand over the side one could touch some unearthly substance. There was in it an effect of inconceivable terror and of inexpressible mystery. The few stars overhead shed a dim light upon the ship alone, with no gleams of any kind upon the water, in detached shafts piercing an atmosphere which had turned to soot. It was something I had never seen before, giving no hint of the direction from which any change would come, the closing in of a menace from all sides.

There was still no man at the helm. The immobility of all things was perfect. If the air had turned black, the sea, for all I knew, might have turned solid. It was no good looking in any direction, watching for any sign, speculating upon the nearness of the moment. When the time came the blackness would overwhelm silently the bit of starlight falling upon the ship, and the end of all things* would come without a sigh, stir, or murmur of any kind, and all our hearts would cease to beat like run-down clocks.

It was impossible to shake off that sense of finality. The quietness that came over me was like a foretaste of annihilation. It gave me a sort of comfort, as though my soul had become suddenly reconciled to an eternity of blind stillness.

The seaman's instinct alone survived whole in my moral dissolution. I descended the ladder to the quarter-deck. The starlight seemed to die out before reaching that spot, but when I asked quietly: "Are you there, men?" my eyes made out shadowy forms starting up around me, very few, very indistinct; and a voice spoke: "All here, sir." Another amended anxiously:

"All that are any good for anything, sir."

Both voices were very quiet and unringing; without any special character of readiness or discouragement. Very matter-of-fact voices.

"We must try to haul this mainsail close up,"* I said.

The shadows swayed away from me without a word. Those men were the ghosts of themselves,* and their weight on a rope could be no more than the weight of a bunch of ghosts. Indeed, if ever a sail was hauled up by sheer spiritual strength it must have been that sail, for, properly speaking, there was not muscle enough for the task in the whole ship, let alone the miserable lot of us on deck. Of course, I took the lead in the work myself. They wandered feebly after me from rope to rope, stumbling and panting. They toiled like Titans.* We were an hour at it at least, and all the time the black universe made no sound. When the last leech-line was made fast, my eyes, accustomed to the darkness, made out the shapes of exhausted men drooping over the rails, collapsed on hatches. One hung over the after-capstan, sobbing for breath; and I stood amongst them like a tower of strength, impervious to disease and feeling only the sickness of my soul. I waited for some time fighting against the weight of my sins, against my sense of unworthiness, and then I said:

"Now, men, we'll go aft and square the main-yard. That's about all we can do for the ship; and for the rest she must take her chance."

VI

As we all went up it occurred to me that there ought to be a man at the helm. I raised my voice not much above a whisper, and, noiselessly, an uncomplaining spirit in a fever-wasted body appeared in the light aft, the head with hollow eyes illuminated against the blackness which had swallowed up our world—and the universe. The bared fore-arm extended over the upper spokes seemed to shine with a light of its own.

I murmured to that luminous appearance:

"Keep the helm right amidships."

It answered in a tone of patient suffering:

"Right amidships, sir."

Then I descended to the quarter-deck. It was impossible to tell whence the blow would come. To look round the ship was to look into a bottomless, black pit. The eye lost itself in inconceivable depths.

I wanted to ascertain whether the ropes had been picked up off the deck. One could only do that by feeling with one's feet. In my cautious progress I came against a man in whom I recognised Ransome. He possessed an unimpaired physical solidity which was manifest to me at the contact. He was leaning against the quarter-deck capstan and kept silent. It was like a revelation. He was the collapsed figure sobbing for breath I had noticed before we went on the poop.

"You have been helping with the mainsail!" I exclaimed in a low tone.

"Yes, sir," sounded his quiet voice.

"Man! What were you thinking of? You mustn't do that sort of thing."

After a pause he assented. "I suppose I mustn't." Then after another short silence he added: "I am all right now," quickly, between the tell-tale gasps.

I could neither hear nor see anybody else; but when I spoke up, answering sad murmurs filled the quarter-deck, and its shadows seemed to shift here and there. I ordered all the halyards laid down on deck clear for running.

"I'll see to that, sir," volunteered Ransome in his natural, pleasant tone, which comforted one and aroused one's compassion too, somehow.

That man ought to have been in his bed, resting, and my plain duty was to send him there. But perhaps he would not have obeyed me. I had not the strength of mind to try. All I said was:

"Go about it quietly, Ransome."

Returning on the poop I approached Gambril. His face, set with hollow shadows in the light, looked awful, finally silenced. I asked him how he felt, but hardly expected an answer. Therefore I was astonished at his comparative loquacity.

"Them shakes leaves me as weak as a kitten, sir," he said, preserving finely that air of unconsciousness as to anything but his business a helmsman should never lose. "And before I can pick up my strength that there hot fit comes along and knocks me over again."

He sighed. There was no complaint in his tone, but the bare words were enough to give me a horrible pang of self-reproach. It held me dumb for a time. When the tormenting sensation had passed off I asked:

"Do you feel strong enough to prevent the rudder taking charge if she gets sternway on her? It wouldn't do to get something smashed about the steering-gear now. We've enough difficulties to cope with as it is."

He answered with just a shade of weariness that he was strong enough to hang on. He could promise me that she shouldn't take the wheel out of his hands. More he couldn't say.

At that moment Ransome appeared quite close to me, stepping out of the darkness into visibility suddenly, as if just created with his composed face and pleasant voice.

Every rope on deck, he said, was laid down clear for running, as far as one could make certain by feeling. It was impossible to see anything. Frenchy had stationed himself forward. He said he had a jump or two left in him yet.

Here a faint smile altered for an instant the clear, firm design of Ransome's lips. With his serious clear, grey eyes, his serene temperament, he was a priceless man altogether. Soul as firm as the muscles of his body.

He was the only man on board (except me, but I had to preserve my liberty of movement) who had a sufficiency of muscular strength to trust to. For a moment I thought I had better ask him to take the wheel. But the dreadful knowledge of the enemy he had to carry about him made me hesitate. In my ignorance of physiology it occurred to me that he might die suddenly, from excitement, at a critical moment.

While this gruesome fear restrained the ready words on the tip of my tongue, Ransome stepped back two paces and vanished from my sight.

At once an uneasiness possessed me, as if some support had been withdrawn. I moved forward too, outside the circle of light, into the darkness that stood in front of me like a wall. In one stride I penetrated it. Such must have been the darkness before creation. It had closed behind me. I knew I was invisible to the man at the helm. Neither could I see anything. He was alone, I was alone, every man was alone where he stood. And every form was gone too, spar, sail, fittings, rails; everything was blotted out in the dreadful smoothness of that absolute night.

A flash of lightning would have been a relief—I mean physically. I would have prayed for it if it hadn't been for my shrinking apprehension of the thunder. In the tension of silence I was suffering from it seemed to me that the first crash must turn me into dust.

And thunder was, most likely, what would happen next. Stiff all over and hardly breathing, I waited with a horribly strained expectation. Nothing happened. It was maddening. But a dull, growing ache in the lower part of my face made me aware that I had been grinding my teeth madly enough, for God knows how long.

It's extraordinary I should not have heard myself doing it; but I hadn't. By an effort which absorbed all my faculties I managed to keep my jaw still. It required much attention, and while thus engaged I became bothered by curious, irregular sounds of faint tapping on the deck. They could be heard single, in pairs, in groups. While I wondered at this mysterious devilry, I received a slight blow under the left eye and felt an enormous tear run down my cheek. Raindrops. Enormous. Forerunners of something. Tap. Tap. Tap. . . .*

I turned about, and, addressing Gambril earnestly, entreated him to "hang on to the wheel." But I could hardly speak from emotion. The fatal moment had come. I held my breath. The tapping had stopped as unexpectedly as it had begun, and there was a renewed moment of intolerable suspense; something like an additional turn of the racking screw.* I don't suppose I would have ever screamed, but I remember my conviction that there was nothing else for it but to scream.

Suddenly—how am I to convey it? Well, suddenly the darkness turned into water. This is the only suitable figure. A heavy shower, a downpour, comes along, making a noise. You hear its approach on the sea, in the air too, I verily believe. But this was different. With no preliminary whisper or rustle, without a splash, and even without the ghost of impact, I became instantaneously soaked to the skin. Not a very difficult matter, since I was wearing only my sleeping suit.* My hair got full of water in an instant, water streamed on my skin, it filled my nose, my ears, my eyes. In a fraction of a second I swallowed quite a lot of it.

As to Gambril, he was fairly choked. He coughed pitifully, the broken cough of a sick man; and I beheld him as one sees a fish in an aquarium by the light of an electric bulb, an elusive, phosphorescent shape. Only he did not glide away. But something else happened. Both binnacle lamps went out. I suppose the water forced itself into them, though I wouldn't have thought that possible, for they fitted into the cowl perfectly.

The last gleam of light in the universe had gone, pursued by a low exclamation of dismay from Gambril. I groped for him and seized his arm. How startlingly wasted it was.

"Never mind," I said. "You don't want the light. All you need to do is to keep the wind, when it comes, at the back of your head. You understand?"

"Aye, aye, sir. . . . But I should like to have a light," he added nervously.

All that time the ship lay as steady as a rock. The noise of the water pouring off the sails and spars, flowing over the break of the poop, had stopped short. The poop scuppers gurgled and sobbed for a little while longer, and then perfect silence, joined to perfect immobility, proclaimed the yet unbroken spell of our helplessness, poised on the edge of some violent issue, lurking in the dark.

I started forward restlessly. I did not need my sight to pace the poop of my ill-starred first command with perfect assurance. Every square foot of her decks was impressed indelibly on my brain, to the very grain and knots of the planks. Yet, all of a sudden, I fell clean over something, landing full length on my hands and face.

It was something big and alive. Not a dog—more like a sheep, rather. But there were no animals in the ship. How could an animal. . . . It was an added and fantastic horror which I could not resist. The hair of my head stirred even as I picked myself up, awfully scared; not as a man is scared while his judgment, his reason still try to resist, but completely, boundlessly, and, as it were, innocently scared—like a little child.

I could see It—that Thing! The darkness, of which so much had just turned into water, had thinned down a little. There It was! But I did not hit upon the notion of Mr. Burns issuing out of the companion on all fours till he attempted to stand up, and even then the idea of a bear crossed my mind first.

He growled like one when I seized him round the body. He had buttoned himself up into an enormous winter overcoat of some woolly material, the weight of which was too much for his reduced state. I could hardly feel the incredibly thin lath of his body, lost within the thick stuff, but his growl had depth and substance: Confounded dumb ship with a craven, tip-toeing crowd. Why couldn't they stamp and go with a brace? Wasn't there one God-forsaken lubber in the lot fit to raise a yell on a rope?

"Skulking's no good, sir," he attacked me directly. "You can't slink past the old murderous ruffian. It isn't the way. You must go for him boldly—as I did. Boldness is what you want. Show him that you don't care for any of his damned tricks. Kick up a jolly old row."

"Good God, Mr. Burns," I said angrily. "What on earth are you up to? What do you mean by coming up on deck in this state?"

"Just that! Boldness. The only way to scare the old bullying rascal."

I pushed him, still growling, against the rail. "Hold on to it," I said roughly. I did not know what to do with him. I left him in a hurry, to go to Gambril, who had called faintly that he believed there was some wind aloft. Indeed, my own ears had caught a feeble flutter of wet canvas, high up overhead, the jingle of a slack chain sheet. . . .*

These were eerie, disturbing, alarming sounds in the dead stillness of the air around me. All the instances I had heard of topmasts being whipped out of a ship while there was not wind enough on her deck to blow out a match rushed into my memory.

"I can't see the upper sails, sir," declared Gambril shakily.

"Don't move the helm. You'll be all right," I said confidently.

The poor man's nerve was gone. I was not in much better case. It was the moment of breaking strain* and was relieved by the abrupt sensation of the ship moving forward as if of herself under my feet. I heard plainly the soughing of the wind aloft, the low cracks of the upper spars taking the strain, long before I could feel the least draught on my face turned aft, anxious and sightless like the face of a blind man.

Suddenly a louder sounding note filled our ears, the darkness started streaming against our bodies, chilling them exceedingly. Both of us, Gambril and I, shivered violently in our clinging, soaked garments of thin cotton. I said to him:

"You are all right now, my man. All you've got to do is to keep the wind at the back of your head. Surely you are up to that. A child could steer this ship in smooth water."

He muttered: "Aye! A healthy child." And I felt ashamed of having been passed over by the fever* which had been preying on every man's strength but mine, in order that my remorse might be the more bitter, the feeling of unworthiness more poignant, and the sense of responsibility heavier to bear.

The ship had gathered great way on her almost at once on the calm water. I felt her slipping through it with no other noise but a mysterious rustle alongside. Otherwise she had no motion at all, neither lift nor roll. It was a disheartening steadiness which had lasted for eighteen days now; for never, never had we had wind enough in that time to raise the slightest run of the sea. The breeze freshened suddenly. I thought it was high time to get Mr. Burns off the deck. He worried me. I looked upon him as a lunatic who would be very likely to start roaming over the ship and break a limb or fall overboard.

I was truly glad to find he had remained holding on where I had left him, sensibly enough. He was, however, muttering to himself ominously.

This was discouraging. I remarked in a matter-of-fact tone:

"We have never had so much wind as this since we left the roads."

"There's some heart in it too," he growled judiciously. It was a remark of a perfectly sane seaman. But he added immediately: "It was about time I should come on deck. I've been nursing my strength for this—just for this. Do you see it, sir?"

I said I did, and proceeded to hint that it would be advisable for him to go below now and take a rest.

His answer was an indignant: "Go below! Not if I know it, sir."

Very cheerful! He was a horrible nuisance. And all at once he started to argue. I could feel his crazy excitement in the dark.

"You don't know how to go about it, sir. How could you? All this whispering and tip-toeing is no good. You can't hope to slink past a cunning, wide-awake, evil brute like he was. You never heard him talk. Enough to make your hair stand on end. No! No! He wasn't mad. He was no more mad than I am. He was just downright wicked. Wicked so as to frighten most people. I will tell you what he was. He was nothing less than a thief and a murderer at heart. And do you think he's any different now because he's dead? Not he! His carcass lies a hundred fathom under, but he's just the same . . . in latitude 8° 20′ North."

He snorted defiantly. I noted with weary resignation that the breeze had got lighter while he raved. He was at it again.

"I ought to have thrown the beggar out of the ship over the rail like a dog. It was only on account of the men. . . . Fancy having to read the Burial Service over a brute like that! . . . 'Our departed brother' . . . I could have laughed. That was what he couldn't bear. I suppose I am the only man that ever stood up to laugh at him. When he got sick it used to scare that . . . brother . . . Brother . . . Departed . . . Sooner call a shark brother."

The breeze had let go so suddenly that the way of the ship brought the wet sails heavily against the mast. The spell of deadly stillness had caught us up again. There seemed to be no escape.

"Hallo!" exclaimed Mr. Burns in a startled voice. "Calm again!"

I addressed him as though he had been sane.

"This is the sort of thing we've been having for seventeen days, Mr. Burns," I said with intense bitterness. "A puff, then a calm, and in a moment, you'll see, she'll be swinging on her heel with her head away from her course to the devil somewhere."

He caught at the word. "The old dodging Devil," he screamed piercingly, and burst into such a loud laugh as I had never heard before. It was a provoking, mocking peal, with a hair-raising, screeching over-note of defiance. I stepped back utterly confounded.

Instantly there was a stir on the quarter-deck, murmurs of dismay. A distressed voice cried out in the dark below us: "Who's that gone crazy, now?"

Perhaps they thought it was their captain! Rush is not the word that could be applied to the utmost speed the poor fellows were up to; but in an amazing short time every man in the ship able to walk upright had found his way on to that poop.

I shouted to them: "It's the mate. Lay hold of him a couple of you. . . ."

I expected this performance to end in a ghastly sort of fight. But Mr. Burns cut his derisive screeching dead short and turned upon them fiercely, yelling:

"Aha! Dog-gone ye! You've found your tongues—have ye? I

thought you were dumb. Well, then—laugh! Laugh—I tell you. Now then—all together. One, two, three—laugh!"

A moment of silence ensued, of silence so profound that you could have heard a pin drop on the deck. Then Ransome's unperturbed voice uttered pleasantly the words:

"I think he has fainted, sir—" The little motionless knot of men stirred, with low murmurs of relief. "I've got him under the arms. Get hold of his legs, someone."

Yes. It was a relief. He was silenced for a time—for a time. I could not have stood another peal of that insane screeching. I was sure of it; and just then Gambril, the austere Gambril, treated us to another vocal performance. He began to sing out for relief. His voice wailed pitifully in the darkness: "Come aft, somebody! I can't stand this. Here she'll be off again directly and I can't. . . ."

I dashed aft myself meeting on my way a hard gust of wind whose approach Gambril's ear had detected from afar and which filled the sails on the main in a series of muffled reports mingled with the low plaint of the spars. I was just in time to seize the wheel while Frenchy, who had followed me, caught up the collapsing Gambril. He hauled him out of the way, admonished him to lie still where he was, and then stepped up to relieve me, asking calmly:

"How am I to steer her, sir?"

"Dead before it, for the present. I'll get you a light in a moment."

But going forward I met Ransome bringing up the spare binnacle lamp. That man noticed everything, attended to everything, shed comfort around him as he moved. As he passed me he remarked in a soothing tone that the stars were coming out. They were. The breeze was sweeping clear the sooty sky, breaking through the indolent silence of the sea.

The barrier of awful stillness which had encompassed us for so many days as though we had been accursed was broken. I felt that. I let myself fall on to the skylight seat. A faint white ridge of foam, thin, very thin, broke alongside. The first for ages—for ages. I could have cheered, if it hadn't been for the sense of guilt which clung to all my thoughts secretly. Ransome stood before me.

"What about the mate," I asked anxiously. "Still unconscious?"

"Well, sir—it's funny." Ransome was evidently puzzled. "He hasn't spoken a word, and his eyes are shut. But it looks to me more like sound sleep than anything else."

I accepted this view as the least troublesome of any, or at any rate, least disturbing. Dead faint or deep slumber, Mr. Burns had to be left to himself for the present. Ransome remarked suddenly:

"I believe you want a coat, sir."

"I believe I do," I sighed out.

But I did not move. What I felt I wanted were new limbs. My arms and legs seemed utterly useless, fairly worn out. They didn't even ache. But I stood up all the same to put on the coat when Ransome brought it up. And when he suggested that he had better now "take Gambril forward," I said:

"All right. I'll help you to get him down on the main deck."

I found that I was quite able to help, too. We raised Gambril up between us. He tried to help himself along like a man, but all the time he was inquiring piteously:

"You won't let me go when we come to the ladder? You won't let me go when we come to the ladder?"

The breeze kept on freshening and blew true, true to a hair. At daylight by careful manipulation of the helm we got the foreyards to run square by themselves* (the water keeping smooth) and then went about hauling the ropes tight. Of the four men I had with me at night, I could see now only two. I didn't inquire as to the others. They had given in. For a time only I hoped.

Our various tasks forward occupied us for hours, the two men with me moved so slowly and had to rest so often. One of them remarked that "every blamed thing in the ship felt about a hundred times heavier than its proper weight." This was the only complaint uttered. I don't know what we should have done without Ransome. He worked with us, silent too, with a little smile frozen on his lips. From time to time I murmured to him: "Go steady"—"Take it easy, Ransome"—and received a quick glance in reply.

When we had done all we could do to make things safe, he

disappeared into his galley. Some time afterwards, going forward for a look round, I caught sight of him through the open door. He sat upright on the locker in front of the stove, with his head leaning back against the bulkhead. His eyes were closed; his capable hands held open the front of his thin cotton shirt baring tragically his powerful chest, which heaved in painful and laboured gasps. He didn't hear me.

I retreated quietly and went straight on to the poop to relieve Frenchy, who by that time was beginning to look very sick. He gave me the course with great formality and tried to go off with a jaunty step, but reeled widely twice before getting out of my sight.

And then I remained all alone aft, steering my ship, which ran before the wind with a buoyant lift now and then, and even rolling a little. Presently Ransome appeared before me with a tray. The sight of food made me ravenous all at once. He took the wheel while I sat down on the after grating to eat my breakfast.

"This breeze seems to have done for our crowd," he murmured. "It just laid them low—all hands."

"Yes," I said. "I suppose you and I are the only two fit men in the ship."

"Frenchy says there's still a jump left in him. I don't know. It can't be much," continued Ransome with his wistful smile. "Good little man that. But suppose, sir, that this wind flies round when we are close to the land—what are we going to do with her?"

"If the wind shifts round heavily after we close in with the land she will either run ashore or get dismasted or both. We won't be able to do anything with her. She's running away with us now. All we can do is to steer her. She's a ship without a crew."

"Yes. All laid low," repeated Ransome quietly. "I do give them a look-in forward every now and then, but it's precious little I can do for them."

"I, and the ship, and every one on board of her, are very much indebted to you, Ransome," I said warmly.

He made as though he had not heard me, and steered in silence till I was ready to relieve him. He surrendered the wheel, picked up the tray, and for a parting shot informed me that Mr. Burns was awake and seemed to have a mind to come up on deck.

"I don't know how to prevent him, sir. I can't very well stop down below all the time."

It was clear that he couldn't. And sure enough Mr. Burns came on deck dragging himself painfully aft in his enormous overcoat. I beheld him with a natural dread. To have him around and raving about the wiles of a dead man while I had to steer a wildly rushing ship full of dying men was a rather dreadful prospect.

But his first remarks were quite sensible in meaning and tone. Apparently he had no recollection of the night scene. And if he had he didn't betray himself once. Neither did he talk very much. He sat on the skylight looking desperately ill at first, but that strong breeze, before which the last remnant of my crew had wilted down, seemed to blow a fresh stock of vigour into his frame with every gust. One could almost see the process.

By way of sanity test I alluded on purpose to the late captain. I was delighted to find that Mr. Burns did not display undue interest in the subject. He ran over the old tale of that savage ruffian's iniquities with a certain vindictive gusto and then concluded unexpectedly:

"I do believe, sir, that his brain began to go a year or more before he died."

A wonderful recovery. I could hardly spare it as much admiration as it deserved, for I had to give all my mind to the steering.

In comparison with the hopeless languor of the preceding days this was dizzy speed. Two ridges of foam streamed from the ship's bows; the wind sang in a strenuous note which under other circumstances would have expressed to me all the joy of life. Whenever the hauled-up mainsail started trying to slat and bang itself to pieces in its gear, Mr. Burns would look at me apprehensively.

"What would you have me do, Mr. Burns? We can neither furl it nor set it. I only wish the old thing would thrash itself to pieces and be done with it. This beastly racket confuses me."

Mr. Burns wrung his hands, and cried out suddenly:

"How will you get the ship into harbour, sir, without men to handle her?"

And I couldn't tell him.

Well—it did get done about forty hours afterwards. By the exorcising virtue of Mr. Burns' awful laugh, the malicious spectre had been laid, the evil spell broken, the curse removed. We were now in the hands of a kind and energetic Providence. It was rushing us on. . . .

I shall never forget the last night, dark, windy, and starry. I steered. Mr. Burns, after having obtained from me a solemn promise to give him a kick if anything happened, went frankly to sleep on the deck close to the binnacle. Convalescents need sleep. Ransome, his back propped against the mizzenmast and a blanket over his legs, remained perfectly still, but I don't suppose he closed his eyes for a moment. That embodiment of jauntiness, Frenchy, still under the delusion that there was "a jump" left in him, had insisted on joining us; but mindful of discipline, had laid himself down as far on the forepart of the poop as he could get, alongside the bucket-rack.

And I steered, too tired for anxiety, too tired for connected thought. I had moments of grim exultation and then my heart would sink awfully at the thought of that forecastle at the other end of the dark deck, full of fever-stricken men—some of them dying. By my fault. But never mind. Remorse must wait. I had to steer.

In the small hours the breeze weakened, then failed altogether. About five it returned, gentle enough, enabling us to head for the roadstead. Daybreak found Mr. Burns sitting wedged up with coils of rope on the stern-grating, and from the depths of his overcoat steering the ship with very white bony hands; while Ransome and I rushed along the decks letting go all the sheets and halliards by the run. We dashed next up on to the forecastle head. The perspiration of labour and sheer nervousness simply poured off our heads as we toiled to get the anchors cock-billed. I dared not look at Ransome as we worked side by side. We exchanged curt words; I could hear him panting close to me and I avoided turning my eyes his way for fear of seeing him fall down and expire in the act of putting out his strength—for what? Indeed for some distinct ideal.

The consummate seaman in him was aroused. He needed no

directions. He knew what to do. Every effort, every movement was an act of consistent heroism. It was not for me to look at a man thus inspired.

At last all was ready, and I heard him say, "Hadn't I better go down and open the compressors now, sir?"

"Yes. Do," I said. And even then I did not glance his way. After a time his voice came up from the main-deck:

"When you like, sir. All clear on the windlass here."

I made a sign to Mr. Burns to put the helm down and then I let both anchors go one after another, leaving the ship to take as much cable as she wanted. She took the best part of them both before she brought up. The loose sails coming aback ceased their maddening racket above my head. A perfect stillness reigned in the ship. And while I stood forward feeling a little giddy in that sudden peace, I caught faintly a moan or two and the incoherent mutterings of the sick in the forecastle.

As we had a signal for medical assistance flying on the mizzen it is a fact that before the ship was fairly at rest three steam-launches from various men-of-war arrived alongside; and at least five naval surgeons clambered on board. They stood in a knot gazing up and down the empty main deck, then looked aloft—where not a man could be seen either.

I went towards them—a solitary figure in a blue and grey striped sleeping suit and a pipe-clayed cork helmet on its head. Their disgust was extreme. They had expected surgical cases. Each one had brought his carving tools with him. But they soon got over their little disappointment. In less than five minutes one of the steam-launches was rushing shorewards to order a big boat and some hospital people for the removal of the crew. The big steam-pinnace went off to her ship to bring over a few bluejackets to furl my sails for me.

One of the surgeons had remained on board. He came out of the forecastle looking impenetrable, and noticed my inquiring gaze.

"There's nobody dead in there, if that's what you want to know," he said deliberately. Then added in a tone of wonder: "The whole crew!"

"And very bad?"

"And very bad," he repeated.* His eyes were roaming all over the ship. "Heavens! What's that?"

"That," I said, glancing aft, "is Mr. Burns, my chief officer."

Mr. Burns with his moribund head nodding on the stalk of his lean neck was a sight for any one to exclaim at. The surgeon asked:

"Is he going to the hospital too?"

"Oh, no," I said jocosely. "Mr. Burns can't go on shore till the mainmast goes. I am very proud of him. He's my only convalescent."

"You look . . ." began the doctor staring at me. But I interrupted him angrily:

"I am not ill."

"No. . . . You look queer."

"Well, you see, I have been seventeen days on deck."

"Seventeen! . . . But you must have slept."

"I suppose I must have. I don't know. But I'm certain that I didn't sleep for the last forty hours."

"Phew! . . . You will be going ashore presently, I suppose?"

"As soon as ever I can. There's no end of business waiting for me there."

The surgeon released my hand, which he had taken while we talked, pulled out his pocket book, wrote in it rapidly, tore out the page, and offered it to me.

"I strongly advise you to get this prescription made up for yourself ashore. Unless I am much mistaken you will need it this evening."

"What is it then?" I asked with suspicion.

"Sleeping draught," answered the surgeon curtly; and moving with an air of interest towards Mr. Burns he engaged him in conversation.

As I went below to dress to go ashore, Ransome followed me. He begged my pardon; he wished, too, to be sent ashore and paid off.

I looked at him in surprise. He was waiting for my answer with an air of anxiety.

"You don't mean to leave the ship!" I cried out.

"I do really, sir. I want to go and be quiet somewhere. Anywhere. The hospital will do."

"But, Ransome," I said, "I hate the idea of parting with you."

"I must go," he broke in. "I have a right!" He gasped and a look of almost savage determination passed over his face. For an instant he was another being. And I saw under the worth and the comeliness of the man the humble reality of things. Life was a boon to him—this precarious hard life—and he was thoroughly alarmed about himself.

"Of course I shall pay you off if you wish it," I hastened to say. "Only I must ask you to remain on board till this afternoon. I can't leave Mr. Burns absolutely by himself in the ship for hours."

He softened at once and assured me with a smile and in his natural pleasant voice that he understood that very well.

When I returned on deck everything was ready for the removal of the men. It was the last ordeal of that episode which had been maturing and tempering my character—though I did not know it.

It was awful. They passed under my eyes one after another—each of them an embodied reproach of the bitterest kind,* till I felt a sort of revolt wake up in me. Poor Frenchy had gone suddenly under. He was carried past me insensible, his comic face horribly flushed and as if swollen, breathing stertorously. He looked more like Mr. Punch than ever; a disgracefully intoxicated Mr. Punch.

The austere Gambril, on the contrary, had improved temporarily. He insisted on walking on his own feet to the rail—of course with assistance on each side of him. But he gave way to a sudden panic at the moment of being swung over the side and began to wail pitifully:

"Don't let them drop me, sir. Don't let them drop me, sir!" While I kept on shouting to him in most soothing accents: "All right, Gambril. They won't! They won't!"

It was no doubt very ridiculous. The bluejackets on our deck were grinning quietly, while even Ransome himself (much to the fore in lending a hand) had to enlarge his wistful smile for a fleeting moment.

I left for the shore in the steam-pinnace, and on looking back beheld Mr. Burns actually standing up by the taffrail, still in his enormous woolly overcoat. The bright sunlight brought out his weirdness amazingly. He looked like a frightful and elaborate scarecrow set up on the poop of a death-stricken ship, to keep the seabirds from the corpses.

Our story had got about already in town and everybody on shore was most kind. The marine office let me off the port dues,* and as there happened to be a shipwrecked crew staying in the Home I had no difficulty in obtaining as many men as I wanted. But when I inquired if I could see Captain Ellis for a moment I was told in accents of pity for my ignorance that our deputy-Neptune had retired and gone home on a pension about three weeks after I left the port. So I suppose that my appointment was the last act, outside the daily routine, of his official life.

It is strange how on coming ashore I was struck by the springy step, the lively eyes, the strong vitality of every one I met. It impressed me enormously. And amongst those I met there was Captain Giles of course. It would have been very extraordinary if I had not met him. A prolonged stroll in the business part of the town was the regular employment of all his mornings when he was ashore.

I caught the glitter of the gold watch-chain across his chest ever so far away. He radiated benevolence.

"What is it I hear?" he queried with a "kind uncle" smile, after shaking hands. "Twenty-one days from Bangkok?"

"Is this all you've heard?" I said. "You must come to tiffin with me. I want you to know exactly what you have let me in for."

He hesitated for almost a minute.

"Well—I will," he decided condescendingly at last.

We turned into the hotel. I found to my surprise that I could eat quite a lot. Then over the cleared table-cloth I unfolded to Captain Giles all the story since I took command in all its professional and emotional aspects, while he smoked patiently the big cigar I had given him.

Then he observed sagely:

"You must feel jolly well tired by this time."

"No," I said. "Not tired. But I'll tell you, Captain Giles, how I feel. I feel old. And I must be. All of you on shore look to me just a lot of skittish youngsters that have never known a care in the world."

He didn't smile. He looked insufferably exemplary. He declared:

"That will pass. But you do look older—it's a fact."

"Aha!" I said.

"No! No! The truth is that one must not make too much of anything in life, good or bad."

"Live at half-speed," I murmured perversely. "Not everybody can do that."

"You'll be glad enough presently if you can keep going even at that rate," he retorted with his air of conscious virtue. "And there's another thing: a man should stand up to his bad luck, to his mistakes, to his conscience, and all that sort of thing. Why—what else would you have to fight against?"

I kept silent. I don't know what he saw in my face, but he asked abruptly:

"Why—you aren't faint-hearted?"

"God only knows, Captain Giles," was my sincere answer.

"That's all right," he said calmly. "You will learn soon how not to be faint-hearted. A man has got to learn everything—and that's what so many of them youngsters don't understand."

"Well I am no longer a youngster."

"No," he conceded. "Are you leaving soon?"

"I am going on board directly," I said. "I shall pick up one of my anchors and heave in to half-cable on the other as soon as my new crew comes on board and I shall be off at daylight tomorrow."

"You will?" grunted Captain Giles approvingly. "That's the way. You'll do."

"What did you expect? That I would want to take a week ashore for a rest?" I said, irritated by his tone. "There's no rest for me till she's out in the Indian Ocean and not much of it even then."

He puffed at the cigar moodily, as if transformed.

"Yes, that's what it amounts to," he said in a musing tone. It was as if a ponderous curtain had rolled up disclosing an unexpected Captain Giles. But it was only for a moment, merely the time to let him add: "Precious little rest in life for anybody. Better not think of it."

We rose, left the hotel, and parted from each other in the street with a warm handshake, just as he began to interest me for the first time in our intercourse.

The first thing I saw when I got back to the ship was Ransome on the quarter-deck sitting quietly on his neatly lashed sea-chest.

I beckoned him to follow me into the saloon where I sat down to write a letter of recommendation for him to a man I knew on shore.

When finished I pushed it across the table. "It may be of some good to you when you leave the hospital."

He took it, put it in his pocket. His eyes were looking away from me—nowhere. His face was anxiously set.

"How are you feeling now?" I asked.

"I don't feel bad now, sir," he answered stiffly. "But I am afraid of its coming on. . . ." The wistful smile came back on his lips for a moment. "I—I am in a blue funk about my heart, sir."

I approached him with extended hand. His eyes, not looking at me, had a strained expression. He was like a man listening for a warning call.

"Won't you shake hands, Ransome?" I said gently.

He exclaimed, flushed up dusky red, gave my hand a hard wrench—and next moment, left alone in the cabin, I listened to him going up the companion stairs* cautiously, step by step, in mortal fear of starting into sudden anger our common enemy it was his hard fate to carry consciously within his faithful breast.

AUTHOR'S NOTE

THIS story, which I admit to be in its brevity a fairly complex piece of work, was not intended to touch on the supernatural. Yet more than one critic has been inclined to take it in that way, seeing in it an attempt on my part to give the fullest scope to my imagination by taking it beyond the confines of the world of living, suffering humanity. But, as a matter of fact, my imagination is not made of stuff so elastic as all that. I believe that if I attempted to put the strain of the Supernatural on it it would fail deplorably and exhibit an unlovely gap. But I could never have attempted such a thing, because all my moral and intellectual being is penetrated by an invincible conviction that whatever falls under the dominion of our senses must be in nature and, however exceptional, cannot differ in its essence from all the other effects of the visible and tangible world of which we are a self-conscious part. The world of the living contains enough marvels and mysteries as it is—marvels and mysteries acting upon our emotions and intelligence in ways so inexplicable that it would almost justify the conception of life as an enchanted state. No, I am too firm in my consciousness of the marvellous to be ever fascinated by the mere supernatural, which (take it any way you like) is but a manufactured article, the fabrication of minds insensitive to the intimate delicacies of our relation to the dead and to the living, in their countless multitudes; a desecration of our tenderest memories; an outrage on our dignity.

Whatever my native modesty may be it will never condescend so low as to seek help for my imagination within those vain imaginings* common to all ages and that in themselves are enough to fill all lovers of mankind with unutterable sadness. As to the effect of a mental or moral shock on a common mind, it is quite a legitimate subject for study and description. Mr. Burns's moral being receives a severe shock in his relations with his late captain, and this in his diseased state turns into a mere superstitious fancy compounded of fear and animosity. This fact is one of the elements of the story, but there is nothing supernatural in it—nothing, so to speak, from beyond the confines of this world, which in all conscience holds enough mystery and terror in itself.

Perhaps if I had published this tale, which I have had for a long time in my mind, under the title of *First Command*, no suggestion of the

Supernatural would have been found in it by any impartial reader, critical or otherwise. I will not consider here the origins of the feeling in which its actual title, *The Shadow-Line*, occurred to my mind. Primarily the aim of this piece of writing was the presentation of certain facts which certainly were associated with the change from youth, care-free and fervent, to the more self-conscious and more poignant period of maturer life. Nobody can doubt that before the supreme trial of a whole generation I had an acute consciousness of the minute and insignificant character of my own obscure experience. There could be no question here of any parallelism. That notion never entered my head. But there was a feeling of identity, though with an enormous difference of scale—as of one single drop measured against the bitter and stormy immensity of an ocean. And this was very natural too. For when we begin to meditate on the meaning of our own past it seems to fill all the world in its profundity and its magnitude. This book was written in the last three months of the year 1916.* Of all the subjects of which a writer of tales is more or less conscious within himself this is the only one I found it possible to attempt at the time. The depth and the nature of the mood with which I approached it is best expressed perhaps in the dedication which strikes me now as a most disproportionate thing—as but another instance of the overwhelming greatness of our own emotion to ourselves.

This much having been said, I may pass on now to a few remarks about the mere material of the story. As to locality, it belongs to that part of the Eastern Seas from which I have carried away into my writing life the greatest number of suggestions. From my statement that I thought of this story for a long time under the title of *First Command* the reader may guess that it is concerned with my personal experience. And, as a matter of fact, it *is* personal experience seen in perspective with the eye of the mind and coloured by that affection one can't help feeling for such events of one's life as one has no reason to be ashamed of. And that affection is as intense (I appeal here to universal experience) as the shame, and almost the anguish, with which one remembers some unfortunate occurrences, down to mere mistakes in speech, that have been perpetrated by one in the past. The effect of perspective in memory is to make things loom large because the essentials stand out isolated from their surroundings of insignificant daily facts which have naturally faded out of one's mind. I remember that period of my sea-life with pleasure because, begun inauspiciously, it turned out in the end a success from a personal point of view, leaving a tangible proof in the terms of the letter the owners of the ship wrote to me two years afterwards when I resigned my command in order to come home. This resignation marked the beginning of another phase of my seaman's life, its terminal phase, if I may say so, which in its own way has coloured another portion of my writings. I didn't know then how near its end my sea-life was, and therefore I felt no sorrow except at parting with the ship. I was sorry also to break my connection with the firm which owned her and who were pleased to receive with friendly kindness and give their confidence to a man who had entered their service in an accidental manner and in very adverse circumstances. Without disparaging the earnestness of my purpose I suspect now that luck had no small part in the success of the trust reposed in me. And one cannot help remembering with pleasure the time when one's best efforts were seconded by a run of luck.

The words, "*Worthy of my undying regard*," selected by me for the motto on the title page, are quoted from the text of the book itself; and, though one of my critics surmised that they applied to the ship, it is evident from the place where they stand that they refer to the men of that ship's company: complete strangers to their new captain, and who yet stood by him so well during those twenty days that seemed to have been passed on the brink of a slow and agonising destruction. And *that* is the greatest memory of all! For surely it is a great thing to have commanded a handful of men worthy of one's undying regard.

J. C.

1920

EXPLANATORY NOTES

1 *Title-page*: the subtitle 'A Confession' and the epigraph do not appear in the serial publications. *The Shadow-Line* and *Under Western Eyes* (1911) are the only two of his fictional works for which Conrad chose an epigraph from the work itself (see p. 82).

2 *Dedication*. Borys was Conrad's older son. See the Introduction for discussion of this dedication (p. xiii). The dedication is not included in the serial publications, and is punctuated, typeset, and lineated slightly differently in A1, giving the name 'Borys' a line of its own. Following some responses to the serial publication of the work, Conrad wrote to his agent J. B. Pinker that 'I am really quite jumpy about this thing, and I think I'll cancel the dedication as I don't want the boy's name to be connected with a work of which some imbecile is likely to say: that it is a "good enough" sort of story in the Conrad manner but not a work to be put out by itself with all that pomp, etc., and to be charged such a price for.' The letter is dated 'early 1917' by G. Jean-Aubry (*Joseph Conrad: Life and Letters*, ii (London: William Heinemann, 1927), 181–2).

3 *D'autres fois . . . mon désespoir*: the quotation is from Charles Baudelaire's (1821–67) sonnet 'La Musique', in *Les Fleurs du Mal* (1857), which opens with the line 'La musique souvent me prend comme une mer!' ('Music often takes me like a sea!') The quotation should end with an exclamation mark, but Conrad's punctuation has an appropriateness that I have been unwilling to alter. The extract quoted by Conrad can be translated as follows: 'At other times, a calm flatness, the great mirror | Of my despair'.

undiscovered country: the first of many echoes from *Hamlet*. In *Hamlet* III. i, the 'undiscovered country' to which Hamlet is referring is death.

the kicks and the halfpence: according to Eric Partridge's *A Dictionary of Slang and Unconventional English*, 8th edn., ed. Paul Beale (London: Routledge & Kegan Paul, 1984), a phrase usually found in the form 'more kicks than halfpence', i.e. more trouble than profit.

4 *steamship . . . blind loyalty*: Conrad's attachment to the unique character-forming qualities of the sailing ship can be traced throughout his writing, but a useful summary of his views on the matter can be found in his 'Memorandum on the Scheme for Fitting out a Sailing Ship for the Purpose of Perfecting the Training of Merchant Service Officers Belonging to the Port of Liverpool' (1920), which is reprinted in *Last Essays* (1926).

an Eastern port: as becomes clear later on, the port is Singapore. Conrad frequently alludes to actual places without naming them in his fiction, and in a letter to Richard Curle late in his life he objected to Curle's having named the port to which the shipwrecked crew row in 'Youth' (1898). See the letter for 24 April 1922, reprinted in Richard Curle (ed.), *Conrad to a Friend: 150 Selected Letters from Joseph Conrad to Richard Curle* (London: Sampson Low, Marston, 1928), 143.

4 *also red, but with a green border and with a white crescent*: Jacques Berthoud explains the colours as follows: red because of its association with the Merchant Service, green because this is the colour of the flag of Saudi Arabia, and the white crescent representing Islam. See Berthoud's edition of *The Shadow-Line* (Harmondsworth: Penguin, 1986), 148.

an Arab . . . and a Syed at that: see note for p. 5, and also Glossary (*Syed*).

Archipelago: the Malay Archipelago.

5 *green sickness of late youth*: the *Shorter Oxford English Dictionary* dates 'green sickness' to 1583 and defines it as 'an anæmic disease which mostly affects young women about the age of puberty and gives a pale or greenish tinge to the complexion; chlorosis'. The dictionary also mentions a figurative sense associated with 'the morbid appetite which characterizes chlorosis'. Conrad's application of the term to a man seems unusual: see the Introduction, p. xxiv.

Kalashes: compare the following from Conrad's 'Youth' (1898): 'Four Calashes pulled a swinging stroke. This was my first sight of Malay seamen.'

The Captain: Captain Kent is modelled on the actual captain of the *Vidar*, a Captain Craig. Conrad's early biographer G. Jean-Aubry located and talked to Craig in 1924 and Craig gave him various particulars, including the following. 'The first time I met Conrad was at the Shipping Office of Singapore about the middle of August, 1887. He pleased me at once by his manners, which were distinguished and reserved. One of the first things he told me was that he was a foreigner by birth, which I had already guessed from his accent. I replied that that did not matter in the least as he had his certificate. (It was quite difficult at that time to find officers in the East who were not over fond of the bottle.) The *Vidar* belonged to an Arab called Syed Mosin Bin S. Ali Jaffree.' Craig also told Jean-Aubry that 'when he went down to the cabin to talk to his first mate, he usually found him writing' (*Joseph Conrad: Life & Letters*, i. 94, 98). Compare note to p. 79, discussing the narrator's diary extracts in *The Shadow-Line*.

second engineer: according to Norman Sherry, 'James Allen and John Niven, first and second engineers on the *Vidar*, had been travelling through the archipelago in her for at least four years before Conrad joined the ship. [. . .] Allen and Niven appear in *The Shadow-Line*. Allen is the young man "with a mist of fluffy beard all round his haggard face", a "confirmed dyspeptic", and Niven is the "fierce misogynist" ' (Sherry, *Conrad's Eastern World*, 31). The *Vidar* was the ship Conrad left before his appointment as captain of the *Otago*. Jean-Aubry reports that Conrad wrote to Niven many years later, and quotes from a letter dated 5 December 1923: 'You could not really have believed that I have forgotten any time in the *Vidar*. It is part of my sea life to which my memory returns most often, since there is nothing to remember but what is good and pleasant in my temporary association with three men, for whom, I assure you, I have preserved to this day a warm regard and sincere esteem' (Jean-Aubry, *Joseph Conrad: Life and Letters*, i. 99).

John Nieven: see previous note.

6 *I believe he would*: in the MS: 'It was said humorously, but I believe he would have perpetrated . . .'

7 *Officers' Sailors' Home*: according to Norman Sherry, the 'Sailor's Home in Singapore' was pulled down in 1922 to make room for a cinema, and no records survive to establish whether or not Conrad stayed there. See *Conrad's Eastern World*, 20.

Chief Steward: Norman Sherry quotes extensively from a letter from W. G. St Clair sent to the *Ceylon Observer*; abridged in the *Malay Mail* Tuesday, 2 September 1924. In it St Clair talks of recognizing the setting and characters in the opening of *The Shadow-Line* when he looked at it in the *English Review*, and he quotes from a letter Conrad sent him subsequent to his contacting the author about the work. According to Conrad's letter to St Clair (dated 31 March 1917), 'The "Home" Steward's name (in my time) I don't remember. He was a meagre wizened creature, always bemoaning his fate, and he did try to do me an unfriendly turn for some reason or other'. St Clair's own letter provides a slightly different perspective. 'The steward of the Sailor's Home, originally Balestier's house, was a retired sergeant of artillery, who combined the supervision of the Sailor's Home with the job of instructor to the old Rifle Volunteers, disbanded about the time Conrad came to the East. His name was Phillips, really a very well-meaning person, whose evangelical activities were mainly devoted to Malay missions.' See Sherry, *Conrad's Eastern World*, 316–17. Zdisław Najder describes Phillips as 'an evangelist and temperance worker and an inspector of brothels—in short a professional do-gooder' (*Joseph Conrad: A Chronicle* (Cambridge: Cambridge University Press, 1983), 102).

8 *East End of London*: at this time the poor or working-class quarter of London.

9 *I could make Hamilton*: Norman Sherry has confirmed that 'there was a C. Hamilton in the East who is mentioned in the *Singapore and Straits Directory*, 1883, the year of Conrad's first visit to Singapore' (*Conrad's Eastern World*, 214). In 'The End of the Tether' (1902) a Hamilton—also described as a 'loafer'—is forced by the Master-Attendant to take command of a ship whose captain has died. In the MS, the word 'make' in this phrase is underlined for emphasis.

Captain Giles: in the letter to W. G. St Clair quoted in the note to p. 7, Conrad writes: 'My Captain Giles was a man called Patterson, a dear, thick, dreary creature with an enormous reputation for knowledge of the Sulu Sea'. St Clair himself remembers Patterson 'as a stout ungainly man often to be seen at Motion's, the chronometer and compass-regulating business in Battery Road' (Norman Sherry, *Conrad's Eastern World*, 317).

9 *rank outsider*: the phrase occurs in Conrad's early 'The Return' (1898). It is applied by the snobbish bourgeois Alvan Hervey to the poet with whom his wife nearly elopes: 'He's an outsider—a rank outsider.' Hervey is as unsympathetic as Hamilton, albeit in different ways. No doubt the outsider Joseph Conrad had reason to be especially unsympathetic to those who used the term. Edward Said has found 'an interesting parallel' between the situation in *The Shadow-Line* and that in stories like 'The Return', and he draws particular attention to the role played in these two works by a letter that either goes astray or that is read when its sender wishes to retrieve it. (See Edward W. Said, *Joseph Conrad and the Fiction of Autobiography* (Cambridge, Mass.: Harvard University Press, 1966), 177.)

10 *'to assist the master'*: here and elsewhere in *The Shadow-Line* 'master' is used to refer to a ship's captain.

11 *Rajah's yacht*: here 'Rajah' almost certainly refers to a Malay dignitary or ruler.

12 *Oh! these nice boys! . . . No! I didn't mean that*: the exchange suggests that 'nice boy' has a homosexual connotation that causes the narrator to laugh but that Giles did not intend and is embarrassed by. John Stape (personal communication) refers to a curiously similar exchange in Conrad's *Heart of Darkness* (1899). The Russian 'Harlequin' is telling Marlow about his long discussion with Kurtz:

> 'We talked of everything,' he said, quite transported at the recollection. 'I forgot there was such a thing as sleep. The night did not seem to last an hour. Everything! Everything! . . . Of love, too.' 'Ah, he talked to you of love!' I said, much amused. 'It isn't what you think,' he cried, almost passionately. 'It was in general. He made me see—things.'

14 *Queen Victoria's first jubilee celebrations*: in 1887, which dates the action of the novella to about the same time that Conrad had his first (and only) seagoing command—of the *Otago*.

17 *dreary lunacy*: the first of a number of references to madness that gain force from the novella's many allusions to and borrowings from *Hamlet*. Cf. Captain Giles's comment on p. 35: 'As to that, I believe everybody in the world is a little mad'.

20 *stuffy philistinish lair*: 'philistinish,' meaning 'without culture' in contemporary English, suggests the class condescension implied by associating the steward with the East End of London (p. 8). Partridge's *A*

Dictionary of Slang and Unconventional English gives 'drunkards' for 'Philistines', which might suit the steward's 'solitary tippling' (p. 22), although Partridge gives no such usage subsequent to the eighteenth century.

that force somewhere within our lives which shapes them this way or that: cf. *Hamlet*, v. ii. 10–11: 'There's a divinity that shapes our ends, | Rough-hew them how we will—'.

21 *He leaned against the lintel of the door*: Conrad regularly misuses 'lintel' to mean 'door-frame', and later editors of his work often correct this usage. See my two short articles, 'Conrad and Lintels: A Note on the Text of *The Shadow-Line*' (*The Conradian*, 12/2 (November 1987), 178–9) and 'More on Conrad and Lintels' (*The Conradian* 13/2 (December 1988), 205–6).

22 *like solid truth from a well*: alluding to the saying that truth is to be found at the bottom of a deep well.

23 *this stale, unprofitable world of my discontent*: cf. *Hamlet*, I. ii. 133–4: 'How weary, stale, flat and unprofitable | Seem to me all the uses of this world!'

24 *He had a Scottish name, but his complexion . . . languishing expression*: the 'but' hints at a racial slur, suggesting perhaps that the head shipping-master has Asian or Jewish blood. Such slurs occur, regrettably, from time to time in Conrad's works and seem especially directed at those of mixed racial identity. Compare the description of 'a certain prominent man in Sta. Marta' in *Nostromo* (1904) 'who was then a person in power, with a lemon-coloured face and a very short and curly, not to say woolly, head of hair'.

quill-driver: pens were originally made from feathers (quills) and the name was retained for steel pens. 'Quill-driver' is thus a dismissive way of referring to a clerk.

Captain Ellis . . . deputy-Neptune: Norman Sherry has confirmed that Conrad based his portrayal of Ellis on the real Henry Ellis, who was the Master-Attendant at Singapore who indeed gave Conrad his first command (of the *Otago*). Sherry's diligent research has unearthed Ellis's memorandum to Conrad confirming him in the appointment and instructing him to proceed to Bangkok 'today' on the SS *Melita*, as well as a letter to the British Consul in Bangkok on the same subject. Both letters are dated 19 January 1888 (Sherry, *Conrad's Eastern World*, 215). Sherry also located a letter sent by W. G. St Clair, and forwarded by publisher J. M. Dent to Conrad, in which St Clair describes Ellis as 'a tall bigboned Ulsterman, rough to look at, but an honest good fellow withal' (ibid. 315). Conrad's response to this description was not positive; writing back to Dent he commented: 'His recollection of Capt. Ellis does not seem very exact. Capt. E. was certainly big but not a "raw-boned Irishman." He was a fine, dignified personality, an ex-Naval officer. But journalists can't speak truth,—not even see it as other men do. It's a *professional* inability, and that's why I hold journalism up for the most demoralizing form of human activity, made up of catch phrases, of mere daily opportunities, of shifting feelings' (Jean-Aubry, *Joseph Conrad: Life and Letters*, ii. 186–7.)

Neptune was the Roman god of the sea, traditionally depicted holding a trident (to which Conrad alludes on p. 25). The term here is humorous: Captain Ellis is or sees himself as second only to the god of the sea.

24 *rule the waves*: here the narrator seems to have moved from Neptune to Britannia—perhaps because Britannia was depicted on British copper coins holding a trident, like Neptune. In the patriotic song by James Thomson (1700–48; music by Thomas Arne, 1710–78) the refrain runs: 'Rule, Britannia! Britannia rule the waves!'

pretended: Conrad's English has many Gallicisms (he learned French before English), and he regularly uses 'to pretend' in the French sense of 'to attempt', as seems to be the case here.

whose lives were cast upon the waters: cf. 'Cast thy bread upon the waters: for thou shalt find it after many days', Ecclesiastes 11: 1.

his temperament was choleric: here used metaphorically to suggest irascibility, but forming a subtle counterpoint to the literal 'choleraic symptoms' manifested by the original steward of the captain's first command (p. 55). Perhaps the variation of spelling is intended to indicate this shift from the metaphorical to the literal.

25 *white wings*: Conrad did not invent this picturesque way of referring to sails seen from a distance; it was apparently a standard term.

the official pen, far mightier than the sword: echoes the proverb 'the pen is mightier than the sword'. The theme is a common one in Conrad's work. See also p. 29.

being a sailing-ship man: see note for p. 4.

26 *I haven't been long getting to the office*: in the MS the captain's reply has a tinge of sarcasm: 'I haven't been long enough out here sir.'

Bangkok: throughout the MS Conrad uses the spelling 'Bankok', as he does elsewhere, and this spelling is repeated in E1. John Stape, who has consulted Zdisław Najder on the matter, reports that it seems most likely that Conrad was influenced by the Polish spelling of the town, as 'Bankok' is not recorded as a contemporary English variant spelling (personal communication). The spelling has accordingly been standardized throughout the text. See also note for p. 55.

the steamer Melita: Conrad travelled on a steamer of this name from Singapore to Bangkok in 1888 to take command of the *Otago* (see note for p. 24). 'Melita' is the older form of 'Malta'.

27 *A subtle change . . . dropped on getting up*: compare what we learn about Captain Ellis's 'official life' on p. 107.

28 *dream-stuff*: cf. *The Tempest*, IV. i. 156–8: 'We are such stuff | As dreams

are made on, and our little life | Is rounded with a sleep.' The depiction of an older generation watching the growth into maturity of a younger one in Shakespeare's final play matches Conrad's concerns in *The Shadow-Line*. There is a stronger echo of this line on p. 42. The novella contains both literal and metaphorical references to sleep and dreaming.

29 *my deep detachment from the forms and colours of this world*: cf. William Wordsworth (1770–1850), 'Lines Composed a Few Miles above Tintern Abbey' (1798), ll. 77–80: 'the tall rock, | The mountain, and the deep and gloomy wood, | Their colours and their forms, were then to me | An appetite . . .' Wordsworth's poem also involves an older man looking back on the time of his enthusiastic boyhood and youth.

31 *not to be surprised*: in the MS 'to be surprised', implying either that Conrad's second thoughts attributed different characteristics to youth or that the complexity of his syntax confused his initial formulation. The force of the whole passage does suggest the young captain's indignant youthful outrage.

32 *Captain Ellis had gone for me bald-headed*: had attacked me in a spirited fashion. The entry for 'bald-headed' in Partridge's *A Dictionary of Slang and Unconventional English*—too long to quote in full here—makes amusing reading.

34 *sink or swim together!*: in the MS this is followed by three additional paragraphs, see Introduction, pp. xxv–xxvi.

And yet he's nearly done it: a representative example of Conrad's difficulty with English tenses: the idiomatic form would be 'And yet he nearly did it'.

35 *everybody in the world is a little mad*: see note for p. 17.

written character: in modern English, a reference or written testimonial. Cf. the 'letter of recommendation' that the captain writes for Ransome on p. 109.

38 *deepest slumber*: in the MS (Conrad's deletions in square brackets) this is followed by:

> deepest slumber—it receded still and soundless like a shadow in the hot night. And the [ships we passed] anchored ships we passed one after another [had the same] were as still and silent as if all the crews were dead. They were like tombs each with the unwinking light of a lantern above their dark solid shapes scattered on the polished level of the roadstead catching here and there the dim gleam of a star.
>
> The hail 'steam launch ahoy!' made me spin round face forward. We were close to a [steamer which was by no] steamer and she was not dark as a tomb. Lights shone . . .

meagre hand: in view of the other echoes of Coleridge's (1772–1839) 'The Rime of the Ancient Mariner' (1798) it is tempting to associate the unpleasant captain's meagre hand with the mariner's 'skinny hand'—

although the captain's close-clipped grey beard is in (partial) contrast to the mariner's 'long grey beard'. As was common at the time, *The Shadow-Line* when first published contained advertisements for books at the end. The first such advertisement in E1 is for *The Shadow-Line* itself, and includes the comment: 'This is a Far-Eastern story of a haunted ship, and might be fitly described as the prose counterpart of *The Ancient Mariner*, though it owes nothing except a hint of atmosphere to that immortal poem.'

39 *the great gilt pagoda*: doubtless the Golden Mount—the chief of many pagodas in Bangkok.

40 *King's Palace*: on the river, in the centre of Bangkok.

42 *the stuff dreams are made of*: see note for p. 28.

rails: a term with a number of possible meanings; as the rails are described as 'polished', Conrad probably has in mind brass railings enclosing a deck.

lobby: Mr Burns's description of the old captain's death seems to establish that the lobby adjoins the captain's cabin, and thus the definition provided by McEwen and Lewis in their *Encyclopedia of Nautical Knowledge* may be appropriate: 'An apartment or passage-way below the quarter-deck forward of the captain's cabin.' Mr Seiji Minamida has pointed out that 'The Secret Sharer' refers to 'the lobby at the foot of the stairs', and he cites a definition from the first edition of *Webster's Dictionary*: 'In a ship, an apartment close before the captain's cabin' (personal communication).

43 *'quick-change' artist*: *SOED* relates 'quick-change' to an actor who shifts costume speedily so as to assume another part. The word 'artist', however, suggests the music-hall rather than the theatre, and it would be interesting to know if Conrad had a particular performer in mind.

44 *His name was Burns*: Conrad based Burns to some extent on Charles Born, chief mate of the *Otago* when Conrad took command of this ship. Twice in the MS 'Born' is corrected to 'Burns'. Versions of the same man also appear in *The Mirror of the Sea* (1904–5), 'The Secret Sharer' (1910), and Brierly's Chief Mate Jones in *Lord Jim* (1900). But all these are in part Conrad's creation rather than faithful portraits of the man. Norman Sherry, for example, has confirmed that Charles Born was actually on good terms with John Snadden, the previous captain of the *Otago*; he nursed him in his final sickness, and forwarded his possessions to his widow. See note for p. 46.

45 *He struck me as rather a cub*: 'An awkward, unformed youth' (*SOED*), but Conrad's usage (the second officer is described as 'cubbish' later in the text) suggests not just youth but a defective character.

46 *the last captain*: it is in his portrayal of the ship's previous captain that Conrad departs most radically from the characters and events associated with his own appointment as captain of the *Otago*. Norman Sherry's

meticulous detective work provides compelling evidence that Conrad's predecessor, Captain John Snadden, who did die and was buried at sea, bore no resemblance to Conrad's fictional portrait. Snadden, it appears, was loquacious not silent, was on good terms with his first mate, was a conscientious captain, and did not throw his violin (which he did possess) overboard! See Norman Sherry, *Conrad's Eastern World*, pp. 220–4.

47 *watch*: the man on watch is on duty for four hours, and is responsible for the ship during this time. A watch is broken up by half-hourly bells, so that each watch runs from 1 to 8 bells.

48 *when the fit took him*: meaning 'when the mood or inclination took him'. In the following sentence, it is thus the violin playing, rather than an actual fit, that is 'very loud'.

photograph: Conrad's short-story 'Falk' (1903) seems to have been based on similar experiences to those described in *The Shadow-Line*. In 'Falk' the narrator has also been 'appointed ex-officio by the British Consul' to take charge of a ship after the sudden death of her captain. On the ship the captain finds 'some suspiciously unreceipted bills, a few dry-dock estimates hinting at bribery, and a quantity of vouchers for three years' extravagant expenditure; all these mixed up together in a dusty old violin-case lined with ruby velvet'. There is also an account-book containing 'rhymed doggerel of a jovial or improper character', and in the fiddle-case 'a photograph of my predecessor, taken lately in Saigon, represented in front of a garden view, and in company of a female in strange draperies, an elderly, squat, rugged man of stern aspect in a clumsy suit of black broadcloth, and with the hair brushed forward above the temples in a manner reminding one of a boar's tusks'.

half-a-crown: a pre-decimalization British coin worth two shillings and sixpence, or one eighth of a pound sterling.

49 *sortilege*: magical powers.

50 *Pulo Condor*: the Archipelago de Poulo Condore is in position 8°42′N 106°36′E. Now called Con Son, it consists of a group of 12 islands east of Cape Cambodia, and was used as a prison for political prisoners during the French occupation. The islands are 490 miles from Singapore, and 520 miles from Bangkok.

such an effective laugh: proleptic of Mr Burns's later loud laugh (p. 98).

51 *he had made up his mind to cut adrift from everything*: the mad captain's final days thus illustrate where the narrator's earlier decision to leave his ship might have ended—as does the situation of both Hamilton and the unnamed hungover guest in the Officers' Sailors' Home.

He meant to have gone wandering about the world till he lost her with all hands: *The Shadow-Line* explicitly refers to literary and mythic accounts such as those of the Flying Dutchman (see note for p. 77) and 'The Rime of the Ancient Mariner', but modern readers should bear in mind that such accounts have a literal purchase too. Sailing ships could get dismasted or becalmed (as in Conrad's 'Falk'), steamships did suffer broken propellers or exploded boilers, and crews did perish in still-floating ships—as the captain is well aware (see note for p. 75).

51 *the breath of unknown powers that shape our destinies*: cf. *Hamlet*, v. ii 10–11 and note for p. 20. Yves Hervouet has argued that the echo of *Hamlet* most probably comes through Anatole France's *La Vie littéraire* (1888–92) in which France, talking of 'l'action romanesque', remarks, 'C'est peu que d'y montrer les hommes: les hommes ne sont rien; il faut y faire sentir *les puissances inconnues qui forgent et martèlent nos destinées*' (see Yves Hervouet, *The French Face of Joseph Conrad* (Cambridge: Cambridge University Press, 1990), 135). The italics are Hervouet's.

He had written to nobody: unlike his model in real life, Charles Born. A touching fragment from the letter Born wrote to the widow of Captain John Snadden has survived, and is reprinted by Norman Sherry in *Conrad's Eastern World*, 319.

54 *they could all be resumed in the one word: Delay*: later editors have sometimes amended Conrad's 'resumed' to 'résuméd'; as is often the case, Conrad is influenced by French usage, and both here and elsewhere the verb 'to resume' is used by him to mean 'to sum up'. The emphasis on delay is another echo of *Hamlet*.

a doctor: Dr William Willis, who was 'Physician to H. M. Legation in Siam', gave Conrad a letter (dated February 1888):

> Dear Sir,
>
> I think it is not out of place on my part that I should state, though not asked by you to do so, to prevent any misapprehension hereafter, that the crew of the sailing ship *Otago* has suffered severely whilst in Bangkok from tropical diseases, including fever, dysentery and cholera; and I can speak of my own knowledge that you have done all in your power in the trying and responsible position of Master of the Ship to hasten the departure of your vessel from this unhealthy place and at the same time to save the lives of the men under your command.

The letter is reprinted by Jean-Aubry (*Joseph Conrad: Life and Letters*, i. 109) and (with a small correction) by Jocelyn Baines (*Joseph Conrad: A Critical Biography* (Harmondsworth, Penguin Books, 1971), 122).

55 *choleraic symptoms*: Norman Sherry reports that a crew member of the *Otago* did die of cholera but before Conrad joined the ship (*Conrad's Eastern World*, 230). The disease that later affects the rest of the crew, given their need for quinine, is clearly malaria. The entry for 'Bangkok' in the 1914 edition of *The Everyman Encyclopædia* includes the following passage: 'The older part of the city is built on rafts, but more civilised methods of town-planning have in recent years made rapid headway, and Bangkok is now supplied with good roads, an excellent tramway system, and many fine modern buildings. . . . The sanitation has improved, though the death-rate is still high.' See also the notes for p. 54 and p. 26.

60 *Having thrown off the mortal coil of shore affairs*: cf. *Hamlet*, III. i. 67: 'When we have shuffled off this mortal coil'.

My command might have been a planet: cf. *The Nigger of the 'Narcissus'*: 'The passage had begun, and the ship, a fragment detached from the earth, went on lonely and swift like a small planet'.

61 *ambushed down there*: that is, lying in ambush down there. *OED* confirms that Conrad's usage is correct. See also p. 67.

What's the good of letting go our hold of the ground only to drift, Mr Burns?: although the question has an obvious literal purchase, it ties in with the work's warnings of the dangers of a more metaphorical drifting (or 'loafing'), associated with the old captain, with Hamilton—and potentially with the narrator himself at the start of the work.

my lonely responsibilities: an interesting passage in the MS that is omitted from all published versions follows at this point. The passage shows Conrad first evoking and then revoking a sense of the supernatural in the reader. The mention of the Bull of Bashan indicates how easily biblical references came to Conrad. Conrad's deletions are in square brackets.

> . . . lonely responsibility; weighed down [by the solitude of] by it in that cabin, gloomy with the lamp turned down and where my predecessor had expired under the eyes of a few awed seamen.
>
> The passage of death made of it like a vast solitude. I took refuge from it in my state-room where [as far as I knew nobody had] nobody had died as far as I knew. After all the passion of anger and indignation I had thrown into my activities on shore the unpeopled stillness of that gulf weighed on my [me like an ???] shaken confidence like a mere artifice of some [forthcoming ??] inimical force—I upbraided myself for the very existence of that unwholesome [sentiment] sensation [.] I resisted it. But that resistance itself was a manifestation of a self-consciousness which was to me a strange experience, distasteful and disquieting. I welcomed a great wave of fatigue that all at once overwhelmed me from head to foot [while] in I struggle[d] against morbidity.
>
> Without taking off any of my clothing—not even removing my cap from my head I ensconced myself in the corner of the couch and crossing my arms on my breast fell into a profound slumber.
>
> I dreamt of the Bull of Bashan. He was roaring beyond all reason on his side of a very high fence striking it with his forehoof and also rattling his horns against it from time to time. On my side of the fence my purpose was (in my dream) to lead a contemplative existence. I despised the brute, but gradually a fear woke up in me—that he would end by breaking through—not through the fence—through my purpose. A horrible fear. I tried to fight [??] against it and mainly to keep it down with my hands. But it got the better of me like a [compressed] powerful compressed spring might have done—violently.
>
> I found myself on my feet, very scared by my dream and in addition

appalled by the apparition of the late captain in front of my open door. For what else could be that dim [??] figure in the [cuddy] half light of the cuddy, featureless, still malevolently silent, not to be mistaken for anything earthly.

Before my teeth began to rattle however the apparition spoke in a hoarse apologetic [?? flesh and blood] voice which no ghost would have [?would] thought it necessary to adopt. Certainly not the ghost of that savage overbearing old [man] sinner who [if he had been able] would have liked to take his ship out of the world with him.

It was but the voice of the seaman on watch who had come down to tell me that there were faint airs off the land. Enough he thought to get underway with.

I told him to call all hands to man the windlass. Before he left the cabin it occurred to me to ask him whether he had much trouble to wake me up.

'You were very sound off Sir' he said [??] with much feeling as he retired. That was it! He must have had to shout pretty loud. He was the Bull of Bashan of my dream, so detailed, so vivid and so concrete as to be more real than the great shadowy peace which met me when I came on deck.

The clink of the capstan forward, the voices of the men aloft ?losing the sails 'ready on the main' 'ready on the fore' floated past my ears like immaterial eerie sounds [???] not of this [words] world. And the gulf, dark still, seemed a mysterious and inaccessible sanctuary in which my orders uttered quietly were like the formulas of a magic rite about to endow the inanimate ship [??? life and motion] with that motion which is life—or the illusion of life.

This was the then moment of which I had day dreams as a boy as a very young man the first and supreme moment when with nothing but the great breath of the world for the agent of my will I should feel my first command move at my word under my feet. But how different it was from those vibrating exulting anticipations of my early years at sea!

And yet those day dreams had been without form or colour anticipations not of circumstance but of pure [feeling] and inward sensation. But who could have imagined the strangeness of it, with no witnesses but the big stars, clear in a black sky, the solitude and the stillness and the remoteness of the spot the uneasy feeling of stealthy departure [on some secret and desperate expedition] from a slumbering coast on a secret and desperate expedition.

With her anchor at the bow . . .

63 *as motionless as a model ship . . . polished marble*: cf. 'The Rime of the Ancient Mariner', ll. 115–18: 'Day after day, day after day, | We stuck, nor breath nor motion; | As idle as a painted ship | Upon a painted ocean.'

64 *The watch finished washing decks*: that is, the man on watch.

65 *an extraordinary and unfair licence*: the phrase is odd and suggests the possibility of a mistranscription. The MS (that part that Conrad dictated to a typist) has 'license'.

67 *ambushed*: see note for p. 61.

69 *The Island of Koh-ring*: nautical Conradians have argued about the identity of this island ('Ko' means 'island' in Thai), which is also mentioned in Conrad's 'The Secret Sharer'. Possible contenders include Koh Rong and Koh Chong, but the most likely is the Island of Kho Rin in latitude 12°48′N 100°42′E. It lies off the last, south-eastern headland of the northern bay at the head of the Gulf of Thailand—just where a ship would enter 'into the larger space of the Gulf of Siam' (p. 68). However, those attempting to base an identification on the description of the island and the ship's route as given in *The Shadow-Line* and 'The Secret Sharer' should perhaps bear in mind a comment made by Conrad about 'The Return' in a letter to William Blackwood: 'facts can bear out my story but as I am writing fiction not secret history—facts don't matter' (letter dated 6 September 1897, *Letters*, i. 382). Jacques Berthoud believes that Conrad's island 'is almost certainly fictitious' (p. 155 of his edition), but most commentators incline to the view that it is based at least in part on Conrad's memory of Kho Rin.

the power to put out of joint the meteorology of this part of the world: cf. *Hamlet*, I. v. 196: 'The time is out of joint'.

72 *The ship's head swung where it listed*: although 'list' seems here to be used in the nautical sense—'to incline to one side, to lean over', the phrase is reminiscent of 'The wind bloweth where it listeth' (John 3:8.), i.e. the wind blows where it wishes.

the ordeal of the fiery furnace: cf. Daniel, 3:23. Mr Burns was described at the onset of his illness as 'radiating heat on one like a small furnace' on p. 55—appropriately in view of his name, perhaps.

malefices: wicked bewitchment.

74 *like bits of copper wire*: compare Captain MacWhirr in 'Typhoon' (1902): 'The hair of his face . . . carroty and flaming, resembled a growth of copper wire clipped short to the line of the lip; while, no matter how close he shaved, fiery metallic gleams passed, when he moved his head, over the surface of his cheek.'

75 *Who hasn't heard of ships found drifting, haphazard, with their crews all dead?*: see note for p. 51. The captain repeats that 'Such things had been known to happen' on p. 84.

77 *North-East monsoon*: E1 and the typescript section of the MS (which Conrad dictated: see 'Note on the Text', p. xxxv) have the opaque 'Nord-East monsoon' (in the MS 'Nord-East' is added by hand). The American serial has the even more puzzling 'Nord-San monsoon'.

Flying Dutchman: Richard Wagner's (1813–93) opera *Der fliegende Holländer* (1841) is based on the legend of the captain of the Dutch ship the

Vanderdechen, who was condemned to sail for ever round the Cape of Good Hope as a punishment for blasphemy, but the legend builds on a number of older myths.

79 *Here is an extract from the notes I wrote at the time*: both the diary extracts (see p. 87 for the second) appear in the dictated part of the MS. In the first extract, the short text introducing it has been written in by hand. In the second extract, the introductory sentence that begins 'Here I must give another sample of it' has been altered from 'Here I must give a sample of it'. Taken together, this suggests that Conrad may have been using previously written material for the diary extracts, possibly even actual diary accounts written during the *Otago*'s first voyage under his command. See note for p. 5 for Conrad's writing habits on the *Vidar*, the ship on which he served prior to the *Otago*.

80 *The effect is curiously mechanical . . . as if somebody below the horizon were turning a crank*: this suggests that Conrad might have had some particular sort of mechanical toy in mind. I am indebted to Stephen Donovan for the following comments.

> The 'crank' would suggest the 'Kinetoscope' (a 'What the Butler Saw' machine which reached London in 1894). This was regarded more as a toy than as a serious invention, particularly after the arrival of projected film in 1896 when smaller hand-held versions such as the 'Kinora' became available for purchase. But larger theatrical entertainments of the 1890s may well have featured mechanical sunrises. The following, from chapter 44 of *The Mirror of the Sea* (1904–5), suggests a familiarity with mechanical toys: 'The vision of my companions passed before me. The whole Royalist gang was in Monte Carlo now, I reckoned. And they appeared to me clear-cut and very small, with affected voices and stiff gestures, like a procession of rigid marionettes upon a toy stage.'

the formidable Work of the Seven Days: see Genesis 2:2, and also note for p. 89.

82 *livid hue*: following these words, MS and A1 have an additional sentence: 'The disease disclosed its low type in a startling way.' However MS reads: 'brought out' for 'disclosed'.

of the Punch type: Punch (who traditionally has a chin and nose that curve out towards each other) is a character in 'Punch and Judy' marionette shows, still to be seen at the British seaside, and his image was reproduced on the front cover of *Punch* magazine.

Gambril: in the MS and the periodical editions this sailor is named Smith.

I expected to meet reproachful glances: cf. 'The Rime of the Ancient Mariner', ll. 214–15: 'Each turned his face with a ghastly pang, | And cursed me with his eye.'

84 *sing out at the ropes*: a traditional sea-shanty was sung to establish and maintain a steady rhythm for specific tasks. Cf. *stamp and go* in the Glossary.

mail-boat track: as mail-boats were frequent, a mail-boat track would be more reliably trafficked, and thus a better place to attempt to encounter another ship. See also Glossary: *mail boat*.

87 *that very evening*: see note for p. 79.

like a decomposition, like a corruption of the air: reminiscent of the images of rottenness in *Hamlet*.

butt-end foremost: the Captain's fear of 'a furious squall coming, butt-end foremost' is somewhat opaque, but it suggests the approach of the 'rear-side' of a storm system rather than its leading edge. The direction in which a storm system is entered affects such things as sea-state and wind direction.

Mei-nam: the Menam river, now known as Chao Phraya, which runs from the Burma–Laos border, crosses Thailand from north to south, and enters the Gulf of Siam through several outlets. Cf. the opening page of 'The Secret Sharer'.

89 *the end of all things*: contrasting with the Creation, 'The formidable Work of the Seven Days', mentioned on p. 80.

90 *we must try to haul this mainsail close up*: this is to 'subdue' it in the face of the imminent storm by hauling it up with the leech-lines so that it is furled against the yard to which it is attached above

Those men were the ghosts of themselves: cf. the ghostly mariners in 'The Rime of the Ancient Mariner': 'We were a ghastly crew' (l. 340).

like Titans: in Greek mythology the Titans were the sons and daughters of Uranus (sky) and Gaea (earth), originally twelve in number. They rose against and castrated their father, but later were themselves deposed by the Olympian gods. Some of Conrad's descriptions here are reminiscent of John Keats's (1795–1821) portrayal of the fallen Titans in 'Hyperion' (1819). Conrad uses two (slightly misquoted) lines from 'Endymion' as epigraph to 'Typhoon' and he corresponded with Sidney Colvin, Keats's biographer. R. L. Mégroz interviewed Conrad in 1922 and reported the novelist's having said that Keats was his favourite poet 'because he is so essentially a genius, and so free from all intellectuality' (*Joseph Conrad's Mind and Method: A Study of Personality in Art* (London: Faber & Faber, 1931), 41).

94 *curious, irregular sounds . . . Tap. Tap. Tap:* a fine example of what Ian Watt, in *Conrad in the Nineteenth Century* (London: Chatto & Windus, 1980), dubbed 'delayed decoding', whereby the reader, along with the narrator or characters, only retrospectively understands the full significance of what is actually happening.

An additional turn of the racking screw: the image is from the instrument of torture, the thumbscrew. Conrad read Henry James's (1843–1916) *The Two Magics* (1898), which included *The Turn of the Screw* (see letter to Ford Madox Hueffer, 20 October 1898, *Letters*, ii. 110–11). But cf. Conrad's short story 'The Return', written before Conrad read *The Two Magics*: 'He perceived himself so extremely forlorn and lamentable, and was moved so deeply by the oppressive sorrow, that another turn of the screw, he felt, would bring tears out of his eyes.' The phrase in *The Shadow-Line* nicely matches the comment in the opening pages of James's tale that 'If the child gives the effect of another turn of the screw' then 'two children give two turns!' The strong hints of the supernatural in James's tale accord with a similarly insistent suggestion of the uncanny in *The Shadow-Line*.

94 *since I was wearing only my sleeping suit*: cf. the captain in Conrad's 'The Secret Sharer' when he meets his double, Leggatt. There is a dreamlike quality to many experiences in both works. In *The Shadow-Line* Gambril is described just below as 'an elusive, phosphorescent shape', reminiscent of the captain's first view of Leggatt: 'Before I could form a guess a faint flash of phosphorescent light, which seemed to issue suddenly from the naked body of a man, flickered in the sleeping water with the elusive, silent play of summer lightning in a night sky'. Leggatt also first appears to be headless, as does the first, doomed steward to the captain when first he comes on board in *The Shadow-Line*.

96 *the jingle of a slack chain sheet*: the sheets attached to the topsail, which would be hauled in to spread the foot of the sail, were originally made of rope, but later of chain. When the ship was becalmed the sheets were not under tension and were thus free to jingle when the ship moved.

it was the moment of breaking strain: see the Glossary. In 'Heart of Darkness' (1899) Marlow notes of *An Inquiry into Some Points of Seamanship* that 'Towson or Towser was inquiring earnestly into the breaking strain of ships' chains and tackle, and other such matters'. F. H. Burgess provides a neat formula for ascertaining the breaking strain of hemp, sisal, or manila: 'square the circumference in inches and divide by three, the result being a good safety margin in tons.'

I felt ashamed of having been passed over by the fever: perhaps a half allusion to the Angel of death, passing through the land of Egypt and smiting the firstborn, but passing over the Jews.

100 *by careful manipulation of the helm we got the foreyards to run square by themselves*: the most likely meaning is that the foreyards are manipulated to be at right-angles to the ship

105 *'And very bad,' he repeated*: in the MS: 'And ve—ry bad' he repeated.

106 *They passed under my eyes . . . bitterest kind*: cf.'The Rime of the Ancient Mariner': 'All fixed on me their stony eyes' (l. 436).

107 *The marine officer let me off the port dues*: in a letter to W. G. St Clair (see note for p. 7), Conrad writes: 'Yes, I remember Bradbury. It was he who

let me off port-dues when I put into Singapore in distress with *all* my crew unfit for duty (1888)' (see Sherry, *Conrad's Eastern World*, 316). This according to St Clair was 'Bradbury, the Assistant Master-Attendant at Singapore'. As Sherry notes, however, Conrad exaggerates the sickness of his crew: he took on only five new crew members in Singapore, and only one of these appears to have come from a wrecked ship. When the *Otago* first reached Singapore, three of its crew were ordered ashore for medical reasons, followed two days later by a man named Pat Conway, who Sherry surmises may be the original of Ransome, although he seems to have been laid low by fever rather than heart disease. See *Conrad's Eastern World*, 248–9.

109 *I listened to him going up the companion stairs*: writing to Sidney Colvin about *The Shadow-Line* in a letter dated 27 February 1917, Conrad claimed, as he had to others, that 'the whole thing is exact autobiography', and commented especially that 'My last scene with Ransome is only indicated. There are things, moments, that are not to be tossed to the public's incomprehension, for journalists to gloat over. No. It was not an experience to be exhibited "in the street."' (Jean-Aubry, *Joseph Conrad: Life and Letters*, ii. 182.) See the note for p. 107.

Author's Note

110 *within those vain imaginings*: the typescript of Conrad's 'Author's Note', taken from his dictation, has 'with' rather than 'within', and this may make better sense.

111 *the last three months of the year 1916*: the comment is wrong on two accounts: first, because *The Shadow-Line* was written in 1915 and not 1916, and second because the writing process took seven rather than three months. See the 'Note on the Text', p. xxxiv. This is not the only time that Conrad misdated the composition of this work; in a letter to Sidney Colvin he wrote: 'I was writing that thing in Dec., 1914, and Jan. to March, 1915' (letter of 27 February 1917, Jean-Aubry, *Joseph Conrad: Life and Letters*, i. 182).

GLOSSARY OF FOREIGN WORDS, GEOGRAPHICAL NAMES, AND TECHNICAL TERMS

The following glossary focuses on the specific meanings of terms as used in *The Shadow-Line* and relies on a number of written sources; the most important of these are Mr Seiji Minamida's '*The Shadow-Line*: Explanatory Notes and Glossary'; 'A to Z of Seamanship in *The Nigger of the "Narcissus"*'; and '*The Nigger of the "Narcissus"*: Explanatory Notes and Glossary' (in *The Journal of the College of Arts and Sciences*, Chiba University, Japan, the first two from November 1988 and the third from November 1987). In addition the following printed sources have been consulted: C. W. T. Layton, *Dictionary of Nautical Words and Terms* (2nd edition, revised by Peter Clissold, Glasgow: Brown, Son & Ferguson, 1967); *Eric Sullivan's Marine Encyclopedic Dictionary* (6th edition, Colchester: LLP, 1999); W. A. McEwen and A. H. Lewis, *Encyclopedia of Nautical Knowledge* (Cambridge, Md.: Cornell Maritime Press, 1953); René de Kerchove, *International Maritime Dictionary* (2nd edition, New York: Van Nostrand Reinhold Company, 1961); F. H. Burgess, *A Dictionary of Sailing* (Harmondsworth: Penguin, 1961); G. O. Watson, *Dictionary of Marine Engineering and Nautical Terms* (London: George Newnes, 1964); Gershom Bradford, *The Mariner's Dictionary* (Barre, Mass.: Barre Publishers, 1972). Jacques Berthoud's notes to his edition of the novella (Harmondsworth: Penguin, 1986) have also been consulted.

aback 'Ship's all aback' (p. 81) means that one or more sails are flat against the mast with the wind on their fore side

aft towards the stern of the ship; the 'after deck' is the deck by the ship's stern

all aback see *aback

amidships that part of the ship midway between bow and stern

anchorage ground suitable for anchoring in; a place set aside for ships to anchor

anchor watch an individual or group responsible for the ship while the ship is at anchor in an open roadstead, charged among other things with making sure that the anchor does not drag

answer the helm the ship answers the helm when it changes direction in response to the movements of the tiller (and thus the rudder)

antimacassars macassar oil was used as a hair dressing; to protect chairs from being stained by it, cloths were used to cover chair-backs, hence antimacassars

bar a bank of e.g. sand across the entrance to a harbour, created by currents and tides or artificially, that serves as a partial breakwater

baulk a heavily squared piece of timber

beat to work windward by successive tacks

belaying pin a pin-shaped device set in the pin rails to secure the running rigging

bells see *watch

bend a suit a suit is a complete set of sails; when they are bent they are secured to a yard or other spar

berth (i) a place where a sailor sleeps on ship; (ii) a place in port allotted to a ship where it can tie up and anchor; (iii) metaphorically, a sailor's contracted employment on a ship for a particular voyage

binnacle a stand of wood or metal in which the ship's compass is suspended; a 'compass-lamp' is used to illuminate the compass

block a framed roller through which ropes run

bluejacket British Royal Naval as opposed to Merchant Marine sailor

brace a rope by which a yard is adjusted on the horizontal plane; each yard on a square-rigged ship had two braces by means of which it could be traversed, or rotated in the horizontal plane

break ground a ship breaks ground when the anchor is hauled up

breaking strain the amount of pull or load on e.g. a rope that will cause it to part

break of the poop where the level of the deck alters at the start of the *poop

bridge an elevated structure from which the officer in charge controls the ship

bring up a ship brings up when it comes to a stop

bucket-rack a rack containing fire-fighting buckets, situated along the break of the poop

bulkhead traverse partitions within the ship, designed partly to ensure rigidity and partly (when watertight) to prevent water filling the whole area of the ship in the case of damage to the hull

by the run allowing a rope to run without hindrance

cable both an anchor cable and a telegraph cable

Cape Liant in modern Thailand, outside Bangkok

capstan a device consisting of a vertical barrel revolving around a vertical spindle turned either manually or by an engine, which takes up an anchor or a rope

cast (ship) to alter the ship's heading to the desired direction while she is stationary or at anchor

chain sheet see *sheet

charter-party a legal document produced in duplicate, binding the two signatories to its terms

China Sea that portion of the Pacific Ocean lying to the east of China and present-day Thailand, generally taken to include the Gulfs of Thailand (Siam) and Tonkin

clear for running said of a coil of rope when it can unwind freely from the top

cleat small object with two horns for making fast halyards, etc.

cock-billed the anchors are cock-billed when they are pointing downwards from the cat-head (a beam projecting almost horizontally from each side of the bows of a ship), and ready to be dropped

come aback see *aback

come-to said of a ship when it turns to face the wind

companion stairs/companion way stairs or ladder leading from one deck to another or to a cabin; the 'engine-room companion' is the stair or ladder leading to the engine room

compass-lamp see *binnacle

compressor a device that grips the anchor chain and that thus has to be opened prior to releasing an anchor

Consul-General an agent appointed by a sovereign state (here Britain) in a foreign country to protect the interests of citizens and to assist in commercial dealings between the two countries

coolie native carrier

cowl a (normally metal) fitting for directing an air-stream towards a particular destination; often used to refer to the hood-like top on a ventilator shaft

coxswain the individual who is in charge of and steers a boat (as against a ship)

dead before straight ahead; the more usual expression is now 'dead ahead'

dead water the eddy water, resembling whirlpools on each side of the ship's stern, produced as she moves forwards

dégagé easy; unconstrained

discharge legal confirmation that a sailor has fulfilled his contractual duties and is free to enter a new agreement

dry-dock a dock that can be pumped dry so as to allow work to the ship's hull; when a ship is dry-docked it is ready for such work

forecastle the forward part of the weather deck, and that part of the ship where the crew's quarters are situated

foreyard see *yard
forward towards the bow of the ship
furl to wrap a sail close up to its allotted yard and to secure it by means of stops or a gasket
galley the ship's 'kitchen'
gharry a horse-drawn cart or carriage
grating a hatch or other covering with openings in it
Gulf of Siam now the Gulf of Thailand
Haiphong in modern Vietnam
halyard from 'haul-yard': a rope by means of which sails are hoisted
harbour office where the business of the harbour is administered, under the authority of the Harbour-Master (see *marine superintendent)
Harbour-Master see *marine superintendent
hatch (hatchway) an opening in the deck to allow passage up and down; 'hatch' can also refer to a covering over such an opening
heart applied to a wind, signifies strength
helm down/up to down helm is to push the helm down to the lee side so as to put the ship about or lay her to windward; to up helm is to raise the helm so as to make the ship 'go large' and catch more wind
helmsman the seaman in charge of the wheel who steers the ship
house-flag flag indicating the ship's owner
leech-line halyard fastened to the leech, i.e. the side edge of a square sail
lift a rope linking the ends of the yards to the mast heads, and by means of which the yards are kept square
lubber an incompetent sailor—used humorously on p. 95
mail boat a ship that carries mail, normally as a result of an official government contract
mainsail the chief and lowest sail on the mainmast
marine superintendent/Harbour-Master the official in charge of port regulations and responsible for the proper berthing and anchorage of ships
mast-head the upper end of a mast (technically, that part of the mast clear of all standing rigging)
mizzen-mast/mizzen the third mast from forward of a ship
ormolu gold, or gold-coloured alloy
Palawan in the present-day Philippines
peon a native attendant or orderly
pinnace a boat somewhat bigger than a launch, generally used for harbour work

poop the deck next above the *quarter-deck, or the highest deck aft

port used on p. 88 to mean port-hole; otherwise either a harbour, or the left side of a ship

port bow that part of the front of the ship that is on the left when facing forwards

port quarter see *quarter

punkah a large fan used to ventilate or cool a room

quarter used to indicate direction, a bearing or direction relative to the ship's fore-and-aft line, looking astern

quarter-deck between the stern and the after-mast

Red Ensign a red flag with the union flag in the top left quarter, the official flag of the British Merchant Marine since 1801; not to be confused with the Union Jack, or with the Pilot Jack (the union flag with a white border)

rigging all the ropes and chains used to support or adjust masts, booms, and *yards

right amidships with the rudder parallel to the ship's keel

ringbolt a bolt attached to the ship with a ring to which ropes can be attached

roadstead (roads) sheltered water in which safe anchorage is available

rudder-casing the watertight casing or well in which the rudder head works

scuppers holes allowing water to drain off deck into the sea

set [sail] to unfurl and expand the sails to the wind, so as to start the ship moving

sextant a reflecting instrument used for measuring altitudes and other angles not exceeding 120°

sheet a rope used to control a sail

ship's articles a contract specifying the type of voyage and the conditions of service such as wages

ship's head the bow or fore-part of the vessel

shore-fasts a hawser securing a docked ship to the shore

slat sails slat when they slap against the masts

Solo Sea otherwise Sulu Sea, or Sea of Mindoro, lying between latitude 5°N and 12°N, and longitude 117°E and 123°E

spar a general term for those thick lengths of timber to which ropes or sails are fixed, such as masts, yards, and so on

squall a strong wind, normally one that comes upon the ship suddenly, and that may or may not be in the same direction as the prevailing wind

square (the mainyard) to swing the mainyard (see *yard) at right angles to the ship's longitudinal axis

stamp and go to perform a task while stamping one's foot to the rhythm of a shanty

state-room here the captain's state-room, where the medicine is stored: a cabin additional to that in which the captain sleeps, but for his personal use

steerage way a ship has steerage way when it has sufficient forward movement to allow it to be steered

stern the rear of a ship

stern-sheets here the space towards the rear of the boat where there are seats for passengers

sternway force exerted on the rudder and felt on the wheel, resulting from the movement of the ship

swell a succession of long and unbroken waves that do not result from local meteorological conditions, but from a source (such as wind) some distance away

swing to to move sideways while retaining a constant distance from a point ahead

Syed from the Arabic word for 'Lord': a Muslim honorary title, sometimes carrying the specific claim that the bearer is descended from Mohammed's grandson Husain

tackle an assemblage of blocks and ropes for lifting (e.g. cargo)

taffrail the rail running round the main deck aft of the ship

take the sun measure the sun's position by means of a *sextant

tell-tale compass an inverted compass attached to the beams of a cabin, allowing the captain to check the ship's direction of movement at any time by looking upward

tiffin a light midday meal

Tonkin the north-eastern province of what is now Vietnam

topmast the mast immediately above a lower mast

topsail here the sail above the *mainsail

trap a small horse-drawn carriage

traps a sailor's personal possessions

trim (yards) to adjust the yards so that sails obtain maximal wind

truck circular piece of wood capping a mast; here the very tops of the masts

water-line either the line at which the water meets the ship's side at a particular draught, or a line painted around a ship to indicate the approximate position of her load water-line

windlass winding gear working on a horizontal axis, used for working cable and to raise or lower the anchor

yard a long spar, tapered at the ends, attached at its middle to a mast and running athwartships; used to support, and when necessary to extend, the top of a square sail, and to extend the bottom of the sail above, if there is one